"Cassandra, What On Earth Are You Up To Now?"

Casey turned. A man she'd never seen before stood in front of her. Man? More like a miracle.

He considered her with frustration. "When are you going to stop playing games? And where in heaven's name did you pick up that atrocious accent?"

"From my mother. She has one just like it. Listen, my car broke down, and I need a tow. Can you help?"

"Cassandra—" he continued.

"How do you know my name? Nobody's called me Cassandra since grammar school." She meant to say more but never quite got it out. He touched her gently. With just that contact, Casey found herself suffused with a sweet hesitation, a languid warmth. She looked up at him and forgot everything she'd been about to say.

"Oh, my Lord." The intensity in his eyes grew. "You're not the princess, are you? You're not like her at all."

Dear Reader:

Series and Spin-offs! Connecting characters and intriguing interconnections to make your head whirl.

In Joan Hohl's successful trilogy for Silhouette Desire— *Texas Gold* (7/86), *California Copper* (10/86), *Nevada Silver* (1/87)—Joan created a cast of characters that just wouldn't quit. You figure out how *Lady Ice* (5/87) connects. And in August, "J.B." demanded his own story—*One Tough Hombre*. In *Falcon's Flight*, coming in November, you'll learn *all* about . . .?

Annette Broadrick's *Return to Yesterday* (6/87) introduced Adam St. Clair. This August *Adam's Story* tells about the woman who saves his life—and teaches him a thing or two about love!

The six Branigan brothers appeared in Leslie Davis Guccione's *Bittersweet Harvest* (10/86) and *Still Waters* (5/87). September brings *Something in Common*, where the eldest of the strapping Irishmen finds love in unexpected places.

Midnight Rambler by Linda Barlow is in October—a special Halloween surprise, and totally unconnected to anything.

Keep an eye out for other Silhouette Desire favorites— Diana Palmer, Dixie Browning, Ann Major and Elizabeth Lowell, to name a few. You never know when secondary characters will insist on their own story. . . .

All the best,

Isabel Swift
Senior Editor & Editorial Coordinator
Silhouette Books

KATHLEEN KORBEL
A Prince of a Guy

Silhouette Desire

Published by Silhouette Books New York

America's Publisher of Contemporary Romance

Dedicated to
Lucia for letting me get away with it
and
Ronald Coleman who made me think
of it in the first place

SILHOUETTE BOOKS
300 East 42nd St., New York, N.Y. 10017

Copyright © 1987 by Eileen Dreyer

ISBN: 0-373-05389-4

First Silhouette Books printing November 1987

America's Publisher of Contemporary Romance

Printed in the U.S.A.

KATHLEEN KORBEL

blames her writing on an Irish heritage, which gave her the desire, and a supportive husband, who gave her the ultimatum, "Do something productive or knock it off." An R.N. from St. Louis, she also counts traveling and music as addictions and is working on yet another career in screen-writing.

Royal House of von Lieberhaven

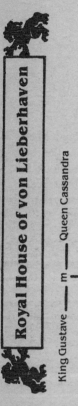
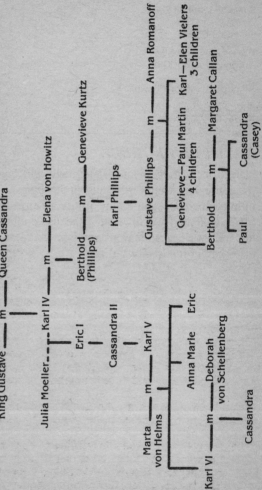

King Gustave — m — Queen Cassandra

Julia Moeller — m — Karl IV — m — Elena von Howitz

Eric I

Cassandra II

Berthold (Phillips) — m — Genevieve Kurtz

Karl Phillips

Gustave Phillips — m — Anna Romanoff

Genevieve — Paul Martin   Karl — Elen Vielers
4 children   3 children

Berthold — m — Margaret Callan

Paul   Cassandra (Casey)

Marta von Helms — m — Karl V

Anna Marie   Eric

Karl VI — m — Deborah von Schellenberg

Cassandra

One

___

Wouldn't it just figure? Stuck in a foreign country where they don't even speak English, and your car breaks down on the way up some ridiculously high mountain. And the next stop is at the top of that mountain. Casey readjusted the strap of her carryall and looked back to where she'd left the little bright red rental car to fend for itself on the negligible shoulder of a narrow, winding mountain road. Then she looked ahead to the tollgate just beyond her.

Moritania. The name of the tiny little country was ornately carved on the entryway. Two sleepy-looking guards manned the station, attired in rather antiquated-looking uniforms and plumed caps. Casey hadn't seen anything so quaint since the Vatican.

Approaching the guards, she turned again to her bag, intent on getting out her passport. She was talking long before she reached the men.

"I can't believe it," she said, riffling through the countless wads of currency and travel brochures that packed the oversized bag. "My first trip out of the States—out of New York, really—and my car breaks down in the middle of the Alps. I was coming up here to see the country—my family's supposed to be from here, ya know—but now I'm going to have to call a garage." Casey didn't notice that her audience was suspiciously quiet. "You do have garages here, don't you?" After seeing those outfits, she wouldn't have been too surprised if they'd said that there was no automation in Moritania at all.

She knew she'd stuck her passport in between her German phrase book and her traveler's checks. Where could it have gone? "Wait, my passport's around her someplace. It's a U.S. passport, and I really wanted to get a Moritanian stamp on it. For my mom. Just to prove the place exists. Who'd believe it?" Casey dug even deeper, the passport still eluding her. "I can't believe that I can't find it. I wonder if I left it at the hotel room with Sandra...."

Her voice trailed off as she finally got her head up to smile at the guards. All thoughts of her broken-down car and missing passport trailed away. The two guards weren't facing her. She wasn't even sure if they were listening. They were both bent at right angles, their eyes resolutely on the ground, their backs as stiff as wallboards.

Casey's eyes followed theirs. "Lose a contact?"

They didn't move. Quaint little country they had here. Maybe it was like Japan, she thought. They couldn't stand up until you bowed back.

She did. They didn't.

"Uh, excuse me?"

No reaction. Casey bent down until she was almost nose-to-nose with one of them. He still refused to face her. "Do you speak English?"

The man came up so fast that he almost collided with her. "But of course, my lady," he stammered, his eyes wide with apprehension. "It is the law." Then he went right back down.

Casey was flummoxed. Now, she realized that she hadn't traveled enough to become an expert on customs. Until she'd won the trip to Europe, she hadn't gone much farther than Brooklyn and midtown Manhattan. But for the life of her she couldn't figure out what this business was all about.

"Maybe I could just call the American consulate," she offered. "For my passport." Then she looked around. "Does a country this size have an American consulate? Does it have a pay phone where I can call the American consulate in the next country?"

"Please, my lady," the gentleman said, his eyes still on the ground. "Let me call."

Casey considered his position. "From there?"

"From the booth. I beg the privilege."

Still confused, she shrugged. It was getting hard not to giggle. "A country without much excitement, huh?"

Twenty minutes later, Casey occupied a chair in the little
booth while the two guards scuttled around trying to find new
and different ways to make her more comfortable. She assured
them that there was only so much comfort one could find at a
border crossing. All she succeeded in doing was making them
more miserable. But when she asked whether the American
consul was coming, or even a tow truck, all they did was ex-
change worried little glances.

"Soon now, my lady," the spokesman assured her. "He
promised."

Casey shrugged again, thinking that she was doing a lot of
that, and crossed her legs, resettling her wide denim skirt
around her legs. Not exactly climbing clothes. But then, Julie
Andrews had done the Alps in a habit.

"This is real *Sound of Music* country," she said, not really
expecting an answer by now. "Of course, you guys were probably raised on Wagner and Romberg."

No answer.

"Romberg," she repeated, trying for some kind of reaction.
"You know, *Student Prince*?"

"Cassandra, what on earth are you up to now?"

Casey lifted her head with a start at the sound of the new
voice. Then her mouth dropped open. Now how had he snuck
up on her?

The guards were back down again, and a new man stood in
the doorway. Man? More like a miracle. He was breathtaking,
the kind of man she was sure she'd never in her life run into on
the streets of Brooklyn. Clad in a hunter's jacket of tweed and
leather and a wool sweater over a snow-white shirt and navy
blue tie, he looked more like an English lord gone to tour his
estate.

Tall, maybe six feet, and slim. Athletic. Casey could imagine him on a polo pony or a yacht, the wind sweeping through
his golden-brown hair. He had a face that would have made
Cary Grant cry: long, with an aquiline nose, a strong chin and
a well-bred brow. It was a cultured face with eyes the color of
a summer sky.

A most practical child, Casey had never been able to figure
how Cinderella could have been swept off her feet within the
space of one dance. If this guy had been the one wearing the

tights, it would have made perfect sense. She was in love before she even knew his name.

He turned briefly and dispatched the guards with a gentle word. The relief on their features was palpable as they straightened and departed.

"How did you do that?" Casey asked, getting to her feet. "No matter what I did they kept checking out their toes. It's kind of unnerving after awhile, ya know?"

Her guest considered her with frustration. "When are you going to stop? You're not going to make them better subjects by playing games with them. And you're certainly playing havoc with my schedule."

"Thanks for the interest," Casey said, smiling dryly. "What the hell are you talking about?"

"And where in heaven's name did you pick up that atrocious accent?"

Casey was bristling now. "From my mother. She has one just like it. Listen, my car broke down and I need a tow. And I forgot my passport back at the hotel. Otherwise I wouldn't have had you paged. Are you with the American embassy?"

He straightened a little, his head tilted at an angle of inspection. "Cassandra..."

"Nobody's called me Cassandra since the nuns... How did you know my name?" She shook her head, the confusion mounting. "Listen, I'll tell you what. If you're not with the embassy, just call me a tow or whatever. If this is an example of Moritanian hospitality, I don't think I want to visit after all. I'd have more fun in the Bronx on a Saturday night...."

Casey had more to say. Something about rudeness and insanity and lack of oxygen at high altitudes. She never quite got it out. As she was speaking, the gentleman's eyes widened with an incredulity that gave her pause. His lips opened in amazement, and he stepped up to her. When he laid a hand under her chin and lifted it, she fell mute.

His eyes caught hers and held them. His hand, graceful and strong, captured her with the gentlest touch. With just that contact, Casey found herself suffused with a sweet hesitation she'd never known. A languid heat, as if his eyes were stealing her strength. She looked up at him and forgot what she'd been about to say and why it had been important.

"Oh, my God," he breathed, the intensity of his gaze growing. His eyes swept her features, her attire, and then came back

to rest on her face. "You're not like her at all, are you? Not at
all."

Casey couldn't seem to drag her eyes away. "I . . . wouldn't
know."

"Who are you?"

"Casey Phillips. Who are you?"

"Eric von Lieberhaven."

Their voices had grown soft somehow, intimate in the little
room. It was Eric who broke the spell first, pulling his hand
away as if he'd been scalded. Casey saw him rub it against his
leg in what she was sure was an uncharacteristic gesture. She
wasn't sure how she knew. She just did.

"But why did they call you?" she asked when he moved far
enough away that she could breathe again. "You never told me.
Do you work for the embassy?"

The smile he gave her was a bright one, rueful and wry. He
had beautiful white teeth and a pattern of crow's-feet from the
sun and wind that adorned his smiles with an endearing
warmth. Casey smiled back without knowing why.

"No," he assured her. "I'm not with the embassy."

He did have an accent, but Casey wasn't sure what kind.
Brooklyn had ruined her ear for distinctions, though she could
instinctively mimic any accent if she wanted. What she wanted,
she realized, was to get to know Eric von whatever better. Fat
chance, from the looks of him. He looked as if he'd been afforded more in life than a flat and a high school education.

Outside, the phone jangled, and one of the guards went to
answer it.

"Your Highness?"

Eric turned to him.

Casey gaped. "Your what?"

"Yes, Franz?"

"It is the palace, Your Highness. They wish you to return
immediately."

Eric nodded, Franz bowed and Casey continued to gape.

"Your *what*?" she repeated.

Eric smiled again. "A matter of formality."

Casey motioned to the guards. "The same kind of formality
that has them inspecting their shoe tops, right? What kind of
highness?"

He shrugged. "If you want the boring facts, I am Prince Eric
Karl Phillip Marie von Lieberhaven."

She gestured to the surrounding mountains. "So you kind of own the place?"

His chuckle was easy and deep. She fell harder. "In a manner of speaking, I suppose. Although I do not stand to inherit the throne. I was a third child."

Casey scowled. "A prince is a prince. Which brings me to my first question. And my second and third. Why did they call you, and how did you know my name? And if they were bowing to you, why were they doing the same to me? Or is this just the most polite country in the world?"

She was rewarded with another chuckle. "Would you care to receive your answers on the way to the palace? I seem to have business to attend there, and I think you might like to come along. There are some people you might like to see."

She was gaping again. She'd never so much as been invited to a formal dinner, much less a palace in a European country, no matter that it was a country just about the size of Queens.

"Why?"

"Do you want your car back?"

"I don't have my passport with me."

His smile broadened. "One of the benefits of 'owning the place.' I can grant you immunity. I ask one favor, though. Don't say anything more to the guards for the moment."

Casey took a look down at the denim skirt and white cotton blouse that had been her traveling attire. Suddenly she would have preferred the habit. She looked as if she was headed to a roundup, especially with her sandy hair in its thick French braid. "Am I appropriate for a palace?" she asked. Then she laughed. "What am I talking about? I don't own *anything* that's appropriate for a palace. But then, I bet you don't have anything to wear to a Mets game, do you?"

His smile grew delighted as he took hold of her arm. "You look quite lovely."

Casey had to laugh. "Be careful," she warned as she followed him out the door. "You're fulfilling every one of my expectations."

Eric managed to pull a straight face for Franz and his associate. "Thank you for being so alert, Franz. You're a credit to the corps."

Franz was so pleased that his nose almost scraped his knees. Casey allowed the prince to help her into the Bronco he was driving and resettled her skirt and carryall.

"Is this what the well-bred prince is driving these days?" she asked. "I was expecting something a little flashier, maybe more along the lines of a Daimler."

He grinned and started the engine, turning the vehicle back through the gate. "I was out hunting. Daimlers just aren't built for the woods."

"So what does one call a man with four names and title?" Casey had the feeling she was babbling, but the situation had gotten beyond her when he'd unleashed those incredible eyes on her. She was strictly on overload now.

"Four names and three titles," he allowed. "Pick any one. I answer to just about anything. Where are you from, Casey? May I call you Casey?"

Casey caught him considering her again and decided that he could call her anything he wanted. "Casey's fine. I'm from Brooklyn, New York. Ever heard of it?"

"Of course. I traveled through it on the way to the airport a few years ago. Kennedy, I believe? I've never seen so many buildings."

She nodded. "That's Brooklyn."

"Have you been to Moritania before?"

She snorted derisively. "I haven't even been outside of the boroughs before. I won a trip to Europe at work and decided to stop by when I saw it on the map. The family story is that my great-great-grandfather came from Moritania. I couldn't believe it really existed."

Casey missed the quick look Eric shot her. "He did?"

She shrugged, looking out at the mountains in an attempt to get her pulse to slow down. He was too close to her, and his cologne was too enticing. She couldn't believe that she was reacting to him like nitro when it got too close to glycerine.

Practical, sensible Casey had always set her sights on the attainable goals. She'd made sure of it. She'd never once fallen head over heels for a suave, handsome prince from a foreign country. But oh, Lord, she had a feeling she was about to now. It just figured.

"That's what my grandfather said. They never talked about it much. They just kept saying that we're Americans now, we should concentrate on being good Americans. We have Romanov blood, too. Russian, Moritanian and Irish. Real Americans."

Eric nodded pensively. "It makes their decision to concentrate on the present an understandable one. The Romanovs certainly had nothing to look back for."

"The only thing I got from that association is a yearning for Fabergé eggs."

"Were you left any?"

She laughed. "All we got was the name. Somebody else got the money. I live in a flat with my mother and work as a secretary for an advertising firm. And I'm going to night school."

"College?"

"Three more years, then law school. I figure I'll be out of that sometime around menopause."

They were coming to the outskirts of a town, the quaint, square-gabled farmhouses giving way to more modern buildings. Casey could see a bit of glass and steel that was reminiscent of New York on a smaller scale. The streets wound in among the steep slopes of the mountains with the taller buildings crowding the base.

Casey still marveled at how houses clung to the sides of these mountains like limpets. There shouldn't have been any way people could have walked up those inclines, much less ride bikes or drive cars. But they did, herding their cattle and sheep and planting their gardens just shy of the tree line. People who had lived the same way for centuries and who had lived that way when her great-great-grandfather had been born here.

The thought gave her an unexpected thrill of belonging—of history past that of her family's time in America. After all, the farthest back she could claim there was the 1880s. Here she could claim back to Hannibal and beyond. These were the same people who had molded mores still practiced in her house. And the man sitting next to her was the heir of the men who had ruled when her family had lived here. Too bad she was too American to give that concept the respect she was sure her great-great-grandfather would have afforded it.

"If you'll pardon my saying so, Eric," she said, deliberately foregoing the title to see what he'd do, "you haven't answered my questions."

He didn't seem to notice her breach of conduct. His gaze firmly on the road ahead, he nodded, almost to himself. "I know. If you'll be patient, there's something I want to show you at the palace first."

Casey couldn't help but grin. "The floors, right? The penalty for being caught on foot without a passport in this country is a good wax and shine of the ballroom."

"You've read Cinderella once too often," he scoffed.

Not often enough, she said to herself. "Do you have little princes of your own?" Nothing like getting right to the point. As if it would make any difference. Grace Kelly she wasn't.

Eric laughed, that same soft rumble that had tickled her before. "None. My mother considers me the black sheep of the family. I've been so busy at the banks that I haven't had the time to settle down with a good wife."

"Hard to find that certain girl who can keep a home and grace state functions, huh?" She couldn't believe she was egging him on this way. But there was just something about her Brooklyn upbringing that made her go on the offensive when she felt intimidated. And how she felt intimidated! Her hands were sweating. The problem was that it wasn't his station in life that was doing it.

He laughed again, his eyes still on traffic. "Cheeky lot, you Americans."

"That's what kept getting us in trouble with the English."

She snuck a look over to feast on his smile. It just made her hands sweat more.

"Did your family talk much about Moritania?" he asked, swinging his gaze around just in time to catch her. Casey looked down abruptly, transferring her attention to the bag in her lap.

"Nope. Not a word. I thought it was a family joke until I saw the map. Which reminds me—" She made a sweeping gesture. "We've been by one town and two castles so far. We're running out of country. Just where is this palace of yours?"

His smile grew rakish. "Afraid I'm going to kidnap you?"

This time she faced him, her eyes giving no quarter. "Do princes still do that sort of thing here?"

For a moment Eric held her gaze, his own eyes suspiciously bright. Then he turned to the road again. "Not in the last hundred years or so. We just ply our women with wine and take them on the royal yacht."

Casey took a look around at the close-packed mountain peaks and laughed. "Yacht?"

"The French are nice enough to let us use the Mediterranean."

"Of course."

Just when she was sure they were heading into Italy, Casey noted that Eric was slowing for a side road. Not just a side road, one with another elaborate guard box. Obviously not the driveway to the local budget motel.

"The palace," he allowed, nodding and waving to the guard as the gentleman bowed in return. "It's actually the old hunting lodge, but we find it a lot more comfortable than the traditional castle that was built in the twelfth century. We let the tourists have that one."

They wound their way along a wide road that cut into a forest of the hugest, most stately trees Casey had ever seen. Every so often, for the next quarter of a mile, she could catch a glimpse of gables and old stone. But it wasn't until they made the final turn into the circular drive in front of the palace that she saw the whole building.

"Hunting lodge?" she asked, her eyes as wide as her mouth. "Who did you put up here, the Allied forces?"

The trees parted to reveal scrupulously maintained lawns that gently rose to the estate, a huge old building of high shingled roofs and old oak beams. Stone walls held a succession of tall, sparkling windows that reflected the lawns from the jumble of wings that made up the great building. It even had a turret or two.

The impression Casey got was of genteel age, of grace and loving care. The immense windows marched down each wall in lovely geometrics. The steps up from the driveway led to a great double door of heavy carved oak, crowned by a complicated crest carved in marble. Just the sight of it gave her the most intriguing feeling of belonging.

"It's not much," Eric said, grinning as he pulled the car to a stop before the great stairs, "but we call it home."

Casey couldn't help but shake her head with a rueful smile. "It's just a pity the conditions some people have to endure."

His laughter was delighted. "Shall we?"

When Eric helped her out of the car, Casey noticed a ring on his right hand, a heavy, ornate gold signet ring that had undoubtedly been passed from generation to generation. It made her envious. He had everything his heritage entitled him to. She had a couple of bitter old aunts and the memory of once having seen the woman who claimed she was Anastasia. Oh, well, not much she could do about it except enjoy every minute she spent under this exalted roof and then report back to Sandra when she resurrected the little red car.

Eric handed her up the steps before him as a silent groom appeared from somewhere and took the Bronco away. Casey half expected him to sweep the cobblestones behind them. When they reached the door, it magically opened, another liveried servant bowing and smiling as he passed them on.

"Rolph," Eric said, easing Casey along when she slowed, "is Her Majesty the queen available for visitors?"

"I shall check for you, Your Highness. Refreshments?"

He stole a look at Casey, who was rubbernecking the paintings on the walls with undisguised avarice. After a moment he nodded. "Yes, I believe they will be needed. In the Great Hall, if you please."

Rolph dispatched a discreetly questioning look, but bowed and moved away. Casey was still trying to take in the extent of the entryway.

Train stations were smaller. The walls extended up some thirty feet, decorated with what looked suspiciously like old masters and terminating in a high, vaulted ceiling that some brave painter had gotten his hands on. It was all light and froth, cherubs and swirling gold banners swimming around a vault of milky white. The floors were of pristinely kept white tile, and the effect was one of immense space, the inside of the building mirroring the image given by the outside. Quiet, understated grace and wealth. No need for ostentation here. It only made her want to see more.

"Like your decorator," she finally managed, casting a sidelong glance over to where Eric was enjoying her reaction.

"Moritania might not be big—" he bowed a little in acknowledgment "—but it is a country rife with good taste. I'd like to show you something, if you don't mind."

"The only thing you could show me to beat this would be the Sistine chapel."

Walking to the right side of the hall, Eric opened a great oak door. Casey walked past him into an even more impressive room. It was long, with six matched sets of crystal chandeliers and floor-to-ceiling windows that reflected in the mirrors along the opposite wall.

"Been to Versailles, had they?" she breathed, coming to a stop.

Eric wouldn't let her. Instead, he took her by the elbow and gently propelled her down the parquet flooring. "I'm sure you don't know," he was saying, "but my brother just died recently...."

Casey immediately turned to him. "Oh, I'm sorry. I didn't."

He nodded with a sad little smile. "He was much older than I, and his heart was bad. The upshot of it is that next week his daughter, my niece, will become the new queen of Moritania. She is his only child, and his wife is also dead."

Casey had no idea where the conversation was leading. He seemed so reluctant to tell her that she knew it was something important to him. She couldn't think of anything more to do but nod.

Then he stopped walking. Turning to her, he took hold of both of her arms, his eyes trying to communicate something of import. They had softened. Casey felt even more confused.

"What, Eric?"

"The portrait here at the end of the Great Hall has just gone up. It is a painting of the next queen of Moritania, Her Royal Highness the Crown Princess Cassandra."

He turned her to face the painting. Casey's jaw dropped. Looking back at her from the canvas was a woman with delicate features, a gently molded face with deep, wide-set hazel eyes and a small, straight nose. A small mouth curved just at the ends as if she was amusing herself immensely with a private joke. Diamonds and rubies glittered in her mane of tawny hair, thick and styled sleekly away from tiny ears where teardrop earrings hung.

Casey turned to Eric and then back to the picture and then back to Eric again, unable to speak. Then she turned once again to the portrait and finally admitted what he'd been trying to prepare her for. She was staring at a portrait of herself.

"And here I thought losing the car was going to be the high point of my day."

Two

———

Behind Casey, Eric chuckled. "Pretty impressive, don't you think?"

Casey tilted her head to the side, trying her best to be objective. She'd never seen herself in satin and jewels before, and to be frank, it was an image she didn't mind. That stray Romanov blood peeking through, she guessed.

"She's prettier than I am," she finally ventured.

"Don't believe it," he told her. "She just has different priorities."

Casey had to grin, turning her head again. "And a great house."

She was about to ask about the rest of the puzzle when she was interrupted by an imperious voice coming from the doorway. It echoed through the room like the memory of an earlier century.

"My dear Cassandra, there you are. Aren't you quite ashamed of yourself for running off?"

Casey turned to see an elderly woman considering her with stern eyes. Elderly, maybe, but definitely unbowed. The woman before her stood ramrod-straight, as if refusing to allow herself to be overtaken by age. Her iron-gray hair was meticulously groomed, her designer suit impeccable and attractive.

Casey had an image of the woman in high-necked satin and lace and a set of crown jewels and knew she was meeting somebody's queen.

Her Brooklyn upbringing and Irish blood responded.

"Mortified," she said, nodding easily. Maybe she'd have been more intimidated if the combination of her bloodlines hadn't destroyed her fear of titles. The Russians had them and couldn't use them, and the Irish had no use for them at all.

Eric stifled another grin as he stepped in, walking briskly over to his mother. With a sidelong glance, he begged Casey to follow. She did, her curiosity overwhelming even her rebellious nature.

"And well you should," the woman said, nodding back. "To take Eric away from his duties is—"

"A pleasure, Mother." He smiled, bending just a little to kiss her cheek. "I was merely murdering innocent birds with the bank's new board of directors."

She continued to glare, although her eyes softened suspiciously when they came into contact with her second son. Casey recognized the look. It had been the only way her own grandmother had been able to display affection. Harder to spot and more precious when given. Must have been part of that imperial training.

"This is not Cassandra, Mother," Eric continued, his hand on his mother's arm.

His mother's glare grew even more impatient. "Don't be impertinent, Eric. I, for one, am tired of your niece's little games."

"No more than I am," he assured her. "But this young lady is not she. Introduce yourself," he suggested, turning to Casey.

Casey stepped forward, knowing better than to hold out a hand. "My name's Casey Phillips, ma'am. I'm from Brooklyn, and my car broke down outside the border crossing. Eri— your son was kind enough to give me a lift to call for help."

Eric turned to Casey for the rest of the introduction. "Casey, may I present my mother, Her Royal Highness Marta, dowager queen of Moritania."

The queen squinted at her, then peered, her eyes like a wary hawk's. "Brooklyn," she snapped.

Casey nodded. "New York. America. I'm here on vacation. It's, um, a pleasure to meet you, ma'am."

For a long moment, nothing else was said. The three of them stood in a kind of tense tableau as Eric's mother studied Casey at her own leisure.

Behind them, another servant edged through the door.

"Shall I serve here, Your Highness?" he asked diffidently.

The queen never turned, never took her eyes from Casey. "In the Rose Room, Gustave."

Gustave bowed and backed out.

"The eyes . . ." she finally said slowly. "They're quite different." She didn't say exactly how. "And Cassandra would never let herself be seen in such a getup."

Casey couldn't help a heartfelt scowl. So much for being invited for the weekend. The rest of her wardrobe wasn't a whole lot different.

Eric intervened. "Cassandra has a well-documented weakness for recognizable labels."

Hers was recognizable, Casey thought with a private grin. Everybody in *her* neighborhood knew who J. C. Penney was.

"You'll join us for some tea, young lady," the queen said. Not so much an invitation as an order, but the matter was moot for a queen. Who would ever think to turn her down? Just for a moment, Casey was tempted to decline, just to see what the old lady would do, but she was too curious to walk away right now. She wanted to learn about this mysterious twin of hers. And, she had to admit, she wanted to spend just a little more time studying the cool blue of Eric's eyes.

"Yes." She nodded. "Thank you."

Eric flashed her a smile of wry gratitude before ushering his mother out before him.

The Rose Room wasn't rose. It was more an eggshell white, with tapestries for decoration and a harp in the corner. Furniture somebody had actually sat on in the seventeenth century and hidden during revolutions and wars filled more parquet flooring, which was covered with a plush Oriental carpet in maroons and beiges.

The queen settled herself on a frail little love seat and motioned Casey to an adjoining wing chair. With the cosy marble fireplace next to them, it was quite an intimate little corner of a huge palace. Casey had the feeling that the queen had assembled it this way.

"Do you play the harp, ma'am?" Casey asked, watching as the servant assembled tea from a trolley behind the queen. Eric pulled up a satin-covered chair and sat alongside his mother.

"Heavens, no," the woman said. "My daughter did, though. Quite well."

Did. And there was a shadow in the stern blue eyes. Eric's family went young, it seemed.

"How did you come to visit Moritania?" she asked, accepting a cup and spoon from the servant.

Casey stole a look at Eric, but he was receiving his own cup. Royalty first, it seemed.

"Well, I won a trip to Europe and saw Moritania was near one of the areas where I was staying. I'd heard about the country from my grandfather as a child. He said that his grandfather came from here."

"Indeed. What was his name?"

Casey accepted her own cup and spooned in a healthy dollop of sugar. No artificial sweeteners around here. "Phillips."

The royal head came up a bit. "Phillips? That is not in the least Moritanian."

"I know. We figured he was renamed by one of the guys at Immigration who couldn't pronounce his real name. Happened all the time back then."

"He must have known the royal family," Eric said, smiling gently.

His mother dispatched another glare. "What trade did the gentleman practice in Moritania?"

Taking a careful sip from the fragile bone-china cup, Casey shrugged just as delicately. "I really don't know. We don't know much at all about him before he hit the shores."

The royal eyebrow arched. "Indeed. Do you know what trade he practiced once he did . . . hit the shores?"

Both Casey and Eric grinned at that. "Yes, ma'am. He was a gentleman's gentleman."

This time Eric's eyebrow lifted, his mouth struggling with an amused little grin. "It was probably his family's trade here, then. Which supports my supposition."

"Eric, really," the queen scolded him, her attention focused demurely on her tea.

It took Casey a couple of minutes to follow his line of reasoning. When she did, her head turned a little, wishing that from where she sat she could still see the portrait of the new queen of Moritania far down the palace hallway.

"You mean I have another royal line in me?" she demanded, not at all sure whether what she felt was pleasure or consternation.

"It's quite possible," Eric allowed. "It's not unheard-of for servant to have ended up founding a dynasty on the wrong side of the blanket."

She nodded pensively. "God knows half the American claim to royal heritage originated that way."

"Mine, too," he said, grinning with even more amusement. His mother was doing her best to ignore him.

Casey almost dropped her cup. "Excuse me?"

Eric laughed, and Casey felt it deep in her chest like a flutter. "My own great-grandfather was the illegitimate son of the king. We ended up with the throne when the old guy ran out of legitimate issue during a rather inconvenient war. My ancestor filled the gap so well that he was invited by the country to make it official."

Casey grinned, too, sharing not only the joke but the feeling of kinship with the handsome prince. "How intriguing. Must make for a great family crest."

She'd forgotten the queen. An outraged little cough brought her abruptly back.

Eric laughed again. "You can't intimidate this girl, Mother," he warned the old woman. "She's also a Romanov. And you know how those Russians are."

Casey wanted to tell them that it wasn't the Russian blood they should consider but the Irish, but she didn't get a chance. A new minion entered, wearing something akin to a morning coat, and bowed, waiting to be heard.

"Yes, Werner?" the queen asked without turning. He stood behind her, his anxious bureaucrat's eyes turned toward the prince instead. The man didn't seem comfortable meeting people's eyes. His own were poised somewhere about the third button on Eric's shirt.

"I beg your pardon, Your Highness." He spoke up in an appropriately hushed voice that made Casey think of funeral homes. "It is the princess. She is expected at the opening of the new children's hospital She is . . . um, late."

Casey could see the gentleman flinch, waiting for some kind of outburst. When it didn't come, his anxious stare turned toward her instead. She watched him with no more than curiosity as his eyes swept her attire and strayed close to her face. She had the most irrational desire to check her neck for dirt.

"She wasn't there?" Eric demanded, checking the slim gold watch on his wrist.

Werner allowed his gaze to swing to the prince before returning to Casey. "If you'll pardon my saying so, Your Highness..."

This time Eric comprehended the hesitation. "Oh, Werner, this is not the princess. This is Miss Casey Phillips from the United States. Quite a resemblance, don't you think?"

The gentleman's eyes grew very large as he gave a crisp bow, unwilling or unable by training to allow verbal surprise or doubt. "Quite, Your Highness. Welcome to Moritania, Miss Phillips."

He couldn't take his eyes off her. By now Casey was getting used to it. "My pleasure, Mr. Werner." Somehow, with the twang of Brooklyn in her speech, the stilted address sounded slightly ludicrous.

"And the princess..." Werner went on, once more turning to the prince for guidance.

"Should be soundly spanked," Eric answered absently, once again considering his watch. "When was she last seen?"

"Her maid helped her dress this morning, Your Highness. She then left the grounds in the Jaguar."

"That was five hours ago. What about her security?"

"Followed behind. They have not seen fit to report in."

Eric nodded briskly. "Get in touch with them. Have them dispatch the princess to the opening or present themselves up for dismissal."

"Eric..." the queen admonished quietly.

Eric acquiesced to his mother. "I know it's not their fault, Mother. But I, for one, am tired of baby-sitting the next queen of Moritania like a student on holiday."

Before leaving, Werner dispatched one more little nudge. "Also, Your Majesty has an appointment with the arts council."

The queen set her cup down with a brisk nod and got to her feet. "So I do, Werner." Turning, she took in Casey with a regal eye. "We hope you enjoy the rest of your visit to Moritania, Miss Phillips. Eric, please don't forget the benefit this evening."

Eric came to his feet, which brought Casey to hers. She figured if the prince got up it was a sure bet the commoner was supposed to, also.

"Of course, dear," he was saying. "Once we nab Cassandra, we won't let her out of our collective sights. Will we, Werner?"

Werner executed another of those bows. "No, Your Highness."

Werner made his exit only after the queen did. Which left the cosy little room to Casey and Eric. She didn't feel quite disposed to leave yet. Neither, it seemed, did Eric.

"More tea?" he asked with an intimate little smile playing across his lips.

"More information?" she countered with a matching grin.

"Our pleasure," he nodded, playing on the royal "we" his mother had invoked.

"Would it be an imposition to see a few more rooms?" she asked diffidently. "I mean, considering that my family line was evidently founded somewhere in one of them."

Eric laughed as he reached around and lifted the silver teapot to serve. "We'll bring our cups along. A frightful breach of protocol, but what can one expect from Americans, after all?"

"Just a bunch of cheeky colonials," Casey countered, accepting her cup from him. His hands were strong, their touch electric. She suddenly found herself staring down at them as if expecting them to give off sparks.

Eric, on the other hand, found his eyes on her face—on the softer lines of her eyes, the broader smile lines and more expressive mouth. If Cassandra had had the personality to craft that face, she could have been the most popular queen in Moritanian history, instead of merely its most notorious fashion plate. He ushered Casey out of the room, trying to figure out a way to see more of her before she had to go home.

Werner caught up with them in the game room. Game meaning dead animals rather than video. Casey wasn't terribly fond of all the beady stares and antlers that crowded the paneled walls. She'd seen *Bambi* one too many times to be comfortable with the deer, and preferred her bears stamping out forest fires. Eric traced the history of the room from the man who might well have been their common ancestor in the time of Louis XIV, his cultured tones invoking the privileged reminiscences of royalty.

"If it weren't for the present government," he was saying, "you could wander through the palace at St. Petersburg and tell the same kinds of stories."

Casey found herself shrugging, her attention more on his elegant features than the stories. "I'm afraid that once you've grown up without the exposure it's not the same. In my neighborhood, the kids would rather spend their time in a video arcade."

Eric turned, the afternoon light from the leaded windows soft on his face. "And you?"

Casey grinned. "I was video game champ for two months running."

"Video games," he mused, the look in his eyes too intense for the tenor of their talk. "I'll have to try them someday."

She felt the breath escape from her lungs. "Cheaper than stuffing bears."

For a second she saw the surprise in Eric's eyes. It still threw him off balance when someone spoke frankly to him. Then he dissolved into laughter. With an unconscious intimacy, he took hold of her arm and leaned over to drop a kiss on her forehead.

"I must stop in Brooklyn next time I fly into Kennedy Airport," he promised. "I've missed the most wonderful place in America."

Casey came to a shuddering halt at his touch, at the soft brush of his lips against her skin. It was as if she'd been without sustenance for a very long time and had just realized it. Damn, she thought with a growing sense of loss, why couldn't I pick a good boy from Brooklyn to succumb to? I've got to be an idiot and turn to water for a prince in a foreign country. Nothing like reaching for the attainable.

"Call me anytime," she heard herself saying. "The number's in the book." Then she smiled involuntarily, her wry wit saving her. "Under Displaced Royalty."

His eyes sparkled with delight. "With pleasure."

"Tell me something," she said a moment later, looking down the shadowy length of the great room. "Do you mind being third?" Neither seemed to notice that Eric had yet to recover his hand.

"Third?"

Casey nodded, her gaze straying to him, then away. "Do you mind not getting the throne? I know my nana said that her grandfather never quite got over it himself. He very much wanted to be Czar."

Taking a sip of his tea, Eric nodded thoughtfully. "Ah, yes. I can imagine. Actually, I'm quite content. Cassandra was born to nod and wave. I was born to banking, and that is where I am most needed. I don't begrudge her her notoriety in the least.''

''Your Highness.''

Eric turned, his hand still firmly on Casey's arm. Werner was back, looking more anxious than ever. He still couldn't seem to make eye contact.

''Yes, Werner?'' Eric's tone wasn't quite as easygoing as before. Casey didn't realize that it had everything to do with her.

''Your Highness, I thought you would want to be apprised. When we tried to raise the security team, they failed to respond. Their auto has just been located west of Braz.''

Eric stiffened, his grip on Casey tightening. ''And the princess?''

Werner looked as if he wanted to dig a hole through the rug and hide. ''Missing, Your Highness. A search is being mounted.''

''You're sure it's not just another one of her . . . tests?''

''It is always possible.'' The little man looked positively sick. ''But there was blood.''

Casey heard a stifled groan. Eric began to slowly shake his head. ''The economic conference begins tomorrow. The coronation is next week. My God.''

''Yes, Your Highness.''

Without hesitation, Eric snapped into action. ''Not a word to the press. If the guard so much as sneezes at the wrong moment, heads will be on the block. I'll call the bank and tell them that I will be conducting business from the palace for the next few days to accommodate the ministers. Get hold of General Mueller. I wish to speak to him personally. Any unusual communications to the palace are to be funneled through me. Understood?''

Werner snapped off another bow. ''Your Highness.'' Then he whirled around and left.

''Damn her!'' Eric snarled, finally letting go. He began to pace, the filtered sunlight glinting in the rich depths of his hair as he passed the windows. Casey had the eerie feeling that the animals on the wall were watching him with patient eyes. We've seen it all before, they were saying.

''You have enough to do,'' she said hesitantly, hating the sound of her words. ''I'll get on back to the hotel.'' It didn't occur to her yet that she still didn't have a car.

The sound of her voice brought Eric around. His eyes, those glacier-blue lights, fixed on her, studying her with an intensity that was disconcerting. They held her pinned to the spot and unable to think of anything redeeming to say.

"Would you mind waiting a bit?" he asked, his own voice colored by the thoughts whirling in his mind. The plans, the recriminations.

Casey shook her head, unsure and unsettled by the sharp consideration he leveled on her. "Of course not. If it's more convenient . . . I just thought that you'd want to see to the princess."

"I'd like to *thrash* the princess," he snapped hotly, then stopped, surprised that he'd voiced the reaction to an outsider. Only the royal family and loyal servants knew what trouble the Crown Princess Cassandra was. What surprised Eric more was that he felt comfortable elaborating. "If it weren't for Cassandra's insistence on playing little games with her country, this wouldn't have happened. She has the damndest idea that it's still the sixteenth century and she can act accordingly."

"You alluded to that before, I think," Casey said quietly. "When we first met. What does she do?"

He shrugged, pacing again. "She does a little disappearing act sometimes, dragging her security forces off on a merry chase to see if they can find her. Or she shows up unannounced to see if the citizens are following the latest law or whether they appreciate her station. She has most of the people of Braz terrorized."

"But is royalty really that much in control here?"

He nodded with rueful eyes. "Until she gets through with it, I'm sure. Moritania has always gotten along quite well with its royal family, and we with the country. With a place this size, if we didn't, we wouldn't have lasted a generation. She does have more control than most modern monarchs. Or she will next week when she's crowned." His eyes strayed toward the door through which Werner had disappeared, and his jaw tightened. "*If* she's crowned, that is."

"And if she's not?"

"The country is thrown into a fine mess of an economic crisis. The constitution demands that unless a new sovereign is crowned within twenty days of the death of the previous one, all legislation must be resubmitted for evaluation. Usually that gives us plenty of time. With the Sunday coronation, we had five days' leeway."

"It's so important?"

He stopped, leveling those eyes on her once more. "For a country that makes more money than Switzerland in banking, yes, I'd say it is. Our biggest selling point is stability. We haven't had a major disruption in government in nearly three hundred years."

Casey nodded, a bit numbly. "Yes," she agreed, wondering how she never knew that. "I guess it does."

He paced a few more times, then swung around on her, his eyes even brighter. "Would you mind coming along while I make some phone calls?"

"Sure. And if you need any help, let me know." She couldn't help but grin. "I'm the best secretary in midtown Manhattan."

Eric took her by the arm and turned her toward the door. "Casey, you may just have a deal, as you Americans say."

Casey watched in rapt silence as Eric conducted his business. Werner had already prepared what must have been the prince's study, a room of warm woods and hunter greens, for their arrival. Once there, Eric procured another pot of tea and some sandwiches and located the bank officers and the head of the Moritanian Guard.

The country didn't have an army per se. As in Switzerland, the entire male population was considered part of the reserve forces in the event of a war. The guard was simply the long arm of the law, as it were, protecting the palace and any foreign dignitaries working in Moritania and investigating the touchier problems that the police didn't quite know how to handle.

Casey heard Eric swear the general to secrecy in his search and then demand constant updates. She had the most intriguing feeling that she had tripped right into the plot of a thriller, except that everybody looked more exasperated than upset. She guessed that if it had been England the chances of a serious problem would have been a lot higher.

Then the bank business arrived, and Eric moved to that without hesitation, working the computer as a pianist would his keyboard. Casey was duly impressed. It seemed that very little could ruffle the man. He didn't so much as sweat as the reports came in from the field that the princess could not be found. Nor did he loosen his tie nor run his hands through his hair when the bank called to say that the representatives from the other countries were beginning to arrive for the conference and expected to see him that night at the benefit, an evening of opera and dinner at the royal opera house in Braz.

As the afternoon began to wear on, he did begin to pace, his long stride eating up yet another exquisite old Oriental rug and the hardwood floor beneath. Casey sat on the window seat edging the big bay window behind his desk and watched him, sipping quietly at her tea and wondering what she could do to help.

"The general is on line two, Your Highness," Werner announced.

"Will you complete the transaction with the bank for me, Werner?" Eric asked, going from computer to phone.

Werner, loaded down with other reports that were due for the courier, hesitated.

Casey sat down her cup and stood. "Go on, Werner," she said, smiling, "I'll do it."

He dispatched a look that she was sure wasn't in his guide to subordinates' manners, but when Eric waved him on, he went. Casey sat down at the desk and took a moment to study the figures scrawled on the pad by the screen. Eric turned to the phone, his fingers still pointing out different things to her as he greeted the general. She filled in the blanks with practiced fingers.

"Found?" Eric snapped, his attention suddenly on the phone conversation. "Where were they?"

Casey looked up, then went back to her work. Eric had forgotten her. Then she heard a sharp intake of breath and forgot the bank completely.

Eric stood alongside her, grasping the phone as if it were his last handhold on the Eiger, his eyes glittering. She could see the muscles jump along the line of his jaw as he received the news.

"Well," he finally answered. "It's her own damn fault. Of course, we must keep a tight rein on the information. Go right ahead with your investigation—" his eyes strayed to Casey, a new introspection in them "—I'll take care of the other. No matter what, no one else must know that this is what we are about, do you understand?"

He must have received the answer he'd anticipated, because he nodded rather sharply. "Keep me informed."

It was a moment after he hung up before Casey finally gathered the nerve to speak up. "I think all the numbers are in the right spaces, if you'd like to check. I can send it off then."

Eric's head snapped up. He stared at her as if surprised that she was still there.

"Is there anything else I can do?" she asked.

He smiled then, the light in his eyes brightening with a rueful wryness. "That isn't a question you should ask lightly just now."

"Oh?" She felt her heart thud oddly and then chastised herself for it. She was getting far too comfortable in this world of antiques and titles. It was high time to get back to her broken car and her off-the-rack clothes.

But Eric wasn't quite finished with her. Quickly scanning the screen, he punched the information on to the bank and drew her to her feet.

"I need a favor."

Then he led her back to the window seat and sat down beside her. "We have a problem," he began, his eyes still rueful. Casey couldn't believe that he still looked as if he'd just stepped from a fine restaurant. There had to have been more than his share of stress in that last call. She'd seen its impact. He could at least have had the decency to be rumpled by it.

She couldn't help but smile at him. "I also type and take shorthand. I do not get coffee, though."

His smile widened. Once again he had taken hold of her and didn't think to let go. She didn't think to tell him. He held her hand this time, and the warmth of his hand around hers was far too enticing.

"I'm afraid I had something a little more complicated than that in mind, Casey." He took a moment's glance at the mountains that climbed from beyond the window before returning to her. "How would you like to go to the opera?"

"The what?"

"The opera. Gounod's *Faust*. Then a formal dinner."

She shook her head. "Eric, I'm not exactly sure what you're driving at, but your mother pretty much said it all. The getup I'm in is about as got-up as I get. I'm unfit for formal dinners *or* the opera. But thanks, anyway."

Idiot, she thought. You should have said, sure, I'll go. After all, look what Scarlett O'Hara did with just the drapes. Casey's rejection ate at her stomach like a knife.

Even so, Eric's smile refused to falter. "Let me complete my proposal first...."

She laughed with nervous energy. "Never say proposal to a girl from Brooklyn."

"Idea, then." He smiled. "Problem. I just finished speaking to the general, and the news was not all good. The security guards were found, unscathed except for nosebleeds. The princess was not."

Casey's smile froze. "What do they think?"

"No thinking necessary. They found a note. From a dissident group. The princess was kidnapped."

Casey couldn't help her own glance out to the majestic scenery, the closest she'd ever been to heaven. "You have dissidents here?" she demanded instinctively. It seemed so out of place.

Eric found himself smiling again. "My dear Casey, you can't organize a bridge club without dissidents, much less a country. These are a club of rather virulent socialists. They feel the monarchy must be banned."

"Socialists," she echoed rather stupidly.

He shrugged. "In a country with no unemployment, it is a bit difficult to comprehend. At any rate, they promise the princess will be safe if we free some of their friends in neighboring countries and proclaim to the world that a socialist government will be set up instead of Cassandra being crowned." His smile returned again. "Unfortunately, the way Cassandra has been behaving, I can hardly blame them."

"You don't seem terribly worried."

"Neither did the general. He knows these groups better than I, and he says that the princess is as good as rescued. The problem, of course, is that with the economic conference beginning tomorrow, we cannot allow word of this to leak out."

"Stability and all...." Casey nodded, getting her first glimmer of what Eric had in mind. Her eyes widened, her mouth dropped, and she took a look around the room.

"The opera?" she repeated slowly, her stomach and heart all of a sudden crowding her throat.

"If you wouldn't mind."

"But, Eric," she protested instinctively, "it couldn't possibly work. Listen to me. I sound like Rocky, not the future queen of Moritania. Me pose as Cassandra? Not even Hollywood would buy something that weird!"

"We'll say you lost your voice. You can nod and wave, can't you?"

She showed him.

He nodded briskly. "Excellent. We'll fit you in one of Cassandra's dresses, and I will escort you. No one will know."

Her eyes grew bigger. "You're nuts."

He shook his head without noticeable agitation. "Merely rather desperate."

"I don't know a salad fork from a tuning fork! What if I butter my bread in the soup bowl or fall asleep at the opera?"

"Cassandra has been known to do worse. All you have to do to create the correct impression is flirt shamelessly with everyone under the age of eighty."

Casey groaned. "I wouldn't know how to flirt if I saw a demonstration on videotape."

She didn't notice that his smile was a wry one. "I believe you greatly underestimate yourself." How could he begin to explain to her that her fresh exuberance was far more enticing than Cassandra's calculated cunning could ever be?

"Oh," he added, certain that he had a victory. "One more thing. You must act properly bored with Rudolph Van Dorn, Baron of Austerlitz."

Casey looked up, anticipating impending doom. "Who's he?"

Eric smiled. "Your fiancé."

She closed her eyes, capitulating. "Forget what I said. You're not the one who's nuts. I am." The breath she took to gather courage was a tremulous one. "I think I'm going to do it."

Three

Do I like the opera?"

"You detest it."

"Thank God." Casey reached out hesitantly to pick a long white kid glove from the bureau where it was laid out for her. Holding it as if it was a dead mouse, she turned back to Eric. "I was afraid I was going to have to say something obscene like 'My dear, don't you just adore the mezzo?' I'd rather slit my throat."

Eric's smile was delighted. "After an evening of *Faust*, you may end up doing just that."

"How long do I have to get ready?"

He checked his watch again. "About two hours."

She nodded, her eyes back on the royal-blue satin gown that lay spread out before her. "It might take just about that long." Her bravado briefly giving out, she turned to him, the glove following like a ruffled wind sock. "Oh, Eric, I really don't think this is going to work. I'm going to fall off my heels or insult a world leader or something. Tell them that Cassandra is indisposed."

With a hand on each arm, Eric faced down her rising panic with gentling eyes. "You'll be marvelous. Just follow my lead and we won't have any problems at all. If you don't make an appearance tonight, there won't be any way to fight the kidnapper's propaganda when it hits the media. We have to try."

"But I don't *look* like her!"

He reached up to brush an errant strand of hair from her forehead. "You don't dress like her, that's all. And with Maria's help, no one will ever know the difference. Trust me, Cassandra. No one but us will know."

She shook her head, her eyes wide. "Both of us are nuts."

"Possibly." He nodded, and Casey had the unsettling impression for a moment that he wasn't talking about their upcoming escapade. "But it's the only idea I could come up with on short notice. Please don't back out on me now."

She found herself ensnared within the clear assurance of his eyes. She'd never known anyone like him. He was so filled with purpose and confidence, so sure of them both that she felt helpless to do anything but be pulled along in his wake. Those eyes were sapping her panic again, soothing her and exciting her all at once.

"I wish I were back at the hotel," she whined with a heartfelt scowl, dropping the glove back in its place.

The next instant her head popped up and her mouth dropped. "Oh, my God. The hotel. Eric, Sandra was expecting me to get back an hour ago. What am I going to do?"

This was obviously news he hadn't anticipated. "Sandra who?"

"My friend. She and I have been traveling together. We were out late last night at a *hofbrauhaus* and she didn't want to see Moritania. She's waiting back at the hotel for me and the car so we can drive on to Switzerland tonight."

Eric let go of her for a moment, turning away to consider the new wrinkle in the plan. It didn't take him long. Before Casey could think up eight or nine arguments against not returning for Sandra, he turned back to her with a sly smile.

"Do you think she'd mind a short stay at the palace instead? I'm afraid she can't go along tonight, but Maria can see to her needs while we're out."

Casey almost laughed out loud. "Where's a phone? I'll call her."

Casey was sure that Sandra would still be expecting some kind of punch line when the chauffeured limousine came by to pick up her and the luggage, but at least it was all settled. She turned away from the short, rather disjointed phone conversation to continue transforming the ugly duckling into some semblance of a swan.

Eric presented a small, squat woman with rather heavy features and a sweet smile. "This is Maria. She is the Princess Cassandra's personal maid, and has been apprised of the situation. Outside of the military, no one but Maria, Werner and myself knows of your real identity. Of course, that's allowing for the fact that by morning every one of the servants will undoubtedly have figured it out. But they're unquestionably loyal. I hope this will be contained."

Casey wasn't sure Eric saw the brief scowl that crossed Maria's eyes. It seemed that princes didn't always appreciate their staff's loyalty as much as they thought.

"I'd put my life in Maria's hands before I'd put it in the general's," Casey said honestly, and was rewarded with the beginnings of a smile. "Now then, Your Highness," Casey said with an air of finality, "don't you have some dressing to do yourself?"

Eric smiled, a brief shadow over his eyes the only betrayal of his task ahead. Casey wanted very much to tell him it was going to be all right. She had a feeling that one didn't do that in front of the maid. Oh well, there was a lot to learn.

"Everything's going to be all right," she said anyway, as much for herself as for him.

His smile brightened as he bent to drop another kiss on her forehead, this one of gratitude. "You're right, of course. It's a brilliant plan. I only hope Cassandra behaves herself until we manage to get her free."

Maria's eyes rolled ever so slightly behind the prince's back, and Casey found herself stifling a giggle. "See you in an hour or so, Eric," she said, edging him out the door.

Then she turned back to the maid and a room that looked like one giant pink satin ruffle. Pink flowered wallpaper, pink canopied bed, pink ruffled tablecloths and dust ruffles on every stick of furniture in the room. It made Casey think of an exploded bottle of gooey pink stomach medicine.

"Your bath is drawn, Your Highness." Maria offered with a diffident bow. "Do you require assistance dressing?"

Casey gave her a wry smile. "Not since I've been three, thanks. Do you have to call me Your Highness?"

The little maid nodded. "Yes, ma'am. The prince insisted."

Casey nodded back, her eyes still wandering over the pink wasteland. Cassandra truly didn't have her tastes, and that was a fact. "Okay. Well, Maria, pull up a chair or something. I'm going to have to wash my hair before I do anything else. Half the topsoil of Austria is in it."

"Do you—?"

"No. I do that myself, too."

An hour later, Casey realized that what she couldn't do herself was manage to get her hair to look anything like Cassandra's. Along with all the pink was a gaggle of pictures of the princess, riding her horses, playing tennis, sailing the yacht, encrusted with family jewels at some soiree. In every one, her hair was sleek and leonine-looking. Not a stray hair to be found, even in the wind. Casey couldn't imagine how that could ever be done, if her hair was anything like Casey's.

For all the brushing, all the twisting and pinning and curling, her hair simply wouldn't behave. She stared briefly at the brush in her hand as if that were the traitor, and let out a healthy shriek of frustration, coming inches from hurling the thing at the mirror.

Maria saved mirror and brush.

"If you'll allow me, Your Highness. This is my responsibility always. It becomes easier to do if you put on the crown first."

Casey looked up. "The crown?" Her voice sounded very small.

"Yes, Your Highness. The dowager queen's tiara tonight, if I am correct. Diamonds and sapphires."

She was correct. By the time Sandra was ushered into the room thirty minutes later, Casey stood tall and regal in the blue satin gown, the tiara in place within the sleek chignon, the matching necklace and bracelet already donned. Casey didn't want to so much as move, sure that at least one clasp was faulty. She was just pulling up the white kid gloves when her friend arrived.

"Oh, I'm sorry. This must be—"

The tall brunette stopped in her tracks, looking from Casey to Maria and back before she could manage another word.

"Casey?"

Casey grinned brightly, turning so that the full satin skirt whispered around her. "None other. Like it?"

But Sandra hadn't taken it in. "Casey?"

"No," Casey said, scowling. "Catherine the Great. Sit down before you fall down, Sandy. Maria, this is my friend Sandra Vitale. Sandy, my new friend Maria."

Maria dropped a quick curtsy. "A pleasure, *fraülein*."

Sandy stared a little more. "Wanna tell me what's going on?"

"Did you like the ride?"

She nodded.

"If you liked the car," Casey said, grinning with an energy born of equal parts exhilaration and terror, "you'll love the prince."

As if called once again just by her words, Eric appeared in the doorway, attired in white tie and tails. Casey's knees almost gave out at the sight of him.

Sandra wheeled around just as he arrived, and her mouth dropped again. "Who are you?"

He smiled, and Sandra went dumb. "You must be Sandra. Welcome to Moritania. Has Casey explained the situation to you yet?"

Sandra couldn't even seem to draw breath.

"Don't mind her," Casey advised him. "She startles easily. Besides, I haven't had a chance to fill her in yet."

Eric nodded pleasantly. "Well, we only have about ten minutes before the car comes around. And you and I have much to discuss, Casey."

She nodded back, a sudden tightness in her chest. Eric looked as if he'd stepped out of the pages of a men's magazine. Casey had always liked formal wear on men. It added such an air of rakish elegance to them. But Eric, more elegant than anyone she'd ever seen, transcended the clothes. He moved gracefully in the sleekly cut clothes, filling them to breathtaking perfection. And she was going to be on his arm all night. Good thing she wasn't supposed to talk. She didn't think she was going to have the breath to anyway.

On his arm. Oh, Lord, she couldn't do this. She couldn't face those people and pretend she was somebody she wasn't. . . .

Maria spoke up with the assurance of her position. "Excuse me, Your Highness. The princess has her earrings to put on yet."

"Earrings?" Casey asked, despairing at the thought that she had yet more precious stones to safeguard.

"Princess?" Sandra squeaked. Then she did sit down abruptly in one of the pink chairs.

Maria was going to assist Casey in their insertion when she stopped. "Which, er, site, Your Highness?"

Casey's fingers went to her ears and the three holes she and Sandy had made for various earrings. Maria cast a baleful look over at Eric.

"See if you can find a set that covers the extras," he suggested. "Any more quaint American tortures you've inflicted upon yourself, Cassandra?"

Casey grinned. "I bite my nails to the quick, but that's what the gloves are for."

"Well, make certain that you stay right with me the entire evening so that I can continue to prompt you. There are simply too many customs and protocols that you aren't acquainted with to brief you accordingly. I don't suppose you speak German?" Her baleful look was answer enough. "French? Italian?"

"Fettucine Alfredo?"

Eric nodded fatalistically. Sandra's head had turned back and forth so often she looked as if she was at Wimbledon. Casey presented her ears for Maria's ministrations, the new tenor of the conversation churning in her stomach. Dress-up time was over. It was on to the ball, and she didn't speak German or Italian. She didn't know which fork to eat with or when to applaud at an opera. Or if you did at all.

When all was finished, Casey presented herself for inspection. Eric stood before her, his face composed in a studious frown, searching, she supposed, for errors. The terror of anticipation grew.

She was wrong. Eric was struggling to cover his true reaction. Casey did, indeed, look enough like Cassandra to fool just about everyone. The face, the hair, the elegant clothes, all were perfect. But once again Eric was struck by the difference. Casey's hazel eyes shone like a child's with pleasure at her accomplishment. Her whole face radiated a warmth he'd never known from her namesake, a fresh, infectious vitality. Even the great size of Casey's eyes, reflecting her stark terror at the sudden undertaking, was beguiling.

He wasn't at all sure whether anyone else would notice. But he did. It made him realize that he wasn't sure if he really wanted to rescue the real Cassandra. If he did, this one would have to leave and he would be left with the cool isolation of his life.

Trapping Casey's eyes with the sweet sky of his, Eric approached her. He took her gloved hand in his own and bent over it, brushing his lips over her knuckles. Casey felt the whisper of his touch all the way to her satin-clad toes and knew that her eyes had involuntarily widened even more. She knew, too, that Eric couldn't help but see her helpless fascination when he straightened and sought her gaze once again.

"Her Highness is especially beautiful tonight," he said softly, his voice excluding the other people in the room.

Casey's eyes were radiant. "We thank the prince for his kind words," she answered, only a modicum of humor in her breathless voice.

"I know it sounds trite, Casey," he said, his eyes darkening with sincerity, "but you are doing my country a great service. We will never be able to thank you enough."

She managed a reply over the lump in her throat. "It's kind of my country, too, isn't it?"

"There is one thing," he said, the expression in his eyes playful, his hand still holding hers. "The Princess Cassandra has never been afraid of anything in her life."

Casey found herself offering a tremulous smile. He'd caught her wondering whether there was any way she could keep from walking out that door. "Just do me a favor and remind me of that when somebody wonders why I'm not paying attention when they address me in Italian. Or French."

Eric's eyes praised her as his words couldn't. "Think we'll carry it off, Maria?" he asked, his hand firmly around Casey's now.

Maria crossed herself. "God willing, Your Highness."

He smiled. "Indeed. Well, my dear, this is one show that cannot begin without us. Shall we?"

Casey slipped her hand into the crook of his arm and swung out the door before she had the chance to back out. "See you later, Sandy. Maria will take care of you till we get back."

When the rustle of Casey's dress receded down the long hall, Maria walked up to the girl who was still seated in stunned silence. Sandy looked up at her helplessly.

"You come with me," Maria told her. "We get some tea and talk about what goes on in this crazy palace, *ja*?"

With a very weak smile, Sandy got herself off her chair and followed out the door. *"Ja."*

The royal opera house was situated on one of those winding streets in Braz, a great mammoth creature of white marble that reminded Casey a little of Sacré Coeur in Montmartre. The inside seemed to have been decorated by the same muralist who had done the palace. Here, his art was wasted on ceilings so high that the cherubim couldn't be told from the seraphim. The grand stairway was crimson-carpeted, and the furniture in the lobby was French and frilly.

Casey had barely made it in the front door before she almost gave herself away. Her head went straight up in the classic tourist position, her eyes threatening to pop at the opulence she was to enjoy that evening due to the benevolence of the Moritanian people. Eric caught her just in time. With his hand to the small of her back, he gave her a little nudge in the kidneys.

"You've seen this before," he whispered in her ear as everyone in the room was bowing their hellos. "And you find it quite boring."

Casey smiled dryly, her hand to her throat in a gesture that she hoped would excuse the odd movement. "Of course I do."

Her eyes were on all the people caught in their deep obeisance as she and Eric passed. It made her want to giggle. As a rule, people didn't bow to secretaries in Manhattan, and the fact that it was happening here struck her as a bit ludicrous. So did the host of eyes that couldn't manage to look her in the face. She was sure it wasn't her décolletage, since she didn't have any. Must be the temporary title. If Eric's hand hadn't been so firmly in place to administer reminders, she would have been more tempted to tell these people that it was impolite not to look someone in the eye.

They reached their box without Casey tripping over the carpet, and stepped to their seats which had been crafted like small portable thrones. Casey quelled another urge to giggle. Eric kept her from sitting down until homage was paid by those already seated below and around them.

"Bow your head," he murmured, bowing his own with a smile as he gave a little wave.

Casey followed suit, feeling as if she was atop a float in the Rose Bowl parade. The audience straightened and waited. At another cue, Casey took her seat next to Eric.

"I'm beginning to feel like Jerry Mahoney," she complained under her breath.

Eric looked over. "Who?"

She grinned. "A ventriloquist's dummy. He made a lot of money, but he never had anything to say for himself."

If Queen Marta had not arrived just then, Eric would have burst out laughing. Everyone rose again in respect for the old woman, and the ritual was repeated.

Casey saw the queen peer questioningly at her, then at Eric. Obviously not much got past the old gal.

"Cassandra." She nodded, the arch of her eyebrow the only thing that gave away the fact that she knew exactly what was going on. "Nice to see you could join us."

Casey just nodded and smiled.

"Did Werner tell you that Cassandra has lost her voice, Mother?" Eric asked easily.

"He did."

Eric nodded. The queen nodded. Casey offered another pale little smile.

Only a few minutes later, the lights dimmed and the curtain went up. Eric surreptitiously slipped his hand in Casey's and gave it a squeeze of reassurance. Somehow, neither of them thought to let go during the first act of the opera.

Casey would have had enough fun just watching the audience, the building and the other royals during the opera. But she had to grudgingly admit that as the opera wore on, she became involved in that, too. She didn't know the language, couldn't understand a word that was sung, but there was something universal in the actions and the dilemmas that unfolded on the stage.

By the time the last strains of music echoed away into the vaulted ceiling, Casey found that the tight fear that had lived in her chest ever since Eric had first proposed this masquerade was beginning to ease a little. Her sense of well-being lasted only as long as it took to get to dinner.

They weren't just at the head of the table, they were seated on a dais so that every one of the hundred or so guests could see any mistake she made. Casey walked in alongside Eric, his hand once again firmly in the small of her back, the audience once again bowing, eyes downcast. There were Moritanians present, as well as the foreign bankers who were coming to the conference tomorrow. The wealthy and titled from neighboring countries and a few international celebrities were also in attendance. And all of them had come to see her.

"Your Highness." A bejeweled woman in her forties greeted her with a curtsy as they reached the dais. "I understand you've been a bit under the weather. I do hope you're feeling better."

Casey nodded and made a little rasping noise to go with her apologetic smile. A gloved hand went to her throat again. The woman responded with concerned eyes.

"I cannot begin to tell you how grateful we are that you attended the benefit," she gushed.

"It was a favorite cause of the late king," Eric put in, perfectly at ease. Casey wondered what would make that man sweat. She had the uncomfortable feeling that she was about to, herself. She wondered if she could escape to the solitude of the bathroom for a minute.

Then she wondered just where royalty went to the bathroom at these things. Did they use the public facilities, with a lady-in-waiting parked outside to make sure nobody viewed the royal bodily functions, or were you supposed to just wait until you got home? It certainly was a question she should have asked beforehand.

"Eric." She had enough forethought to make the word a low rasp.

He turned to her, somehow without excluding their hostess. She didn't quite know how to ask. Looking into the perfectly serene regard of those blue eyes, she lost her courage. With a wave of her hand, she changed her mind and let him return his attention to the woman.

That was when disaster loomed the second time. The hostess was reaching out to catch someone's attention in an attempt to make introductions to the prince and princess. When Casey caught sight of who it was, she almost passed out.

James McCormac. Star of screen, theater and Casey's bedroom walls all during her teen years. A ruggedly handsome man who had always had the knack of appealing to a woman's softer side, he had single-handedly carved out Casey's expectations of a man. The fact that she was going to meet him almost destroyed her.

Eric almost didn't catch her reaction in time.

"Her Royal Highness, Princess Cassandra," the woman was saying, her own eyes on the craggy features and gently silvering hair, "may I present James McCormac."

Casey's hand went out and her mouth opened. "Oh..."

Eric turned just in time, knocking into Casey with a force that took her breath away. The "O-o-o-o-h, my God, you're James McCormac!" about to come out died in a series of strangled little coughs. Eric succeeded in saving her from falling forward into the centerpiece as he covered the unfortunate lapse.

"Oh, Cassandra, excuse me," he purred. "Are you all right? You looked for a moment like you were choking."

Her answering glare was more than appropriately heartfelt.

"Jim," he said, smiling easily, turning back to the star. "Good to see you again."

Again. Not only was Casey expected to look reasonably intelligent in the presence of her childhood idol, she was supposed to have known him before. Marvelous.

"You're going to be sitting with us tonight?"

"That's what I understand, Your Highness. It will be my pleasure," McCormac said. Casey could hardly keep herself still at the resonant music of that familiar voice. When he turned to her with those incredible brown eyes, she wanted to run for the ladies' room. But she hadn't figured out just what she was supposed to do about that, had she?

"Your Highness." He bowed easily, his smile familiar and flattering. "It's a pleasure to see you again. You're looking more beautiful than ever."

She resorted once again to nodding and smiling. He didn't seem to mind.

"Oh, look, Cassandra," Eric said with some relish. "It's Rudolph. And I thought he wouldn't be able to make it tonight."

Casey turned to see a younger version of Herbert Hoover walk up, all spit, polish and starched collars. She wanted to laugh. Cassandra was going to marry this guy? He looked as if he was just about as much fun as a trip to the dentist.

Deciding that she was probably staying right in character, she walked over to James McCormac and slid her hand through his arm. Then, motioning to the table, she walked away with him.

"You probably ripped wings off insects when you were a kid, didn't you?"

Eric looked over to where Casey slumped in the seat next to him. They were riding through the winding roads back to the palace, the car as silent as the Alpine night.

"You did perfectly well tonight. Even Mother was impressed."

She snorted, sliding a finger up under her tiara to scratch at the pins holding it on. "Mother didn't have to walk into an ambush armed only with a tiara and a case of laryngitis."

Eric laughed, slipping an arm around her sagging shoulder. "Didn't you enjoy yourself? The opera was fairly good; the food certainly was. And, to be frank, the company was far superior to that at some of the benefit functions we must attend."

"James McCormac," she groaned, her eyes rolling heavenward. She'd done everything but drool down his shirtfront. It just wasn't fair. She'd dreamed about meeting him since the day she'd turned twelve, and Eric had stolen her moment of glory by not preparing her for it. It didn't matter at the moment that there wasn't any way he could have.

"You don't like James McCormac?" he asked.

She scowled again, her head back, her eyes on Eric. The shadows softened the contours of his face and all but hid his eyes. He still made her heart skip beats.

"Maybe you wouldn't find this in your frame of reference," she said, "but I've fantasized about James McCormac since I first went to the movies. He shows up tonight and I turn into mush."

Eric smiled down at her. "If you'd like, we'll invite him to the palace. He loves to use our stables when he's in the country. Cassandra has been known to ride with him."

Casey sat upright abruptly. "Are you crazy?"

"You keep asking me that."

"Cassandra is an exquisite rider, correct?"

He nodded, a smile playing at his lips.

"Well, pal, I can just about stay on. Brooklyn isn't exactly noted for its riding academies."

His smile grew. "You don't like to ride?"

"I've wanted a horse longer than I've wanted James McCormac."

Without their realizing it, they had pulled up to the front steps of the palace. Now the chauffeur bent to open the door for them.

"We'll finish the discussion inside," Eric said as he helped an exhausted Casey from the auto. The dress whispered against the cobblestones, and the faint lights caught in the jewels. Casey's throat gleamed a pearl white in the night air. It never occurred to her that she looked stunning. It occurred to Eric.

"Donna Reed," Eric said with a private little smile as he poured each of them a brandy a few minutes later.

Casey looked up from where she was trying to unwind her hair from the crown. It was getting too uncomfortable. "Pardon?"

He walked over and sat next to her on the soft leather couch. They had decided to sit in his study for a few minutes. "You said that you'd always dreamed of meeting James McCormac. I always dreamed of meeting Donna Reed." He handed her her glass and began to swirl the contents of his own, his eyes introspective. "I suppose as a boy I always wished she were my mother. She was always so . . ."

Casey waited for the rest, but after a moment Eric shook his head and took a drink.

"Loving," she finished for him.

He turned to her, surprised.

She smiled, wishing she could wipe the ghost of loneliness from his eyes with just a gentle hand. "My nana was raised in the imperial court. Your mother reminds me very much of her. A good mother, but one who doles out affection carefully. It must be difficult to understand as a child."

His voice, when he answered, was very quiet. "Were your parents the same?"

Casey shook her head. "No. My mother thinks that hugs should be world currency. And my father was famous for what we called attack kisses. He'd pick you up on the run, plant a kiss and be off."

"He is gone, too?"

She nodded, missing the big, gruff man. "About three years ago."

For a long moment, Casey considered the tawny liquid in her glass. Eric watched the shadows pass over her eyes and thought of the fresh air she'd swept into this stuffy place.

"Casey Phillips," he said softly, a hand beneath her chin. She lifted her face, her wide eyes mesmerizing in the half-light of the room, her lips soft. "Thank you for what you have given us. What you've given me. I'll never forget it."

Casey fought a surprising urge to cry. It was over, then. In the morning she'd give back the clothes, the bedroom and the laryngitis and go on to Switzerland to continue her trip. But she'd have to say goodbye to Eric. Suddenly the trip seemed empty.

"I won't, either, Eric. You've given me quite a day."

His eyes locked with hers, he offered a small, wry smile. "Even the kidney punch when you tried to shake McCormac's hand?"

She smiled back, her lips tremulous. "Even the goose-liver paté and caviar I had to choke down that I would have rather fertilized a garden with."

Without his realizing it, his face grew close to hers. She could feel his soft breath on her cheek. "I'm going to miss you, Casey. I wish you didn't have to go."

Casey found herself fighting the tears that welled in her eyes. "I do, too."

Once again, she was heard. As if it was preordained, both were startled to hear a knock on the door. Eric straightened to check his watch and shot Casey a puzzled look.

"Who could it be at this hour?"

She shrugged, hiding the tears with a nod toward the door. "One way to find out."

"Yes?" he called, setting his snifter down. Casey took the opportunity to drain hers, hoping it would ease the pain in her chest. It didn't.

Werner poked his head through the door. "I beg your pardon, Your Highness. We have some distressing news. The princess has been taken out of the country."

Eric came to his feet, his eyes on Casey. "That changes things, doesn't it?"

Werner's eyes followed. "I'm afraid it does, your Highness."

Casey found herself staring up at Eric with a mixture of dread and anticipation. They still needed her. She didn't have to leave yet, after all.

Four

Casey woke the next morning wondering where she was. It wasn't home, she thought, her eyes closed as she stretched beneath the deliciously warm linens. Not enough noise. At home there were sirens and traffic and airplanes on final approach. All she could hear here were ... birds.

The trip. She was still in Europe. Was today Germany, Austria, Switzerland? After five countries in almost as many days, it was hard to keep track. She was covered in eiderdown, those lovely marshmallowlike comforters that enveloped a person more comfortably than a mother's hug.

Austria. They'd been in Austria. But weren't they supposed to head to Switzerland? She opened her eyes then and saw the pink. It was all she needed to remember.

She sat bolt upright to see that Maria had already been in. A set of clothes was laid out for her, including some beautiful peach silk underwear. Maria must have gone through the suitcase Sandy had brought last night and decided that absolutely nothing it contained was suitable. Casey felt uncomfortable at the idea of somebody else seeing her things. After all, not all of her underwear was in the condition that peach stuff was. And her favorite flannel nightgown had more than one worn spot. By now all the rest of the staff probably knew about it. Maybe even Eric.... She wondered whether Maria was supposed to report back to him.

Casey's thoughts wandered a bit as the notion conjured up pictures of Eric from the night before: circulating through the crowd in those impeccable clothes, protectively watching over Casey as they passed one crisis after another. Sharing his most private recollections with her in the still of the early-morning hours.

She had the unshakable feeling that this wasn't the kind of thing he did with just anyone. Why her, then? Was it because she reminded him so much of his niece? She wasn't so sure about that. He hadn't exactly professed an undying loyalty to the young princess.

Casey wanted to think it was because he was comfortable with her and valued her response. Did he start at her touch as much as she did at his? she wondered. Did he see her eyes as clearly as the sunlight when he thought about her?

Casey shook herself abruptly. This is not a Broadway musical, she admonished herself, throwing the covers aside. You don't get the prince in the third act simply because you're useful in the first. Grow up and get on with it.

She wondered where a person got fed around this place. Her stomach was telling her that it could use more than the goose-grown wallpaper paste she'd fed it the night before. Maybe Sandy would like to make a foray into the kitchen with her.

Casey swung out of the high old bed and padded across to the door. Sandy's room was across the hall. She'd been asleep when Casey'd finally gotten up to bed. Casey hoped she was ready to get up. She wasn't sure, since she didn't have a watch, but she thought it was still fairly early.

"Come in," Sandy answered to the quiet knock on the door. Casey walked in to find her friend dressed and sitting by the window.

Sandra looked up suspiciously. "Who won the '86 World Series?"

Casey snorted and closed the door. "Don't be silly. The Mets did. In the seventh game."

Sandy nodded. "Just wanted to make sure. Maria explained the whole situation to me last night, and I'm still confused."

Pulling up another chair next to Sandy, Casey sat down. "Think how I feel. I can't even wear my own clothes."

At this Sandy had to grin, gesturing toward the beautiful blue satin gown Casey wore. "Don't be ridiculous. With outfits like that, who'd want to wear their own clothes?"

Casey grinned back. "Did you get a load of that room I'm supposed to live in?"

"It *is* a little much."

Casey disagreed. "The *wallpaper* is a little much. The whole thing put together is a disaster. Where does she get her taste?"

Sandy's gaze strayed out the window. "She makes up for it in other areas, like her clothes. And her uncles."

Casey could hardly argue. "Yeah, he's real hard to look at, isn't he?" She didn't realize how suddenly wistful her voice sounded.

"I can tell you're having trouble with it. How was the party last night?"

"Come down to the kitchen with me and I'll tell you. I'll even tell you who I met."

Sandy turned to her again, cautious. "The kitchen? Are you supposed to go there?"

"I'm the Crown Princess Cassandra," Casey reminded her. "I can go anywhere I want."

Sandy nodded. "Good point. Let's go."

They'd gotten to the door when Casey thought to ask. "Do you have any idea where it is?"

Sandy grinned. "It's the one place in this maze I do know how to get to."

Casey did think to dress first, in a pair of gray wool slacks and a matching patterned sweater, but she didn't bother to do more than comb out her hair. She and Sandy sneaked down the back stairs, guided by the enticing smells of baking bread and the sounds of lively chatter.

When they appeared at the door, though, all noise ceased. The servants who worked in the great kitchen all came abruptly to attention and bowed, their eyes speculative enough that Casey had the feeling that they did, indeed, know by now that she was an imposter.

"You wish to inspect, Your Highness?" one senior-looking gentleman in white asked with hesitant deference. The rest of the staff looked as if they'd seen the ghost of Christmas past. It was obvious that the kitchens weren't a favorite haunt of the princess.

"No," Casey said, coming in. "I was starved and smelled the wonderful baking smells down here. I don't suppose you have any coffee and pastries or anything, do you?"

"But, Your Highness," the gentleman objected gently, his well-bred eyebrow arching with suppressed amusement at the broad accent. "It is only eight o'clock. You don't ever request your breakfast before ten. And you prefer it in your room."

"A change in habit can be good for the soul," she assured him blithely, feeling more at home here than among all the well-dressed people she'd mingled with the night before. "I won't tell anybody if you don't."

He bowed, still very unsure. "Very well, Your Highness."

Suddenly Casey started to sneeze. The staff looked as if they were about ready to drop to their knees to pray for her health. Holding up a hand, she tried to stop long enough to look around.

"Somebody's cleaning," she accused, sneezing again.

The culprit brought forth her bucket. "I was just going upstairs with my supplies, Your Highness. Is there a problem?"

Casey nodded, sniffling against the frustrating tickle in her nose. "Pine cleaner," she allowed. "I'm allergic to it. If you don't mind, don't clean my room with it for the next few days."

That seemed to appease everyone, and once the bucket of cleaner was gone, Casey's nose became reasonable enough that she was able to eat.

For the first few minutes, the staff was extremely uncomfortable having the two young women eating in their kitchens as they worked. It's probably like having someone you don't anticipate go through your underwear, Casey thought, taking a first bite from a cinnamon roll.

"Oh, my God," she breathed, her eyes lighting with the delicate taste. "Who made these?"

All activity stopped again. Casey looked up, motioning with the half-eaten roll. "Who made these?"

A great, broad woman stepped forward, her gray hair in a bun and her hands folded beneath her apron. Casey had a quick image of a nun on the playground at school. Except that this woman looked very nervous indeed.

"I baked them, Your Highness," she admitted in a soft voice, dropping a quick curtsy. "Is something wrong?"

"You bet there's something wrong." Casey grinned. "I'm going to end up gaining ten pounds by the end of breakfast, if I have my way. These are wonderful!"

The woman's face crumbled into a relieved little smile. She didn't seem terribly used to praise.

"I bet you make great blintzes," Casey went on, finishing off the cinnamon roll with dispatch and reaching for another. "My nana used to love blintzes."

"You would like me to make some?"

Casey's eyes rolled heavenward at the thought. "I haven't had good blintzes in ages. Do you make soda bread, too?"

The confused look on the woman's face was a giveaway.

"No, I guess not. That's Irish. I'll have to show you how. Great for breakfast, you know."

Within five minutes, Helga had the recipe for soda bread and Casey had finished off two more rolls. Sandy was still waiting to hear about the party.

"Your Highness, there you are."

Casey looked up to see Maria approaching in what for Maria was a dead run. The little woman scuttled past the rows of dangling copper pots and gleaming ovens to where Casey and Sandra sat.

"I was hungry—" Casey began.

Maria waved her explanations aside. "The prince is looking everywhere for you. There is a problem he needs to discuss with you immediately."

Casey looked around. "He couldn't come here for me himself?"

At this, Maria looked honestly perplexed. "A prince does not search through the servants' quarters, Your Highness."

"Oh," she answered with an arched eyebrow. "Excuse me. Can I at least finish my breakfast?"

"It is most urgent, ma'am."

With a resigned shrug, Casey got to her feet to follow. But as she passed the table where Helga pounded on bread dough, she leaned over.

"It's kind of, well, stuffy up there," she admitted under her breath to the surprise of the pastry chef. "Would you mind if I came back later for another roll or two?"

Helga didn't say a word. She merely patted the stool next to her station and smiled. Casey smiled back and followed Maria out.

Eric was once again pacing in his office when Casey and Sandra appeared. Casey noticed that he was in a navy pin-striped suit today, the banker off to business. Only this banker stopped her in her tracks. She wished he'd give her a minute to just feast on his eyes. They were so bright in the morning light. Crisp as autumn.

"Ever been to the kitchens?" she asked instead, the emotions he provoked scaring her. "Pretty nice down there."

He gave her a wry smile. "So that's where she found you. I was wondering."

"Did you think I'd sneak away in the night?"

"It's been known to happen."

"Not by me," she replied, grinning raffishly. "All that pink put me in a coma."

His answering smile was dampened. "Casey, there is a new problem."

"I did sleep well, thanks," she answered, wondering why she felt so compelled to antagonize him. He'd been nothing but kind to her. "And you?"

His eyes briefly touched hers, and she had the nagging feeling that there was something he wished he could say. But the moment passed, and his attention shifted.

"Fairly well. I was awakened this morning with the news that the dissidents have already made their statement that they have Cassandra."

Casey shrugged, seeing his strain now in a set of lines at the corners of his mouth, a tightening of his jaw. He had a habit of shoving his hands in his pockets as he walked. She wondered if it was to assume an air of indifference he didn't feel.

"You knew it was bound to happen," she offered more gently, wanting to reach out to him.

Eric nodded, his gaze returning to her. She felt that blue light like a shaft of sunlight on her face. "They produced pictures. Very convincing ones. And today is the first day of the economic conference."

It didn't take Casey long to follow his train of thought. "So what does a princess wear to the opening ceremonies of an economic conference?"

That brought him to a halt. "I'd wanted to have more time to brief you," he said. "To get you better acquainted with royal protocol before you had to interact on your own."

"On my own?" Casey's stomach dropped. "Aren't you going to be there?"

Eric shook his head. "Not like I was last night. I can't be by your side every minute this afternoon. And there is the press to contend with."

"Can I at least still have laryngitis?"

His smile was heartfelt. "The royal physician has been on the wire services already with the full story."

Casey nodded, trying to think fast. "Just how long do you think this whole thing is going to go on?"

Eric shrugged, coming up to her. "Not long, surely. The general assures me that it shouldn't be long before Cassandra's found. He, of course, cannot enlist aid from any outside sources, but he says that the kidnappers left a rather easy trail."

"Does this guy know what he's doing?" she asked.

"Under normal circumstances. My brother appointed him as a favor, but we've never had much quarrel."

"You've never had a princess kidnapped, either," she reminded him.

Eric didn't have much of an answer.

The opening left Casey even more drained than the benefit had. She felt like an understudy who had to fill a lead without benefit of rehearsal. Come to think of it, she didn't even know all the lines. At least her only job at the function was to nod and wave. She did do that well, facing the swarming press with the proper modicum of imperious disdain and greeting the gathered delegates with elaborate body language. But once she'd cut the proverbial ribbon, she sat back in silence to listen to what the princess was supposed to know about once she took power as the queen. The fact that she fell asleep during one of the long introductory speeches on interest rates and loans to third-world nations was excused by the fact that she was on medication for her indisposition. Finally, Eric collected her for the ride home.

"There's got to be a better way to make a living," she groaned as the chauffeur started the car.

Eric laughed. "You're a natural, you know?"

"No," she disagreed. "I'm a wreck. And Cassandra's shoes are too small."

He took hold of her hand with unconscious ease. "I don't know what I would have done without you, Casey."

She looked at him beneath the netting of the black-and-red hat she wore. "You would have dressed Maria up in black and a veil and said she was in mourning."

Eric smiled down at where Casey's head rested once more against the seat. Then, lifting her hand to his lips, he kissed it. "Anyone can impersonate a queen," he assured her, his eyes oddly intense in the shadows. "It takes a special woman to make a confirmed bachelor realize his loneliness."

For a very long time, Casey couldn't think of anything to say. She was trapped within the sudden exhilaration, the heart-pounding fear Eric's words had given her. She couldn't drag her eyes away, couldn't seem to smile or frown or speak. She was too afraid that he'd take back what he said and that she'd be left with half-realized longings.

"Eric," she finally managed, lifting her head and pulling her gaze from him, "do we have to go back right away?"

"What do you mean?"

She gave a little shrug, her heart still crowding her throat, eyes resolutely on the red linen of her suit. "The palace. Maybe you're used to it, but all those servants popping up when you don't expect them makes me a little claustrophobic."

Eric looked out at the late afternoon scenery, at the fiery sun crowding the mountaintops with fire, and smiled to himself. "Where would you rather go?"

"What about some cozy little coffeehouse?"

"Without advance notice?" He smiled ruefully. "Unthinkable. It would cause an unforgivable furor."

"I guess that means McDonald's is out of the question."

"No," he decided suddenly, reaching for the car phone. "I know just the spot."

They made one stop, where the chauffeur picked up a wicker basket from a corner store and townspeople watched respectfully from a distance, their smiles possessive and shy. Then the car turned onto a back road that wound its way into the countryside, neatly slipping in among the towering mountain peaks.

Casey slipped off her hat and held it in her hands, watching quietly as the farms and woodlands passed by them. Eric found no need to initiate conversation, and the silence deepened between them, a richly comfortable fabric that united them within the cocoon of the limousine.

Casey thought of passing time, of how by the same time next week she would be back at her desk at Wade, Simpson and Associates, the memories of these days solely hers. Due to the Russian and Irish blood in her she carried a fair dose of fatalism, and it manifested itself in her grieving for past beauty while still savoring it.

Time was fleeting, and her moment of beauty would be gone all too soon. Eric would return to his reality and she to hers, and they would never see fit to meet again. Unless, of course,

Cassandra was kidnapped again. But Casey had the feeling that once Eric got his errant niece back he wasn't likely to let that happen again.

Eric thought of the delicious opportunities in chance. No more than three days ago he had been settled in a life-style designed from birth, orchestrated by only a limited amount of choice. As the second son, he was not born to rule. He had become the banker because banking was the military service of Moritania. It held the country's fortune and defended it against encroachment.

He had become an excellent banker because it was in his blood to lead. But he had remained a bachelor because, until he'd chanced upon the sandy-haired American with the free spirit, he had never met anyone he could say excited him. His circle of acquaintances was determined by bloodline and financial success, not necessarily personal dynamism. He'd never really had the opportunity to meet anyone who could manage to thumb her nose at everyone and everything as it was needed.

Casey was like a new light in his life, a means by which he could view his world from a different perspective. Hers were eyes unspoiled by advantage or prospective gain, and more and more he found himself wanting to share their view. He wanted to be able to continue basking in the freshness that had so long been missing from his world. A freshness that translated into a potent sensuality she didn't even realize she had.

The limo slowed a bit at another guarded gate and then swept on past, down a broad meadow that was lined with old oak trees. There were no farmhouses here. It was, however, well groomed, the broad lawns close-cropped and the trees trimmed as they swept toward the enclosing mountains.

"Is this where you were murdering helpless birds yesterday?" Casey asked, awed by the pastoral beauty around her.

Eric smiled over at her. "As a matter of fact, yes."

"And to think," she said with a little smile, "my relatives probably used to poach here."

The sound of his chuckle warmed her to a new smile. "If they were any kind of self-respecting Moritanians, they did," he assured her. "There's a spot a little farther on that's a favorite refuge of mine. We can enjoy our booty there."

Casey's idea of a refuge was a library room where everybody had to be quiet at once. Eric's was an immense expanse of garden, the product of centuries of development and care. Shrubbery bordered the area in precise geometrics, and a thousand well-mannered flowers spread a riot of color and scent over the center, right up to the exactly trimmed gravel walks and lily-laden ponds. From where they stepped from the car, Casey couldn't see the end of the gardens. They seemed to stretch on forever, a haven of solitude and birdsong where the world was kept at bay and reality in abeyance.

Unable to even wait for Eric, she wandered down the paths, drinking deeply of the mingled fragrances of roses and holly-hocks and dahlias—flowers she'd seen only in parks, in pictures in a book. She and her mother had grown some pretty scrawny chrysanthemums and tomatoes on the roof of their apartment building, all the while dreaming of lush gardens just like these. To have been dropped right in the center of all this, and not to have to share them with anyone else was as much of a dream as dressing up as a princess.

Casey didn't get any farther than the first arbor. Kicking off the black-and-red pumps that were beginning to cramp her feet, she sat herself down on the polished wooden bench beneath the clematis. The summer surrounded her and soothed her agitation.

"You found it." Eric smiled down at her.

Casey looked up with amazement in her eyes to see the deep gold of the late sun glint from his hair and warm the planes of his cheeks. He stood before her, basket in hand, looking like a schoolboy on a picnic.

"How did you manage to tap into my daydreams?" she demanded with delight. "This is the exact spot where I imagined I married James McCormac when I was twelve."

He laughed, the hearty music ringing out over the nodding flowers, and set the basket down. "This is the arbor I always escape to when the pressures get to me."

Taking a seat next to her, he spent a moment reacquainting himself with the place. Casey looked over to see the magic take hold in him and ease the lines around his mouth. His smile broadened dreamily as he surveyed what was his.

She didn't wait for him to come back from his reverie. Suddenly it seemed important that nothing interrupt his peace of mind. He had so little of it, she was sure. Even less with the kidnapping and the schooling of a barbarian in the ways of the royal family. Reaching into the basket, she drew out a bottle of chilled white wine and some cheese and set it between them. Then she reached in again for a couple of tins that completed the cache.

"Caviar?" she asked with a wrinkled nose. "I guess that's for you."

Eric looked over, the light in his eyes oddly intense for the peace he'd gained in the garden. "For you, actually," he said, a sly humor edging into his eyes. "You eat it every day."

Casey shook her head. "Not me, bucko. The only eggs I eat come from chickens, and I'm not overly fond of those. Ever since my first biology class in reproduction, I haven't been able to go near a fish egg. Not that I've ever had the opportunity until last night...."

He reached over to take the tin from her hand. "A class Cassandra should have attended, I suppose. She eats the damn things like jelly beans. Morning, noon and night. Beluga caviar, specially imported by one of our little gourmet shops just for her."

Casey held the offending food out to him like a dead mouse. "Then may she eat it in good health. I'm perfectly happy with the more mundane food groups."

With a corresponding smile, Eric made it a point to drop the tin back in the basket.

"How long of a break do we have?" Casey asked as Eric brought out the corkscrew—gold, she noted—and went after the wine.

"Break?" he countered with a sidelong look. "This isn't a break. I'm teaching you about protocol."

"I know all about protocol." She sneered, holding out the glasses for pouring. "You're the last one to show up, the first one to leave, and nothing gets done until everybody bows to you. Oh, yes, and you look down your nose like this—" she demonstrated with just a slight exaggeration "—at anyone asking a personal question."

Eric found himself laughing again. She was so right, and he'd never even thought about it before. The cork escaped with a definite popping sound, and he began to pour, his one hand around Casey's to hold the glass still.

"It's easy to see that there's imperial blood in you," he admitted, leaning closer than was necessary. Casey could feel his breath sweep her cheek. The warmth of his hand seemed to infuse her more thoroughly than the dying sun. "It's a good thing there isn't too much, though. You might begin taking yourself seriously like the rest of us."

Casey looked up at him in disbelief. "You don't really take all of it seriously, do you?" she asked.

Once again, when his eyes lifted to hers, she felt snared. Trapped in the reflection of the sunset in his eyes, eyes that were like pools of water on the edge of the sky. Her heart quickened and her chest tightened. The hand he held in his began to tremble without her even realizing it.

"Not so much since you've been here," he answered in a very soft voice. Once again they seemed to trap an electricity between them, and the air shimmered with anticipation. "Except for one thing."

She couldn't take her eyes away. Couldn't take her hand away, even though it was suddenly on fire like the rest of her. "What?"

The smile that edged into his eyes held surprise as much as pleasure. Eric set the bottle down and took the glass from Casey's numb fingers. Then, taking her face in his gentle hands, he bent to kiss her.

"I'm very serious," he finally said, lifting his head to consider her, "about you."

Five

Casey sat bolt upright, then fled the bench.

"Oh, no, you don't!" she objected with a voice that was just a bit too shrill. "No, you don't." She couldn't seem to stand still, striding over to the flowers and then back again, terror propelling her. Eric's kiss had set off the most delicious shower of sparks in her, chills that surprised her like a bright starburst against a night sky.

"No I don't what?" Eric asked with passive amusement.

She turned on him, leveling an accusing finger. "I've only known you a day. This kind of thing just doesn't happen in a day. I can't... You can't..." She turned away again, the promise in those laughing blue eyes steeling her outrage. What outrage, she demanded of herself? What she felt was stark fear of possibility. The too-good-to-be-true syndrome. Every nerve ending in her body was screaming at her to sit right back down on that bench. She wanted more.

Behind her, Eric didn't even stir. "In the last twenty-four hours," he said without agitation, "I've been more alive than I have in the last thirty-five years. What do *you* think I should do about it?"

She turned, her eyes wide, her breathing shallow. "I'm going home next week, Eric. Back to Brooklyn, remember? I'm the one who doesn't know what to call a duchess or what wine goes with chicken. I can't tell you who painted one of the pictures on your walls, or which king named your chairs. Hardly the person your mother the *queen* would choose to be seen consorting with her son. Besides, isn't somebody going to say something about a man having an affair with his niece?''

Eric's smile broadened. Casey's eyes widened in true outrage, this time at herself for voicing the thoughts that had been hovering just beyond consideration since she'd first set eyes on him.

"Oh, my God!" she wailed, setting off another march. "You've got me talking affairs now. Listen to me. Lord, my mother would slap me for even talking like that! Nobody in her family even mentions that word out loud.''

"The Romanovs were always having affairs.''

"Not in my house, they weren't!''

Eric finally got to his feet, the filled wineglass in hand, and approached her. Catching her in midflight by the wrist, he inexorably turned her to him. "Here,'' he offered, that wry humor still crinkling the corners of his eyes. "Have a sip of this. It might put things into better perspective.''

"Better than what?'' she demanded, even though she accepted the glass. Her eyes still challenging his, she took a sip and then another. The wine was smooth, refreshing and cool. Before she knew it, she'd finished the glass. Eric didn't say a word. He simply retrieved the bottle and the other glass and went about providing refills.

"How about a slice or two of cheese?''

Casey eyed him suspiciously. "Are you always this cool?''

His smile broadened over the rim of his glass. "Always. It's the mark of a good prince.''

"I guess that's admirable,'' she admitted grudgingly. "Must not help your stress level much, though.''

Eric laughed, drawing her back to the bench. "Stress is an American invention.''

Casey suddenly found herself again seated next to Eric, his proximity doubling the wine-induced heat. She felt too much at ease with him, too seductively comfortable. Before she knew it, she was going to be expecting him to be there all the time.

"Oh, you're right,'' she scoffed. "Heads of small European countries have no stress. They say change of job is a big stress producer. I can't imagine what change of head of state produces.''

He shrugged, slicing up the cheese. "Countries go on. Moritania certainly does." Then, turning, he held out a slice to Casey. "Fragonard."

Casey's head came up. "What?"

Eric's smile was intimate, gentle. "The man who painted most of the pictures in the front hallway. Fragonard. Somebody had a real weakness for him. And Queen Anne."

"She painted, too?"

He unceremoniously stuffed the wedge of cheese in her mouth. "No. She made furniture."

Casey found herself smiling now, too.

"Do you find me so disagreeable?" he asked, almost offhandedly.

Casey met his eyes without flinching this time. The truth was, finally, the truth. It was what could be done about it that was the problem. Taking the time to retrieve her cheese and take a delicate bite, she briefly studied the brickwork beneath her feet. "Just about as disagreeable as Cassandra finds caviar."

Pursing his lips with quiet satisfaction, Eric nodded, his eyes on his wineglass. He swirled it a little so that the wine rocked back and forth, distant sunlight sinking into the clear liquid and shimmering. Then he looked at Casey, and, in his eyes, she saw the fires that Eric seemed to always keep banked. They flared now, warm and sweet, a bottomless blue that held his secrets, contained his passions and remained very much his own. Casey knew without having to ask that this side of Eric was not one many people saw. She wondered, in fact, if any did.

"You've given me laughter, Casey," he said. "That's a precious gift. You keep surprising me. And I find when I lay in bed that I ache for the feel of you next to me."

"Eric, please don't...."

He held up a hand. "I want you to know that I've never said this to anyone before." A self-deprecating grin lit his features. "I don't make it a practice to lure susceptible young females to my bed." For a moment, his eyes drifted back to his glass. "To be perfectly honest, I had no idea I was going to tell you this. I didn't even have a clue I was going to kiss you."

When he turned his eyes back to her, Casey felt the sharp tug in her chest at the vulnerability there, the memories of loneliness and separation. Even though she was of the working class, in many ways Casey had it better than Eric.

As the moments passed, her resolve began to waver. The shadows had crept up to claim their corner of the garden, and the dusk breeze was growing chilly. Casey didn't feel the drop in temperature. She only felt the intensity of Eric's silence and her own inability to provide an answer.

Finally she sighed. "I'll tell you what. Could we maybe have this conversation again when Cassandra has her little fanny on that throne? Until then, I'm afraid that we could cause more problems than we'd solve by testing these, uh, waters." She faced Eric with silent entreaty and found that he understood.

"You have the control to be a princess," he admitted wryly. "Perhaps more control than I do. We'll work together."

Casey couldn't help a sharp little laugh. "That's what got us into trouble in the first place."

Even so, when they had gathered their things to leave, Eric stopped a moment and took Casey in his arms. She didn't stop him. The sure feel of his arms around her, the tensile strength of his long body against hers, stilled her. The searching heat of his lips compelled her. She brought her own hands up, holding him to her, and savored the delicious fire his kiss ignited in her.

A small breeze lifted Casey's hair. The evening birds were beginning to chatter in the trees, and somewhere Casey heard the bells on the grazing cattle. But when Eric finally pulled back, she saw and heard only him.

"We'd better get back," he said quietly, his finger straying over the outline of her lower lip, his eyes devouring hers in the dim light. "We have some time to do more instruction before the dinner tonight."

Consciously willing the fire to bank once again in her, Casey turned down the path with him to where they'd left the limo. They walked hand in hand, with Eric swinging the basket in time with their gait.

"Eric," Casey said a moment later.

"Mmmm."

"The limo's gone."

He nodded without noticeable agitation. "You didn't really expect him to have to wait for us, did you?"

She turned on him. "Well, if we have another appointment, how do you expect to get back to the palace in time?"

His grin was complacent and sly. "We walk. Don't you walk in America?"

"Only when the objective is in sight. You're less likely to get mugged."

"I don't think we have to worry about being mugged here," he assured her, turning into the lane where the late, lamented limo had sat. "Poached, perhaps. But not mugged."

"All right," she conceded. "I give up. Just how far away is the palace?"

Now he smiled, his even white teeth gleaming against his tanned skin. "You'll see."

She saw. They topped the rise to find that they were in the palace's backyard. Backyard being a relative term, of course. They still had a good quarter mile to walk, through a maze of hedges, fountains and reflecting pools and more flower beds, all illuminated with the most cunningly recessed lighting to make it look like a fairyland, mysterious and beautiful in the purpling dusk. The roses smelled stronger here, too. There must have been an immense garden nearby.

"Who does your yardwork?" Casey asked, coming to an amazed halt at the sight of the huge mansion rising from the far side of the terraces, patios and gardens. It was something out of a history book.

"A team of about thirty."

"Thirty." She turned on him with wry eyes. "My mother would die if she saw this."

"Maybe someday she can," he offered.

Casey shook her head. "She hasn't been out of Brooklyn her entire life. That's why Sandy came with me on the trip. I couldn't talk her into it. Besides, this is the last time for a while I'm going to be able to afford to do this."

She didn't notice the quick glance he dispatched as they walked on.

"Tonight is the dinner for the economic ministers," Eric said instead. "Pretty boring stuff."

"As boring as today?"

He laughed and squeezed her hand. "Hardly. Besides, if you nod off tonight, I'll be alongside to give you a nudge."

"I'm developing a bruise from the last nudge you gave me. Why don't you delegate somebody with less enthusiasm for the job?"

"Oh, I can't," he said. "That would absolutely shatter royal protocol."

"I'm absolutely shattering royal protocol by just being here," she reminded him. "Isn't there some kind of law about impersonating a princess?"

He chuckled. "It's been done all throughout history. Churchill even had it done during the war."

"And here Mark Twain thought he had an original idea. So why can't Werner do the nudging?"

"Because it is not allowed for anyone to touch a member of the royal family except under prescribed conditions."

She stopped, really amazed now. "Not touch them? For heaven's sake, why?"

With another wry smile, Eric shrugged. "Royalty is royalty because we're set apart. There are even rules about when we can be spoken to."

"Now she had a disgusted scowl for him. "Like, 'Um, excuse me, Your Royal Highness, I beg the privilege to say Fire!'?"

His laughter was delighted. "Something like that."

"I was wondering why there was a circle of space around me. I just thought it was because of all the people Cassandra had put off."

They were walking again, their steps matching easily, the evening sky before them deepening to a peacock blue that cradled a lone star and a rising moon. Casey clutched at the moment with frantic yearning, wishing she could make it last forever. She had never known such peace, such exhilaration.

"It's a tradition that's centuries old," Eric explained. "From the time when rulers were omnipotent and often thought deified. They also had quite a few people to keep in place to protect their thrones. This was a way of keeping them at arm's length, I guess."

Hearing that hint of melancholy return to Eric's voice, Casey looked over. His eyes were on the great house where he was born and had lived his whole life.

"Not as much of a problem these days, I'd think," she observed.

"No," he answered quietly. "Not much. We don't even have much of the aristocracy left to entertain us. Just the customs."

"Do you have many friends?" she asked.

He nodded, surprised a little by the question. "A few. Back in England. I went to Eton for my schooling. And there are my teammates in polo and rugger."

She found herself squeezing his hand more tightly, offering her own friendship with the simple gesture. "That's not the way I'd run *my* country," she assured him with a definite nod of the head. "It's too isolated."

"After seeing New York," he retorted easily, "I'd have thought you'd like a little more isolation."

"Moderation in everything," she intoned piously.

With a chuckle, Eric slipped a companionable arm around her shoulder.

They had reached the first terrace before he spoke again. "How about a little accent coaching?"

Casey shot him a sharp look. "Why?" The tone of her voice was suspicious.

He shrugged with just a bit too much nonchalance. "You can't have laryngitis forever."

"I don't plan for my throat to clear up until I cross back over that border," she assured him.

"Just try it," he insisted. "For fun. 'The rain in Spain comes mainly on the plain.' "

She snorted, a bit unkindly. "Shouldn't I be learning how to say that in German?"

"Not necessary. One of Cassandra's pet projects is to see that English is Moritania's primary language. She'd already convinced her father to make it the new official language."

"How convenient. It wouldn't do any good, though. I'm sure Cassandra has definite speech patterns. I'd have to listen to those to even get an idea."

Her words were like a signal she didn't comprehend. Stopping in midstride, Eric grinned like a schoolboy and pulled her close for an enthusiastic hug.

"You're brilliant!" he announced with a delighted smile. "The tapes will be in your room within the hour."

"What tapes?" she demanded, feeling decidedly unsettled.

The tapes of any number of Cassandra's official functions, it turned out. On videocassette, on cassette tape, on compact disc. The woman had an obsession with her public image, and Casey, Sandra and Maria were forced to watch her repeatedly as they readied for the dinner.

"Haven't I seen this somewhere before?" Casey demanded as she scowled at the smiling, distant figure on the film.

"Yeah," Sandra agreed. "On Broadway. I think she played *Evita*. I'm surprised people have actually been fooled by you. You're not nearly enough of a witch."

Maria went on pressing and straightening without any change of expression.

"My dear people," Casey intoned, mimicking the accent and posturing for all she was worth. "It is our great pleasure to bestow on our uncle His Royal Highness Prince Eric the Order of Eternal Patience for putting up with our unspeakably juvenile behavior."

Sandra laughed. Maria almost choked.

"The chin a bit higher, Your Highness," she said with a carefully straight face. It was the merry sparkle in her eyes that gave her away.

Casey lifted her chin a little, looking far down her nose, much as she had for Eric. "Like this?"

Maria looked. "Like that, *ja*. Now you are like her. Was Your Highness an actress in this Brooklyn?"

This time Sandra almost choked. "No, Maria. She was just a troublemaker."

"I'm part Romanov," Casey said defensively. "Condescension is in my blood."

"You're not going to do something stupid, are you?" Sandy asked a moment later, after Maria had stepped out of the room.

Casey looked over from where she was still struggling with her dress. Maybe Cassandra was made for strapless. She most definitely was not.

"Something stupid like what?" she asked.

Sandy took a moment to answer. "This is all pretty heady stuff, pretending you're a princess. Nobody back on the block is going to believe it, that's for darn sure. And the prince is awfully handsome."

"Awfully," Casey agreed in a strangely subdued voice.

"And you have a knack for fantasy, you know?"

Casey's answering smile was a sad one. "Just because I was twenty-one before I finally admitted that James McCormac wouldn't marry me?"

Sandy's pale gray eyes were eloquent in their concern. "I just don't want you to be hurt. It doesn't take you long to fall."

Casey couldn't think of anything to do but study the way her hands rested in her lap. "You're right there," she said very quietly. "Took me all of one day this time."

She heard Sandy sigh. "I knew it. Casey, he's—"

Casey didn't even look up. "He kissed me today."

That stopped Sandy. "Please tell me you hated it. He has buckteeth and bad breath."

Casey just dispatched a dry scowl.

Sandy sighed again. "And?"

"I fall fast," Casey allowed. "But I've never thrown myself at somebody's feet." Then she had to grin. "With the possible exception of James McCormac, of course. I came real close last night.''

"Casey," her friend pleaded, "be serious."

"What do you want me to do?" Casey demanded. "Walk away? Throw my drink in Eric's face when he tells me he cares for me?"

Sandy's eyes grew large. "He said that?"

Casey's eyes were on her hands again. Maria had applied fake nails, so that more and more of her was disappearing under Cassandra's facade. The whole situation was getting more and more alien, and it was becoming increasingly difficult to keep an even keel. "He said that he's been more alive since he's known me than in the last thirty-five years." Her voice dropped almost to a whisper. "And that he, uh, wanted me."

That brought Sandy to her feet. "Oh, my God...."

"Cool your jets," Casey retorted dryly. "Neither of us is going to do anything about it." She sighed with a shake of her head. "I can't even believe I'm talking like this. I feel like I'm becoming somebody else."

Sandy came over to her friend and crouched down beside where she sat, both of them in expensive silk gowns and coiffed hair that made them look as if they belonged here more than in their native streets in New York. When Sandy took hold of Casey's hand, Casey looked up at her, sudden tears glittering in her hazel eyes.

"Just be careful, honey," Sandy said. "You're the one who has to go home, not him."

And Casey nodded, the new pain exquisite in her chest. "I know," she said. "I know."

The soft rap on the door brought them both to their feet, Casey dabbing at her moist eyes with a tissue.

"Come in," she called.

The door opened to reveal Eric, in a dinner jacket this time. Cool, handsome, suave. Casey couldn't seem to speak for a minute.

He intuitively understood and entered, a bright smile of greeting on his face, his hands outstretched to the two women.

"Ladies," he said, "you look marvelous. It will be a pleasure to escort you this evening."

"You're just saying that because it's true." Sandy giggled, slipping a hand in the crook of his arm. Then, turning to Casey, she made a face. "Brooklyn was never like this."

"Well, you know what Dorothy said to Toto," Casey said, mimicking Sandy's move on Eric's other side. "We're not in Kansas anymore."

"Cassandra also never quotes movies," Eric warned her with a mischievous grin. "She finds them a waste of time."

"Does she read?"

He shrugged. "The odd cereal box, I'm sure."

Casey groaned. "Marvelous. That just about leaves the state of the hemline and horse etiquette."

"Do you know anything much about horses?" he asked, easing comfortably into his new role as Casey's straight man.

"Yeah." She smiled sweetly. "Where to sit."

He nodded placidly. "Should make for an evening of stimulating conversation."

"I'm still not recovered," she objected as they headed on down the great echoing hallway that bordered the royal apartments.

"Not according to Maria." He smiled slyly. "She said you sounded quite...inspired."

Casey smiled right back. "You try and get a peep out of me, and I swear I'll moon every one of the ministers at that dinner. And *that*," she assured him, "will make for a stimulating evening of conversation."

Eric watched Casey glide into the great banquet hall and thought how she was beginning to grow into her assumed role. Heads turned as she passed, smiling and listening as if she were hanging on every word said to her, and whispers followed her. He knew he should have warned her to close off a little, slip a bit of ice into her demeanor, but it was such a joy to watch what the monarchy could be like that he forestalled it.

"She is so lovely tonight, Your Highness," the Baroness von Richter confided as the two observed Casey courting two of the more taciturn ministers on the other side of the room.

Casey's eyes sparkled as she listened to the one gentleman describing his homeland. She urged him on with a nod of the head, and a hand to the arm, and suddenly the old man, who hadn't spoken more than a few words to Eric in the ten years he'd known him, was opening up like a schoolboy. Standing next to the plump baroness, Eric found himself shaking his head with something akin to wonder.

"It must be the drugs she's on, my dear Eleanor." He smiled gently. "I've never known Cassandra to be so generous."

The baroness allowed herself a small chuckle. "I would never suggest that the princess should succumb to laryngitis more often...."

He smiled right back, embellishing the lie without effort. "Exactly."

It didn't really occur to Casey that she was having an easier time of it tonight. She knew that the champagne she drank before dinner had the most enticing fizzle to it, and that when she caught sight of herself in the far mirrors she couldn't quite believe that it was she in rose silk and diamonds.

And most of all she felt the unspoken support of Eric, no matter where he stood in the room. She knew that if she came within a foot of making an indiscretion, he would be at her side to bail her out. Whenever she turned to see where he was, his eyes were on her, that crystal blue compelling her as if there weren't another soul in the room.

"Your Highness." One of the strolling waiters approached bowing, his silver tray held rigidly in place. "Hors d'oeuvres."

"Oh..." she began to mouth, seeing the little piles of glistening black on each little cracker. The sight of it made her stomach turn. Then Eric caught her eye with a silent admonition. The charade could only be stretched so far, she thought.

She managed a sick little smile and reached for a cracker. Everyone around her immediately followed suit. Casey smiled again at them, trying to put off the inevitable as long as possible. She couldn't. They were waiting politely for her.

Closing her eyes, she popped it in and swallowed.

"My dear Princess." A voice spoke up at her elbow with all the upper-crust nasal condescension it could muster.

With a startled little gulp, Casey turned to answer. She found a small woman smiling, an hors d'oeuvre in hand, little color or intelligence in her eyes. She reminded Casey of that kind of pinched-nosed dog her mother said always bit.

Casey smiled, quelling a sudden stab of fear. Was she supposed to know this woman? Would she call up memories to share that Casey wouldn't recognize? Take a deep breath and nod, she told herself, just like all the other times, and hope that those vile little eggs stayed where they were.

She smiled with a bit more enthusiasm and nodded.

The woman hardly needed encouragement. "I must say that I cannot understand what your fascination is with the English language," she said. With a clipped and precise accent, she had all the hallmarks of a European native. Was she one of the aristocracy who survived into the modern era? Casey wondered.

Waving off her own remark with a gloved hand, the woman dove on. "Not precisely English anymore, anyway, is it? Of course, my Hans said that it was all because you were courting the Americans. I cannot ever imagine why. They're barbarians, hardly worth considering. Just because they have hamburgers and blue jeans, everyone thinks they are worth nothing short of devotion. It's an abomination, if you ask me, to usurp the majesty of German. Even the beauty of Italian for... for that..."

Casey forgot the caviar. All she could think of was how close she was to apoplexy. What a smarmy, self-righteous, condescending witch! There were so many things she wanted to tell her, so many threats and curses she'd like to hurl on her head for her archaic, self-serving attitude. A barbarian, was she?

But when she opened her mouth to offer a rebuttal, Casey saw the faces turned expectantly toward her. The waiter still hovered, certain she would want more caviar. Casey looked back at the smug and nasty little woman and tried again.

Nothing came. She choked, terrified of making a fool of herself in front of these people. What if they found out not only that she was not the princess but that she talked like the very people this woman was so spiteful toward? The fact that she was so terrified of someone this stupid only made her angrier.

"Of course," the woman went on, ignoring the definitely scarlet tint to Casey's cheeks, "I can understand that one must conduct world business, but really. I cannot think of any one custom, or person for that matter, that the U.S. has to offer that could possibly be... well, worthwhile...."

"Cassandra, dear, I need to speak to you for a moment."

Feeling the gentle hand on her arm, Casey whipped around. She was sure Eric saw the wild rage in her eyes. He just smiled as if nothing had happened and turned to her assailant.

"If you'll excuse us, Countess."

The countess blushed, stammered and curtsied. Eric seemed to have a foolproof way of shutting up foolish old women.

"She's not worth it," he whispered under his breath as he led a scarlet Casey out to the renewed bows of their guests. "Just an old busybody."

Casey still couldn't manage a response, angrier at herself than at the busybody.

"Cassandra?" he asked solicitously as they neared the door. "Are you all right?"

She glared straight ahead, her color now closer to purple. They had almost made it to the door and safety.

"Say something."

Casey stopped just shy of the door, then turned to find Eric and the rest of the guests awaiting her answer. When she finally found her tongue, the results echoed from the rafters.

"Off with her head!"

Six

How can you possibly be so in control?'' Casey demanded of Eric.

"Years of study," he said, smiling gently.

The two of them walked the gardens at the back of the palace. It was late, the dinner having been over for a few hours, and Sandy was already in bed preparing for the hangover of the year.

"I almost decked that old lady," Casey admitted with a rueful shake of her head. "In fact, if she were here now, I'd probably still deck her."

"It wouldn't change her mind."

"It would support her claims." Casey lashed out at the soft night air, some of the anger still lingering. "Barbarians, indeed. Americans didn't invent the Inquisition or start World War II."

He couldn't help but grin. "But they did invent plastic lawn flamingos and Fred Flintstone."

"Bad taste doesn't make you a barbarian," she informed him archly. "If that were true, most of the European aristocracy would be guilty. I should have decked her."

"You should have done just what you did."

Casey had to grin. "What, a bad imitation of the Queen of Hearts? Is that what Cassandra would have done?"

"It's exactly what Cassandra would have done, and worse. You conducted yourself admirably tonight," he said, bringing her to a halt by one of the reflecting pools. Only the half-moon found its way into the water tonight. The unseen flowers permeated the soft night air with a thousand seductive fragrances.

The crown jewels still glittered at Casey's throat, and her hair was swept up in a soft mass off her neck. She looked the essence of sleek style. But her eyes, those deep pools that could entice a man to his death, still reflected the thrill and terror of what she'd just done more clearly than the water reflected the moon. It was that intensity, that clarity, that attracted Eric more than the classic beauty they'd transformed her into ever could.

He found his hands on her bare arms, his thumbs sliding up and down over the smooth skin.

"Tell me something," she said more quietly, her now-serious eyes looking into his.

His voice was barely more than a whisper. "Anything."

Casey found herself wanting to penetrate that cool demeanor, the tailored exterior of Eric von Lieberhaven that hid so well the person he didn't get to be. The little boy who'd longed for a normal mother, the man who had too few friends and too much responsibility. The prince who was fascinated by the freedom of a commoner.

"Don't you ever...oh, I don't know, let loose? Rip off that tie, slip on some old jeans and just raise a little hell?"

His answer was a bit wistful. "Oh, I think Cassandra raises enough hell for the both of us."

Casey couldn't help but scowl. "And what excuse did you use before she came along?"

He didn't seem to understand.

"For a younger son," she said softly, trying her best to make him understand, "you seem to have shouldered quite a load."

Eric smiled. His duties had been decided before he'd ever been born. "I have no choice. I have a responsibility to my country."

She nodded with an impatient little shrug. "And what about your responsibility to yourself?"

His gaze strayed back to the palace, that building that was so integral to the fabric of his existence. "I went to England to school. I got away for a while."

"What about now?" she asked. "What do you do now?"

"I play polo," he said. "And rugby."

"And have you ever done anything just for the hell of it?"

Again he didn't quite comprehend.

"Would you ever consider just telling off some old busybody just because it made you feel better?"

Eric didn't have to consider the question before shaking his head.

Casey sighed. "Do you even own a pair of jeans?"

"No."

She shook her head, frustrated that this man who gave so much could think so little of himself. Surely he should be able to inject a little spontaneity, to offset some of the crushing stress of his position. A bit of momentary madness.

The impulse was born even before Casey finished the thought. She could barely suppress the sudden smile. "You really should try it."

"Try what?"

Casey shrugged, easing a little closer to better her balance. Eric got the wrong idea and nestled against her, the fabric of his slacks whispering against the silk of her dress. She brought her hands up to his chest.

"Surprise," she said, with the innocent eyes of a siren. "You know, a little fun."

He bent his head a little lower, the soft timbre of his voice rippling along Casey's skin like a sultry breeze. "What kind of fun?"

Her smile blossomed, all mischief and glee.

"This," she said, and pushed.

Eric landed in the reflecting pool with a great splash and an outraged howl. Casey's laughter pealed out over the sleeping gardens.

"You little witch!" he yelled from his ungainly position, the water lapping against the sodden white linen of his once-pristine dinner jacket. His wet hair tumbled over his forehead. His pants were soaked and his shirt was plastered to his chest. The outrage on his face sent Casey into another paroxysm of laughter. Lights began to flick on at the other end of the garden.

"Why the hell did you do that?" he demanded, struggling valiantly against the laughter that was catching up with him.

"Just to see what you would look like," she admitted, still struggling for breath. Actually, he looked sexier than ever. The way that linen clung to his body showed her just how lean and athletic it was. Rugby must really make a man out of you. "It makes me nervous when somebody doesn't ever get mussed up."

"Is that so?" A smile now tugged at the corners of his mouth as he reached around to dig a sopping handkerchief from his pocket and mop his dripping face. "This was silk, you know."

"And you don't have another one to your name," she goaded.

Although Casey couldn't say how he managed it, Eric tucked the handkerchief away with a great deal of aplomb. "You could at least help me back up."

She held out a hand. She shouldn't have. Eric no sooner took hold of it than an identical smile appeared on his face, that of a pirate catching sight of a fat prize.

"Oh, Eric, no..." she began to protest. She never got the chance. Suddenly she was the one howling and Eric the one laughing. She landed right on top of him.

"You're right," he admitted after due consideration. "It is quite a sight." He reached up to brush the damp tangle of hair back from her forehead.

"This wasn't my dress," she protested instinctively, looking down at the damp mass of silk that did no more now than vividly outline her figure.

"And Cassandra doesn't have another," he said, grinning and wrapping his arms around her.

She laughed, rivulets of water sliding down her throat to mingle with the precious gems she'd borrowed. The evening breeze raised goose bumps in the wake of the water, and she nestled back against Eric's warmth.

"You get the hang of this stuff pretty quickly," she accused, still giggling.

He chuckled, too, not making any move to better his position. The two of them rested along the side of the pool, up to their waists in water.

"That's what I get for getting involved with a barbarian."

Casey let out another howl and turned in his arms, fully intent on giving him the due she'd been unable to give the old lady for the same kind of crack. Eric anticipated her.

Before she could retaliate, he pulled her to him. She gasped and struggled in vain to back off. It didn't do any good. With a deliberate smile, Eric brought her to him, his one hand cradling the back of her neck, the other firmly around her waist. His eyes open and laughing, he bent to kiss her, and she forgot about the cool breeze. He was igniting goose bumps all his own.

The soft command of his lips stole her resistance. The enticing rasp of his cheek against hers brought her hands up to circle his neck, and she ended up kissing him back. She heard his sharp intake of breath as she opened her lips to him. She felt his hand move from her waist, trailing the most delicious shivers with it. Her heart began to thunder in her ears, her breath stolen by the sweet play of his hands against her body. She could smell the heady tang of his cologne mingle with the flowers that surrounded them and taste the last of the brandy on his tongue.

Never in her life had Casey lost reason to the sensation of a man's touch. Never until tonight. When Eric's fingers reached for the soft swell of her breast, she could do no more than sigh, moving against him. His touch, so sure and sensitive, sparked lightning in its wake. Casey's hold on him tightened, her body aching to mold with his, to savor the textures, the strength, the hard angles of him. When Eric suddenly straightened, Casey was surprised by the sharp loss she felt.

She looked up at him, her lips still parted and swollen, her eyes wide and dark with his power over her. She was about to say something, but his eyes were suddenly past her.

Then she heard the discreet cough and considered diving underwater.

"We heard shouts," the voice behind her explained diffidently. "Is Your Highness all right?"

Eric never batted an eye. "Quite all right, thank you." He nodded evenly, never changing his hold on Casey or moving to get up. For her part, Casey couldn't manage any more than a stricken stare into Eric's soggy lapel, her back stiff with discomfort.

"Very well then, Your Highness," the voice said at descending levels. He must be bowing again. "If you won't be needing anything else."

A strangled little sound escaped Casey at that.

Eric smiled an easy dismissal beyond her shoulder. "I don't think so, Rolph. Good night."

"Good night, sir."

Silence returned at intervals.

"Is he gone?" Casey finally managed.

Eric grinned. "He's gone."

She dropped her head onto his chest and groaned. "I'm gonna die. The whole palace will know by morning."

"Probably within the hour," he allowed, still smiling with satisfaction.

That provoked another groan.

"I'm sure the servants have figured out that you're not my niece," he assured her, snuggling back into an intimate embrace, his head just over hers. "They won't mind our having an affair."

Casey's head came up, almost sending his teeth through his tongue. "Don't start that again," she warned.

"You started it," he retorted, his eyes all affronted innocence. Even so, his index finger sought out the puffy edges of her lips, which still betrayed his attention. "After all, you're the one who is responsible for the position in which I find myself. Not to mention the very enticing suggestion to enjoy a little fun."

His eyes returned to hers, soaking up the languid heat that still simmered there. Casey felt herself awash in that delicious blue, sinking without a trace within his charm.

"Well," she managed with a rather shaky voice, reaching up to pull his hand away, "you've had your moment."

Even soaked and dripping, Eric was able to retain his urbane air. He made waterlogged look like the upcoming fashion trend, and it was threatening Casey's breath again. Without blinking an eye, he turned the hand that had captured his and brought it up to his lips.

"But we might not find ourselves in such a conducive position again for so long," he murmured, his breath warming her palm and stirring the embers back to blazing life.

"Conducive to what?" she whispered, trying without much luck to keep an even keel.

He smiled and kissed her palm again. Casey couldn't feel the water anymore. Her body was alternately freezing and burning, the sharp yearning leaping like a brushfire in her. She felt herself lifting her lips to him again, letting them open to seek his warmth....

"Your Highness."

This time even Eric hadn't heard him. The two of them started like rabbits caught in a bright light.

"You do have some guts, Rolph," Casey rasped with a little shake of her head, still not able to face him.

"I truly beg your pardon, Your Highnesses. I was told it was vital I fetch you both."

"Thermonuclear war, I hope," she grated, her embarrassment complete.

Nothing fazed Rolph. "No, Your Highness. General Mueller. He awaits the prince in his office."

Eric's head came up at that. "The general?"

"Yes, Your Highness. He said it was important...." Or I wouldn't have bothered you, his pause said.

"All right, Rolph. Tell him we'll be there," Eric said, finally moving to get out of the pool. When he observed the condition the two of them were in, he amended his statement. "When we've had a chance to make ourselves presentable."

"Very well, Your Highness."

A good servant was a discreet servant, it seemed. By the time Casey made it up to the bedroom there was already a change of clothing set out for her and a bath drawn. She was relieved that Maria hadn't seen fit to stick around for the gory details. She was having trouble enough with them herself. Stripping off the ruined designer original, Casey found herself thinking about the man who was changing just down the hall from her.

It wasn't fair. It just wasn't fair. She was going to be twenty-five next July, and in all those years she had never found herself at a man's mercy. It had always been with a clear eye and a firm foothold in reality that Casey had viewed the men she'd dated. She had never found one to set off the proverbial fireworks or even to compel her so that she couldn't wait to be with him again. That had all come to a screeching halt the moment she'd laid eyes on Eric.

It wasn't enough that he was just about the most handsome man she'd ever laid eyes on. No one she'd ever gone to school or worked with could compare in any way. From the aquamarine of his eyes to the lean lines of his body, he was simply too good-looking to be true. If he'd lived in her neighborhood, the only way he'd still be single by the age of thirty-five would be if he were the parish priest. How the world's most eligible women had failed to net him by now mystified her.

But that had nothing on the fact that he seemed just as mystified with her. Her, Cassandra Marie Phillips, the daughter of a cabdriver and a grade school teacher. She, who'd dutifully ignored whatever lessons in gracious living her grandmother had tried so hard to instill on those painfully uncomfortable visits to the old woman's home. A man with more names than she had shoes was talking about having an affair with her.

Still shaking her head, Casey slid into the steaming water in the old claw-foot tub. It wasn't that she'd ever considered herself ugly. She figured she could stand up with the best of them in the neighborhood, especially if you went in for Tyrolean looks. She'd had dates to the prom and an offer to go steady while in high school.

But she wouldn't put herself up with any of the women she'd met at these dinners. They were world class, wearing their diamonds as if it was their right, easily conversing in any of four different languages about art and politics and the latest in society news. Casey could discuss Keith Hernandez's batting average and the cost of a snow cone on Coney Island. And she could only do that fluently in Brooklynese. She hated fish eggs and preferred the company of the staff to the guests. Eric had no business being attracted to her.

It did occur to her to wonder whether he might be putting on an act to better facilitate her cooperation. He did, after all, take his responsibility to his country very seriously. But that doubt didn't linger long, though whether from honesty or wishful thinking she didn't know. She simply couldn't accept the idea that a man with such sweet eyes could be so deceptive.

The next problem, of course, was what to do about his offer. Should she throw caution to the wind this one time and give in? The brief time she spent in his arms tonight promised a fulfillment she'd never dreamed of, never hoped for. She knew that she was finding life away from him less and less appealing. She knew that she celebrated his laughter and shared the pain that she allowed so fleetingly. And she knew that he made her feel more special than any of those jewel-encrusted women who could claim him by rights.

But, dear God, what would happen when she had to leave? Would it be easier to have committed herself to him during the time they had together—no more than a few days at best? Or would she survive more easily if she kept her distance, only suspecting what he could give her rather than being sure of it and missing it even while she held him in her arms.

Who was she to even consider it, anyway? An affair, even with a prince, was not something she took home to her mother. It would be something she would have to keep as her own for the rest of her life, unable to share it even with Sandy, because even Sandy wouldn't understand.

Casey opened her door to join Eric and the general without having come to any decision. As the time passed, the weight of it grew within her like a soreness that wouldn't go away.

She walked into the paneled office in tailored slacks and a silk blouse. She would have much preferred the denim jump suit she'd packed.

When Eric answered the knock on the door, he smiled at her appearance. She'd haphazardly pinned the curls back from her face, damp tendrils still clinging along her forehead and neck, and chosen to rest her feet from Cassandra's pointed pumps. The heather slacks and shimmering ivory-and-blue blouse that so flattered her lithe figure were complemented by bare feet.

"Come in, Casey," he said, guiding her in. "I was just speaking with the general. General—" he turned to the distinguished gentleman who was even now standing at Casey's approach "—Miss Phillips."

Instead of bowing like the servants or reaching for her hand like Eric, the general executed a swift click of the heels and a nod of the head. He was dramatically silver-haired and well tailored, a man carefully appropriate to his station.

"Fraülein," he said in precise tones, "it is a pleasure to meet you. The prince was telling me what a service you have performed for our small country."

"No problem," she said, smiling a bit uncomfortably. "I always did like to play dress-up."

"The general was just telling me, Casey," Eric was saying as he moved back around to his desk, "that a new communiqué has been received from the kidnappers. Brandy?"

"Would Rolph have to come in to pour it?"

The general stared. Eric chuckled.

"I'll pour it if you'd like."

"Will I need it?"

He nodded. "Probably."

"Thank you, then. A brandy would be lovely." She sat down in one of the leather chairs without waiting for an invitation. The general sat more slowly in his, his still-raised eyebrows the only indication of his surprise at her appearance.

"They do keep odd hours," Casey said, restraining an urge to yawn, "don't they?"

"To keep us off balance," the general assured her.

She nodded as if she understood. "What do they want now?" she asked. "Safe passage to Disneyland?"

Once again it was the general who didn't seem to understand. Eric handed Casey her glass of brandy with a wide smile and perched on the corner of his desk.

"Actually, it's beginning to look better," he admitted. "They've retreated from their earlier demands."

Casey took a sip and thought that she really didn't like brandy, either. Too bad the prince didn't have beer in one of those little cut-glass decanters on his sideboard. "Why?" she asked.

Eric's smile grew sly as he took his own sip. "I have a feeling that Cassandra's making their life miserable. They've offered to let us have her back for a million Swiss francs—flat fee. No announcement, no coronation cancellation." His second sip was longer, and he came away with an even more delighted smile. "You know, I have a feeling that if we just left her there, by the end of the week they'd pay us to take her off their hands."

Casey scowled. "Don't get any ideas. I already owe her one dress."

"The general and I were just discussing that," Eric ventured, leveling those resistance-sapping eyes on her and setting down his glass.

"I don't think I want to hear this," Casey assured him, fighting a new urge to get up and run.

"The kidnappers are still eluding our grasp."

Casey turned to the general. "I thought this was going to be a piece of cake," she protested.

He frowned. "A piece of—"

Casey waved aside his confusion. "Easy," she clarified. "I thought this was going to be over before any of us knew it."

He studied his fingertips with regretful eyes. "I regret to say, *fraülein*, that the leadership of the group seems to have undergone a surprise change. We are dealing with someone we hadn't anticipated, and I fear he managed to move a step beyond our grasp."

Why did she feel as if the quicksand had just reached her hips? The more she helped, the more difficult the operation seemed to become and the more participation was required from her.

"Eric, I have to remind you . . ." She'd turned just in time to see him pull something out from a drawer. "What's that?"

"Try it on," he suggested, holding it out.

Casey shied away as if it was a snake. "No, thanks. I don't like the looks of that."

"It's only a crown."

She snorted. "That's what van Helsing told Dracula about the crucifix. Put it away."

The circlet of diamonds, sapphires and rubies glittered seductively in the soft light as Eric held it out to her. The symbol of everything her family had lost so many years ago, the wealth, the power of sovereignty. That last trace of royal blood, so long dormant in her veins, now called out to it, hypnotized by the lure.

"The coronation is Sunday," Eric was saying.

Casey deliberately shook her head. "I have to be back at work by Friday. Besides, Cassandra really would have my head if I stole her limelight on the biggest day of her career."

"What if we can't rescue her in time? Think of the turmoil."

Still she held fast. "No."

"Casey," Eric pleaded, "you don't understand. The entire economy is at stake. Taping rights have been sold to cable TV. The country will be out millions."

She shook her head, unable to work up the nerve to look at him. "I'll reimburse you. Small weekly amounts for the rest of my life."

The general added his weight. "It is only just in case, *fraülein*, so that the kidnappers cannot possibly have the upper hand."

Then Eric pulled the dirtiest trick he could. Pulling the crown away, he slipped it back into its case in the drawer, just as Casey had asked. A certain amount of light seemed to go out of the room. But then he turned his eyes back on her, and Casey forgot the glitter of those jewels. The jewels in his eyes were far more compelling.

"I can make arrangements with your company," he coaxed. "Stay, Casey. Just a little while."

"You'd go to pretty great lengths to protect your country," she answered. "Wouldn't you?" She couldn't help the note of hurt sarcasm that crept into her voice.

"Yes," he replied honestly. "I would. But I would never go as far as to hurt you."

For a moment it was as if the general wasn't even there. Casey and Eric faced each other, the intensity of their silent communication crackling between them like lightning. Any questions Casey had ever entertained regarding Eric's using her for his country's ends were laid to rest by the stark sincerity in his eyes. She knew that his plea was twofold. The sleight-of-hand idea at the coronation was real enough. But Eric wanted Casey to stay for him as much as for his country.

Emptying her glass with a suddenness that left her watery-eyed, Casey got to her feet.

"Why does it seem like I'm forever giving in to you?" she demanded.

"Because you know it's the right thing to do," the general ventured self-righteously.

"I wasn't talking about that," Casey advised him dryly. He had the good sense to remain quiet. "You might be able to deal with work," she said to Eric, "but you won't have a bit of luck with my mother. I'm going to have to take care of her."

Eric stood to join her. "I don't think you'll regret it."

The smile Casey gave Eric left him in no doubt as to her fears regarding that subject. "Oh, what the hell," she finally sighed, not caring that the general probably knew that she wasn't referring in the least to the charade he had asked her to play. "I might as well practice what I preach and do something just because I want to."

Taking hold of her arms, Eric smiled down at her, his eyes suffusing her with their warmth. "Then I know you won't regret it."

"Don't be so damn smug." She smiled back and left.

Seven

———

Reports from the palace in Moritania today once again categorically deny as absurd the claims by the Moritanian Socialist Movement that they have the Crown Princess Cassandra held captive. A videotape of a woman claiming to be the princess has been received from the group at the same time the princess was participating in the state functions this week in coordination with the world finance conference being conducted in the small country."

Slumped in the leather chair in Eric's office, Casey punched the remote control, and the film of her nodding and shaking hands faded from the screen.

"Casey, it's getting out of hand," Sandy said diffidently from the chair next to her.

Casey shrugged. "I know. I should tell them all to take a hike, especially since Mr. Simpson refused to extend my vacation. I could be fired if I stay long enough to be crowned on Sunday. I guess princes don't carry the weight they used to."

"Come home with me tomorrow," Sandy prodded. "Let them play *Prince and the Pauper* with somebody else."

Without really answering, Casey got to her feet. "Let's go get something to eat."

The two of them had sneaked down to the office to watch the TV accounts of the situation while the rest of the palace readied for dinner. Two more days had passed in which Casey had spent the majority of her time at state functions playing charades and trying to ignore how much Cassandra's shoes hurt her feet. She'd called her mother and lied to her for almost the first time in her life, telling her that she'd lost her passport and wasn't sure they were going to let her get home the same time Sandy did, but not to worry. Her mother had worried, naturally. Sandy had rolled her eyes accusingly. All in all, it was making Casey pretty tired and crabby.

The longer she stayed, the more difficult it was becoming for her to go home at all. All she wanted to do was stay in this comfortable limbo where no decisions had to be made about her trip home, her relationship with Eric, her future. They played their games and conspired like children on a summer's evening, going out of their way to deny the transience of their time together.

"The bell will ring in a few minutes," Sandy finally said, not bothering to move. "You know, I really can't believe that somebody hasn't done more nosing around and figured out that you're fishy."

Now Casey was pacing. "An obedient people, I guess."

"No press is obedient," Sandy snorted.

"Well, maybe they're stupid!"

Sandy turned, her eyes a little wide. "Hey, don't take it out on me. I'm just the Greek chorus. Somebody's got to remind you where the reality line lies."

The turmoil bubbled up suddenly, surprising Casey as much as it did Sandy. Whipping around on her friend, she faced her with accusing eyes.

"I'm doing the guy a favor, okay?"

"You're playing make-believe."

"Of course I am!" she nearly shrieked. "He asked me to pose as his niece, so I'm posing as his niece until she's safely rescued."

Sandy got to her feet, just as upset. "I'm not talking about that, and you know it."

Standing her ground, Casey faced her, her eyes defiant. "Tell me what I'm supposed to do, Sandy."

Sandy never hesitated. "Leave. Get the hell out of this fairyland before it destroys you. You don't belong here, Casey. Pretending you do doesn't change it."

"I don't care if I belong here or not," Casey snorted with a wave of her hand.

Sandy's expression grew disbelieving. "You don't, huh? Then why are you practicing royal etiquette every day with Maria? Why did I almost hear you on your knees giving thanks this morning when they said they still couldn't find the princess? You don't want to go home." Pointing an accusing finger, Sandy made her final judgment. "I, for one, am glad I won't have to be here when it all ends." She didn't wait for an answer before stalking out of the room.

It was all Casey could do to remain in one spot. The fury of her anguish filled her with an unquenchable fire. In only a matter of days she had committed herself to something that she knew was a no-win situation. She knew Sandy was right. She could never stay here. She didn't belong in these echoing old halls. But she knew just as surely that, hour by hour, she was losing ground against the persuasion of Eric's gentle charms.

She should get out so fast that she'd leave the front door banging in her wake. But she couldn't watch Eric struggle day after day to maintain a country's precious equilibrium and desert him when she was his best chance of success. She suddenly couldn't bear to let him shoulder the burden alone, at least while she could legitimately be around to help. And, to be brutally honest, she couldn't bear to walk away from the life he'd stirred in her. It was impossible for her to go, but the longer she stayed, the worse she was making it on herself.

Furious tears welled in her eyes as the pain in her chest grew. Whirling around, she turned to the bookcases alongside Eric's desk. A vase. She picked it up, the need for a little destruction urgent. Hefting the large urn-shaped object, she went into a backswing, a sob escaping her.

"No!"

Startled, she turned, the vase still over her head. Eric stood in the doorway, a hand out to her.

"Not that one," he advised gently. "It's a Ming."

Walking over, he relieved her of it. Then he replaced it with a smaller, lighter vase of a darker green.

"Try this one. It's a lesser dynasty."

She should have given up the attempt. Somehow his words only made the frustration worse. With a little cry of rage, Casey hurled it against the far wall. It shattered with a dramatic explosion.

"Better?" he asked with a smile.

She made a furious swipe at the tears that had spilled onto her cheeks. "Who wants to live in a house where you can't even break anything, anyway?" she demanded crossly. "It's like living in a museum!"

Eric nodded. "Precisely."

"There you go again," she accused, the tears flowing faster. "I just busted your vase, pal. Can't you even get mad?"

He reached out to her. "You needed it. What's more, you deserved it. You've put up with an awful lot in the last few days, Casey. I'm awed that you've managed so beautifully this far." Tenderly he brushed away the tears. It only made matters worse. Casey ended up gulping and sobbing, trying to hold off the torrent his gentleness was unleashing.

"You really are amazing, you know," he murmured, easing her closer.

She would have none of it. "Knock it off!" she demanded, her control slipping farther with another major sob. "Just . . . knock it off. I don't want you thinking I'm wonderful."

"Why not?" he asked with a soft smile. "I do."

"Because . . . because it won't do any good. Sandy's right. I'm playing make-believe. I should get my fanny back to New York where I belong."

Without her knowing how, Casey found herself nestled against Eric's chest, his arms around her and his hand against her hair. She cried even harder.

"Don't even say that," he begged, his voice suddenly very quiet.

Casey lifted her head to see the pain in his eyes, the sudden tight set of his jaw. With a little hiccup, the tears just as suddenly died in her.

"Eric . . ."

He smiled then, his charming facade back in place. "Dinner's ready," he said with studied ease. "I came to get you."

She shook her head, the tears still glistening on her cheeks forgotten. She knew him better now, saw the tension he couldn't quite conceal. He was hurting, and it tore at her more sharply than her own pain.

"Wait a minute," she objected, snaring his eyes with her own. "You're not gonna tell me that you'll walk out of here and pretend everything's okay."

"It is," he argued carefully.

"It is not," she retorted just as carefully. "You're upset about something. And you can't tell me that it's going to all be okay if you just pretend you aren't and go out there and play the perfect prince."

The humor in his eyes was tempered by a wistfulness that brought loss to Casey's mind. "Ah." He nodded with another smile. "The famous American stress."

"Eric," she objected with a frustrated shake of the head, "get mad for a change. Throw something. Yell. It's not gonna hurt anything."

"That's Cassandra's forte, thank you."

"No," she disagreed. "She just takes advantage of the privilege. Did your brother ever scream?"

"Never."

"He might have ruled a little longer if he had."

She'd struck a nerve. She could see it in the darkening of the clear quiet of his blue eyes. There was a storm brewing in those calm waters.

"Yelling doesn't change anything. It doesn't get you what you want."

"What could you want?"

"I told you," he retorted, his hands tight on her arms. "You."

"I'm only staying this long because of you. You think I'd go through all this for Cassandra?"

"But you'll still go home."

"You're damn right I will."

Without either of them realizing it, their voices had begun to raise, their eyes sparking with confrontation.

"So you see? If I yelled at you or threw one of the vases, it wouldn't convince you to stay."

"Eric, how could I possibly stay?" she demanded. "Why should I forfeit my job just to drag out the inevitable?"

"Because I'm falling in love with you!"

The sudden silence was complete. Eric wasn't even sure he was breathing. How did she keep surprising him into admitting what he only suspected?

Once he'd said it, he knew it was true. He knew that he wanted this sprite to stay by him, to continue coloring his world with her brightness. But he knew just as well that this wasn't the time to tell her. She was having enough difficulty with the just task of subterfuge.

With an effort, he offered an easy smile. "Now you know why I don't think yelling is a good idea. One tends to say too much."

"You mean you didn't mean it?" she asked in a strangled voice.

He drew her closer. "I meant every word. But from the looks of you, I don't think you wanted to hear that right now."

Her answer was wry. "I guess the next time I goad you into letting off a little steam it'll have to be from a safe distance."

"What's a safe distance?" he asked.

"New York."

His thumb was brushing her cheek again, the movement bittersweet and intimate. Casey wanted nothing more than to close her eyes against it, to give in to the sweet weakness his touch wrought. For a very long moment the shadowy room remained silent, a silence that weighed heavily between the two of them. The atmosphere of a gracious old home, of a class of people her grandmother had known as a child. A class Casey had never considered real as she'd grown up in her crowded Brooklyn apartment.

She didn't belong here. But she was wanting more and more to stay.

"I believe Mother is waiting for us to join her," Eric finally said, his voice as intimate as his touch.

Casey lifted her eyes to his, basking in the mesmerizing blue. "Well, I always said it doesn't pay to keep a dowager waiting."

With a soft chuckle, he bent to drop a kiss. "I'd advise you to never put it quite that way to the queen."

They found the queen in the private dining quarters, a room the size of only half a football field. The formal dining room could have seated the United Nations without much crowding.

Tonight the intimate room with the twelve-foot leaded-glass windows and the claw-footed sterling candelabra was set for only six. Eric and Casey were the last to arrive.

Rudolph, the much-abused fiancé spoke up briskly from where he stood next to the queen. "Cassandra, are you quite all right? Your face is a bit puffy."

"Cold feet, my dear Rudolph," Casey shot back in an arch tone of voice she'd copied directly from the tapes. "Eric has been trying to remind me of my duty to my country next week."

His eyebrows rose with surprise. "You don't want to be crowned?"

"Don't be silly," she retorted, letting Eric lead her to her place and give her over to Rudolph's rather diffident care. "I didn't say anything about being crowned, did I?"

She had scored a point. Rudolph blushed, the queen frowned and Eric hid his smile behind the glass of wine he raised. Sandy, seated to his left, wouldn't be saying much for a while. To *her* right was the still-stunning Mr. McCormac. Casey looked over to greet him and felt her stomach give way. Damn Eric for throwing him into the pot tonight. Her first reaction was still to just sigh and stare, just as Sandy was doing.

"James, my dear," she said, smiling sweetly and leaning across to touch his hand. "It is so good to see you away from the press of a public function. How has your stay been?"

"Profitable, Your Highness," he admitted with a soft chuckle that made Sandy sigh. "There's something about touching base with one's money that stokes a person's feeling of security."

Casey batted her eyelashes, which sent Eric's eyes rolling. "Any service our humble country can be."

"Eric was saying that you hadn't had the chance to ride in quite a few days," he said as the servants began to circulate. James seemed to know just what to do with circulating servants. He moved around their serving with the grace of a ballet dancer. Casey just sat back, hoping for the best.

"A lot to do this week," she admitted. "I sometimes wish I'd decided to be crowned and married in the same dress. The fittings are absolutely draining me."

It was the eye signals from Eric that alerted her to the fact that one particular butler was standing behind her, awaiting her attention.

"Yes?" she snapped without turning. She wished she could remember the man's name.

"Your Highness, I must notify you that we have been unable to obtain your caviar for this evening."

Casey was a hairsbreadth away from giving herself away once and for all by throwing herself at the man's feet and thanking him with all her heart. Instead, she once again sought Eric's guidance. His brows gathered. She turned on the servant in a right snit.

"What do you mean?" she demanded, causing more than one flinch at the table. "There is always a supply kept ready."

The man bowed, and Casey saw the perspiration glistening on his forehead. It made her feel terrible. She didn't want to yell

at this nice man. Maybe she could make it up to him when she
came back out of the phone booth as Casey Phillips.

"It is my responsibility, Your Highness. I assumed that there
was ample supply. When I found that not to be the case, I went
to the shop where the palace obtains its supplies. The owner
apologized, but he also has had an unexplained rush. He
promises to have more in tomorrow."

Only Casey saw the abrupt stiffening of Eric's posture. It
didn't dawn on her to wonder why. Later, she thought, and
turned back to serve the little man's penance.

"Oh, very well. But if it isn't available at this table tomorrow night, you may serve your notice."

His latest bow was quick as he departed.

"You're becoming disconcertingly tolerant these days, Cassandra," Eric observed in a dry voice. "Could it be that the
prospect of marriage agrees with you?"

Casey wondered what *intolerant* would have been like. "I'll
whip him with rushes when the guests have left," she snapped
just as dryly, and went back to her other guests.

"You do a most credible imitation of Bette Davis in *The
Virgin Queen*, my dear," the queen stated dryly after the other
guests had gone.

"Hardly the appropriate film if you're referring to Cassandra, Mother." Eric laughed from where he sat with his brandy.

She ignored the comment. "I must admit I considered Eric's scheme harebrained at first. It seems, however, to be serving for the moment. Have you heard from Mueller, Eric?"

Eric shook his head. "Not since about noon. They'd combed
all of the known lairs for the MSM and come up dry."

The queen nodded with regal dignity. Casey, sitting off by the
harp, couldn't help but wonder if this woman had ever let her
dignity down and just played. Had she giggled like a school-
girl when her young husband proposed, when he first kissed
her? Or did she deign to be kissed? She'd grown up wondering
the same about her grandmother. It had only been as the old
woman had grown frail that she'd unlocked those memories
that had reflected her human side.

"Very well," the queen said as she rose from her chair.
Turning slightly so that she could take in Casey, seated very
carefully in her antique chair, the china cup in her lap, the
queen gave a quick nod of judgment. "When this is over, you

must be our guest for a few days." An eyebrow arched. "The servants rather like you."

Before Casey could thank her, the queen swept out. Casey turned to Eric, the surprise still in her eyes. It was nothing compared to the surprise in his.

"Good God." He whistled, downing his brandy in a gulp. "She likes you."

Now Casey's eyebrow arched. "You make it sound like she shouldn't."

Standing, he poured another dose. "Not shouldn't. Doesn't. My mother isn't one to open up to people very quickly. One of the professional hazards of having power, I guess. She is very...careful. What you received was nothing short of the royal blessing."

"An offer of a visit?"

"Rest assured," he told her, "you're welcome here anytime. She might even take to inviting you to sip tea with her. And she hasn't made that offer to anyone since my Aunt Eleanor died."

Casey looked after the departed queen, then back to Eric with a little shrug. "Why me?"

He grinned. "She might just respect your gumption, my dear Casey. Not many people in this world are comfortable with her."

"Not many people in this world grew up with my grandmother," she retorted easily. "Now *there* was an old lady who could make you feel uncomfortable."

"Are you going riding with James tomorrow?"

"Are you kidding? And blow my cover?"

Eric laughed, taking a seat next to her. Slipping an arm around her shoulders, he prepared to get comfortable. It was not to be, however. A hesitant knock on the door brought his arm back around and him up off the couch.

"Come in."

It was all Casey could do to keep a straight face. She felt absurdly as she had the night her father had caught her necking on the couch with Mike Molloy after the junior dance.

Their guest was the butler who had put his head on the block at dinner that evening, the same one, she now realized, who'd first greeted her in the kitchens. A tall, distinguished-looking man, he carried himself like an army major. He entered and came to a stiff attention.

"You wished to see me, Your Highness."

Eric got to his feet. "Yes, Simmons, thank you. Sit down, if you'd like. I need to ask you a question."

"I'm sorry I yelled at you tonight," Casey apologized without thinking.

Simmons was coaxed into a surprised little smile. "You do have the knack, ma'am. We're all quite proud of you."

Casey didn't consider the various contradictions in his statement when she smiled back. "Thank you. Everybody's been really nice to me."

"And you they," he replied.

Eric finished pouring another dose of brandy and handed it over to the startled servant, an amused little smile playing around his eyes. "This will of course be held in strictest confidence, Simmons."

Simmons took a look at the liquor he held, took his seat and would have promised to have his tongue cut out.

"You spoke of the princess's supply of caviar tonight." Eric waited for a stunned little nod. "This is the first time to my knowledge that you've ever run out."

"Yes, sir," the man nodded emphatically. "I can't understand it myself. We had the full supply in. I checked it no more than three days ago. And suddenly tonight we show up missin' all of it. And the shop—you know the one—says they're out, too. Most unusual, sir."

Taking up his stride, Eric nodded to himself. "Most unusual. Who would have taken that caviar?"

"Oh, no one. No one really likes the stuff but Her Highness—" with a confused little frown, he turned to Casey "—Your Highness." Then he, too, drained his brandy.

"For just this evening, we might refer to the present Highness as Miss Phillips, Simmons."

"Yes, Your Highness."

"Who is allowed in the pantries?"

"The pantries, Your Highness? Why, any of us, you know. The cooks, meself, Rolph, when Her Highness wants a bit of a snack."

"Is there anyone you wouldn't trust implicitly?"

The words brought Simmons to his feet, the accusation sparking outrage. "Your Highness!"

Casey saw the set of Eric's shoulders ease a bit with the protest. She knew he was satisfied, but still wasn't at all sure what the whole inquisition was about.

"Thank you, Simmons," he said, stepping up to face the man, a supportive hand to his arm. "You've been a great help to me. I simply needed a little affirmation, and you provided it. Has anyone but the staff been near those pantries?"

Simmons took a moment to think that one over. "Well, sir, yes, now that you mention it. Werner's been nosing about a bit. Says he hasn't had time to get regular lunches and all, so he snitches a tin or two of something from the shelf."

"Werner." Eric's voice was almost hushed.

Simmons nodded uncertainly.

Eric nodded back, dismissing the man. "Thank you, Simmons. Good night."

Carefully setting his snifter down, Simmons bowed with a tentative smile. "Night, Your Highness—Your, er, Fraülein Phillips."

"Caviar?" Casey asked after the door had once again closed to leave the two of them to the cozy fire and each other.

Eric turned on her, the expression on his face a mixture of triumph and outrage. "Werner," he said, more to himself than to her. "It can't be."

"What can't be?"

He didn't return to the couch, so Casey got to her feet.

"The caviar," Eric prodded. "What do we know about it?"

Casey shrugged. "It's a source of protein, disgusting-looking and one of the few things I'm glad I can't afford."

"And who is addicted to it?"

At that Casey scowled, since she had been the hapless victim of that little passion. "You don't have to remind me. I've been the one taking her medicine while she's vacationing in the mountains."

Eric turned, his eyes bright with discovery. "And if Cassandra isn't eating it, and you certainly aren't—"

"Not unless somebody shoves it down my throat with a big stick."

"Then who is?"

She thought about it. It didn't add up. Simmons had already said that nobody else really liked the stuff. So it all pointed right back to Cassandra—who was missing.

"But how?" she asked.

Eric turned to the phone. "That's what I'm going to find out. I have a feeling that Cassandra is being supplied with her favorite junk food so that she remains manageable, and someone has to be able to get it for her."

"The shop was out, too," Casey remembered. "My God, Eric, you think somebody's been stealing it right from the kitchens to take to her?" Then it really dawned on her. "You think *Werner* has been stealing it?"

"We'll soon find out."

But they didn't. Eric called just about every official in the country, but he couldn't locate Werner. Off for the evening really meant off for the evening for that particular bureaucrat.

Next Eric tried General Mueller. After hearing the theory of the missing caviar, Mueller promised to look into it right away, since the update from his investigating teams hadn't yet produced anything promising.

Eric set the phone down to find Casey next to him, her expression as intense as his.

"What did he say?" she asked.

"He said, 'Good night, Your Highness. Sleep well.'"

Casey scowled. "In for a penny, in for a pound, my dear Eric," she said, mimicking his own speech. "How close am I to freedom?"

Now he was the one to scowl, stepping up to take her into his arms. "You're so anxious to regain it?" he asked gently.

Casey eased into his embrace without even thinking. Looking up at him, she saw the remembrance of their earlier conversations gleaming eerily in his eyes. Frustration, anticipation, a gentle reproach. He was so close to her, his scent filling her nostrils, his solid strength enveloping her. She felt whatever resistance she had left dissolving. All he had to do was hold her against him and she lost all interest in what happened to her namesake. All she could think of was what it would feel like to have this man make love to her. Slowly, gently, with a passion that only she could unleash, even as she had begun to unleash his emotions.

"Posing as your niece *is* a bit restraining," she admitted in a hushed little voice, her face lifting to his. "I can't even play footsies with you at dinner."

"What about now?" he asked, so close now that his breath stirred fire along her throat. She wanted his lips there, his hungry hands. Her body was beginning to thrum with wanting him. Her heart had begun to race.

"Now?" she echoed, letting her hands stray up his back, the expensive linen delicious against her fingers, as it kept her seeking hands from the steely strength of his back. "All I know now is that you'd better kiss me."

NO C̶O̶S̶T̶ **...ON!**
NO P̶... **...SARY!**

PLAY "LUCKY 7"
AND GET AS MANY AS SIX FREE GIFTS...

HOW TO PLAY:

1. With a coin, carefully scratch off the three silver boxes at the right. This makes you eligible to receive one or more free books, and possibly other gifts, depending on what is revealed beneath the scratch-off area.

2. You'll receive brand-new Silhouette Desire® novels, never before published. When you return this card, we'll send you the books and gifts you qualify for *absolutely free*.

3. And, a month later, we'll send you 6 additional novels to read and enjoy. If you decide to keep them, you'll pay only $2.24 per book, a savings of 26¢ per book. And $2.24 per book is all you pay. There is no charge for shipping and handling. There are no hidden extras.

4. We'll also send you additional free gifts from time to time, as well as our monthly newsletter.

5. You must be completely satisfied, or you may return a shipment of books and cancel at any time.

MAKEUP MIRROR AND BRUSH KIT FREE

This lighted makeup mirror and brush kit allows plenty of light for those quick touch-ups. It operates on two easy-to-replace bulbs (batteries not included). It holds everything you need for a perfect finished look yet is small enough to slip into your purse or pocket—4-1/8" X 3" closed. And it could be YOURS FREE when you play "LUCKY 7."

Just scratch off the three silver boxes.
Then check below to see which gifts you get.

YES! I have scratched off the silver boxes. Please send me all the gifts for which I qualify. I understand I am under no obligation to purchase any books, as explained on the opposite page.

225 CIY JAX9

NAME

_____

ADDRESS   APT.

_____

CITY   STATE   ZIP

7	7	7	WORTH FOUR FREE BOOKS, FREE MAKEUP MIRROR AND BRUSH KIT AND FREE SURPRISE GIFT
🍒	🍒	🍒	WORTH FOUR FREE BOOKS AND FREE MAKEUP MIRROR AND BRUSH KIT
●	●	●	WORTH FOUR FREE BOOKS
🔔	🔔	🍒	WORTH TWO FREE BOOKS

Terms and prices subject to change.
Offer limited to one per household and not valid for present subscibers.

PRINTED IN U.S.A.

"I had?" he asked, and then dipped to brush her lips with his, the touch maddening. "Perhaps you're right."

His arms tightened. His eyes lit as he bent to recapture her lips. Casey closed her eyes, sighing against him. His lips tasted and taunted, and when he explored she opened to him, suddenly wondering why she hadn't liked brandy. It tasted so enticing on him.

He kissed her eyes, her cheek, her throat as she drew her head back, her hair tumbling over his hands at her back. Sparks flashed from his touch, skittering over her skin and sinking deep into her belly. She clutched at him as if afraid of falling, her fingers bunching into the fabric that covered his back.

"Eric, is this a good . . . idea?"

His hand strayed along her ribs, igniting chills across the silk-clad skin. She could hardly breathe for the freezing, burning fire he was unleashing in her. It frightened her, not only because she'd never known anything like it before but because she craved it so desperately. His fingers edged up toward her breast and she found herself wanting to urge him on.

"I think it's a wonderful idea," he whispered against her throat. "You can't imagine what it costs me to keep my hands off you."

"And here I thought those cold showers were a holdover from public school."

Eric nuzzled closer against the velvety skin at her throat, his tongue flickering against the soft crescent at its base. Casey gasped at the sudden lightning it unleashed, a liquid fire that swirled all the way to the edges of her fingers.

She never felt the buttons at her throat loosen. She just knew that for a moment his hand left her, and she felt it like the shock of loss. Eric's mouth was still against her skin, tracing tantalizing little kisses along the base of her ear. Casey felt the tight grip his other hand had on her waist, because without it she would have slowly sunk to her knees.

And then she felt his fingers skim her breast. Her breath caught. She arched against the agonizing thrill. He caught her nipple and teased it, his lips dropping to the ridge of her collarbone.

"Casey. . ." he groaned against her, crushing her to him, his patience lost. "I want you."

Casey recognized the power of his arousal against her and knew that her own sanity was vanishing as fast as his. With her last reserves of control, she took a deep breath. "Not here," she managed. "I'd never be able to sit down to tea with your mother again."

She surprised an abrupt laugh out of him. "Ever my practical Casey," he admonished breathlessly, his hold on her tightening.

"I want you, Casey," he repeated. "Now."

Casey felt herself nod, and couldn't believe it. Her lips were open, her eyes wide, her hair and dress disheveled. She felt as if she was sneaking around behind someone's back, but for the first time felt no shame. No guilt. She wanted Eric just as much as he wanted her, and she might never get another chance.

"Upstairs," she offered with a breathless little smile. "I have a bed that's wasted on just me."

With another kiss, he led her to the door. "Upstairs," he agreed.

No one else saw them walk arm in arm up the broad marbled stairs or down the long hall past the royal suites. Casey couldn't prevent the silly grin that kept plaguing the corners of her mouth as she thought about the man who walked next to her. Just the feel of his arm around her waist gave her a bright, giddy thrill, as if she was just soaring over the top in a Ferris wheel. She could see all the world, and it was spectacular.

They padded past the silent doors until they reached Casey's. Loosening his hold on her, Eric reached to open the door. The room beyond was dark, only a ghostly sky visible through the open curtains by the bed. Eric slid his hand along the wall for the light switch as Casey followed him through the door.

He never reached it.

Suddenly a shadow bolted up before them. Casey shrieked. Eric whipped around too late. The intruder's arm arced down, the blunt instrument in his hand connecting against the back of Eric's skull. With a groan, Eric slumped against the wall.

Casey turned toward the door. The intruder caught her by the arm and pulled her to him.

"Help!" she screamed, struggling to get free. "Eric, help!"

Eric didn't hear her.

Eight

—

The first sounds Eric could discern were the discordant sighs and grunts of struggle. It was dark. He couldn't remember much, just that he had landed in an ungainly heap on the floor where he lay wedged against a table.

The floor.

He remembered now. He'd meant to turn on the lights. He'd brought Casey up to her room....

Eric's eyes opened as the remaining memory returned—as did the pain, a tearing sensation at the back of his head as if someone with a pickax was at work. Over by the window he saw the shadows, two of them, tumbling around in silhouette against the gray sky, the sound of their breathing heavy and urgent.

"Casey," he groaned, trying to move in her direction. "God, Casey..."

He heard her muffled answering cry. Someone had a hand over her mouth and was trying to strong-arm her out the window. When she heard Eric she flailed out. Eric heard a resulting grunt of pain, then a surprised whimper from her as her attacker struck back.

Eric made it to his knees, then his feet. The room was spinning, the pain bringing on waves of nausea. One hand on the wall, he stumbled over to where Casey was kicking at her attacker.

Eric almost reached them when his hand made contact with a lamp. Without thinking, he flipped it on, then grabbed it.

Casey's attacker stopped. A heavy man, he wore a stocking mask and gloves. Eric didn't recognize him. But he saw that Casey was beginning to be worn down by the man's superior strength. She was going to be out that window in another minute.

"Let her go," he growled.

The intruder backed toward the window, Casey held firmly in front of him. Eric followed, trying to find an angle of attack. He could see the terror that welled up bright in Casey's eyes. It ignited a rare fury in him.

"Put her down or I'll kill you," he warned once again. The man laughed.

Casey took advantage of her captor's brief attention lapse. Relaxing against his hold, she threw him slightly off balance. When he moved to regain it, she shoved a hand straight up and struck his nose. He let out a howl, freeing one of Casey's hands. It was all Eric needed. Pivoting, he took a great cricket swing with the lamp and shattered it against the man's head.

It would have brought a lesser man down. It just stunned this one. Without letting go of Casey, he swung her at Eric, sending both of them tumbling against the wall. The man scuttled out the window.

Sandy got to the door in time to see Eric and Casey in a jumble on the bedroom floor.

"Really," she observed with an arch look, a hand on her hip. "Can't you two keep it a little more quiet? If the wind's with us, Switzerland probably heard your unbridled passion."

"Security," Eric gasped, trying once again to gain an upright position. "Let out the dogs."

For a moment, Sandy didn't answer. Then the truth sank in with a snap that brought her eyes wide open and a hand to her mouth.

"Oh, my God, Prince, you're bleeding!"

Tears still streaming down her face, Casey managed to get herself up in time to make the same discovery. Without any consideration for the room's real tenant, she whipped the linen tablecloth off the small nightstand and pressed it against Eric's head.

"Sandy, get help!" she snapped.

"Are you all right?" Eric asked, his back against the wall and his free arm around Casey. The other took over the job of holding the cloth. There was real fear in his eyes.

"I get sick at the sight of blood." She sniffed, trying to wipe her tears away. "Are you okay? You're a mess. You were great with that lamp." Another sob escaped her when she tried to grin. She was shaking. "Damn it, he hurt you."

"It could have been worse." Eric smiled, although he wasn't feeling appreciably better. The floor still tilted beneath him at regular intervals. At least he didn't have to move for a while. "You weren't bad yourself. Where did you learn that little move with your hand?"

Casey wiped away tears with the back of her hand. "From a marine D.I. I knew." When Eric's eyebrows raised, she defended herself. "Hey, pal, I live in New York. You learned how to ride horses, I learned how to ride subways. That was one of the lessons."

They held on to each other as they heard the burgeoning sounds of alarm gather in the great house. Suddenly Casey began to giggle.

"What's the matter?" Eric asked.

She motioned to the mess. "This isn't exactly what I had in mind when we came up here."

"I wonder if it was punishment for something."

Now Casey was laughing, the adrenaline still racing through her. "The nuns used to say that we'd get hit by lightning if we were ever caught messing around." She shook her head. "They never said anything about getting a blackjack to the back of the head."

They were so busy laughing that for a moment they didn't see the dowager queen standing in the doorway. When they did, it was to discover the real human fear she couldn't quite hide when she saw her only surviving son slouched in a pool of blood. For a painful moment, Casey was afraid the old woman was going to cry.

Not the dowager queen. "Rolph has called for Dr. Schmidt," she announced, only the quaver in her voice still giving her away. "I . . . presume the cut is superficial?"

Casey had the feeling that she simply couldn't bring herself to voice worse fears.

"I'm sure it is, Mother," Eric assured her in a rather washed-out voice. "It just feels like a bad hangover."

"You're ready to return to your room?"

"I think I'll just stay here for now, thanks."

She nodded, unable to leave yet unable to say more. For the first time, Casey felt sorry for her. There was a certain amount of loneliness in not being able to allow your feelings, especially for the person you loved most in the world. Watching this woman struggle with her control, Casey vowed that she would never raise her children that way. Rather than be an example, she was going to be an attack kisser.

"And you, Miss Phillips," the old woman finally said, turning to acknowledge Casey. "I hope you're quite all right."

"Thank you," Casey managed. "Eric saved me from being hauled out that window. That makes things pretty okay."

The sharp eyes sharpened. "Indeed."

"To think—" Casey scowled in Eric's direction "—I might have had to live on a diet of caviar and water. You saved my life, Eric."

Eric's reaction probably would have been a lot different had his mother not been there. As it was, he settled for a pained scowl. He thought the bleeding was slowing down somewhat. The dizziness was abating a little. It was time to reassert control. Releasing his hold on Casey, he slowly rose to his feet.

The queen's hand was out in protective warning before she could stop it. "Are you sure you—?"

Eric's eyes raised to those of his mother and softened. From where she sat, Casey saw a rare communication pass between them. The changing of the guard. For the first time in their relationship, the mother was not the one in control. She would never again hold the same authority.

"I'm not going to run after the gentleman, Mother." Eric smiled, easing himself down onto one of the ruffled pink love seats. "I'll just sit here until Dr. Schmidt shows up. The security people know where to find me."

His mother appeased, Eric turned to where Casey still huddled on the floor.

"Casey," he said gently, holding out a hand. "Come sit."

She gave him her hand, oblivious to the fact that it was still bloody. Now that all the excitement was over, she could feel the reaction set in. She had almost been kidnapped. Whoever had attacked her had certainly bounced her around enthusiastically enough. Everything was beginning to ache from her ribs to her shins. It would be nice, she thought, her eyes still on Eric's as if for the reassurance of that serene blue, when she could climb between the sheets and consign all that had happened to oblivion. It would be nicer if she could fall asleep in Eric's arms, but one look at the queen quelled that idea.

Casey's attempts to stand were a shambles. With Eric's hand for support, she tried to ease off the floor with half his grace. Instead, she ended up right back on her fanny, her knees as useful as antlers on a frog. She tried again, with much the same outcome. Her efforts only resulted in the reappearance of worry in Eric's eyes.

"I think I'm beginning to fall apart," Casey admitted in a very small voice.

He didn't bother to answer. He just stood up, his injury forgotten, and lifted her onto the seat next to him, holding her together with the force of his own control.

"I feel so stupid," she admitted, not noticing that the tears had returned. "You're the one bleeding."

Suddenly there was no one else in the world. "You're the one who was almost kidnapped," Eric said. "You have every right to feel a bit shaky."

"Shaky is one thing," she scowled. "Nonfunctioning is quite another."

He sat forward in his chair, an arm around her and both her hands in one of his. "I'm sorry, Casey. I would have never asked you to help if I'd known there would be any danger to you."

Casey snorted self-righteously. "There's more danger crossing the street in downtown Manhattan. I'll be fine. Although I've totaled another one of Cassandra's dresses." She exhibited the torn and stained teal-blue silk Eric's hands had so recently traveled over.

"I'll protect you from her," he said softly.

Casey felt so secure within his gaze, so safe and content. If only he didn't have to leave her side. She lifted her hand to the blood matted behind his ear. "Are you sure you're okay?" she asked, her eyes liquid with residual fear.

Before Eric could answer, Sandy reappeared, accompanied by the doctor, a short, florid man with half glasses he delighted in peering over. The queen had evidently decided that it would not be appropriate to be seen in her bathrobe, and was now missing from the assemblage.

Right on the tail of the doctor arrived the general, accompanied by his minions and brusque in his approach.

"Your Highness, the guards just notified me. Are you quite all right?"

Eric looked up from where the doctor was peering at his head. "I'll live, General. I don't suppose they caught the fellow."

The general's military posture showed definite signs of sagging. "I'm afraid not. I shall begin a thorough investigation in the morning concerning how he was able to get so close. I promise you, heads will roll."

Eric winced, whether at the doctor's ministrations or the general's choice of words, Casey wasn't sure. She took his hand without considering the company. He didn't seem to mind.

"He was right here in the bedroom?" Sandy was asking Casey in hushed tones, her eyes wide.

"How did the intruder manage to get into the grounds?" Eric was asking the general.

"The alarm system has been sabotaged," the general admitted. "It was just discovered."

"He had his hairy hands on my throat," Casey told Sandy.

"He wore gloves," Eric reminded her with a slight turn of the head.

"Poetic license," she allowed. "He did have a stocking mask. I don't have a feeling his looks would have improved appreciably without it, though."

Sandy grinned. "A real mouth-breather, huh?"

"It's amazing how thugs look the same the world over."

"A stocking mask?" the general asked.

"Support hose," Casey said, nodding. "His nose was within a millimeter of his left ear."

With a little clucking noise, the doctor finally straightened to deliver judgment. "Not a serious injury, Your Highness," he announced. "Although you will certainly feel some discomfort from it." Only Casey was in a position to see Eric's reaction to the obvious. "However, it will need to be sutured. I can do it right here if you'd like."

Eric cast a jaundiced eye around his niece's bedroom. "No offense, Cassandra—" he smiled dryly "—but I doubt sincerely whether this particular shade of pink is conducive to healing. I'll be more than happy to be treated in my own room."

Casey was glad. The only thing that made her sicker than the sight of blood was the sight of needles. The last thing they needed was for her to do a swan dive when the doctor treated Eric.

"You've already done quite a sufficient amount of damage to my room," she countered for the benefit of the doctor and a few guard officers who'd collected behind the general. "I'll never be able to get the disgusting stain off my wall."

"Don't try," he suggested. "Incorporate it into the decor."

"Would you like a sleeping draught?" the doctor asked, and Casey realized he was addressing her. She hadn't heard it put quite that way since her last gothic read. Didn't this country know about tranquilizers?

"No, thank you," she said, as evenly as possible. "A healthy dose of terror always puts me right to sleep."

Eric cast her a sidelong glance as he got to his feet. The doctor and general each took an arm to help him to his room. He shook both of them off.

"Perhaps your friend would stay with you for a while, Cassandra," he suggested, turning earnest eyes on her.

"I'll be fine," she assured him, her gaze not nearly as frigid as the tone of her voice. "As long as the general remembers to turn the alarm back on."

"I'll have a guard on the door," the gentleman assured her.

"Only if James McCormac volunteers," Casey retorted, and dismissed them all.

"So you've come to your senses and decided to come home with me tomorrow," Sandy said a little while later. "Right?"

Seated by the window, Casey gazed sightlessly out over the darkened expanse of back lawn and garden. The moon hadn't made it up yet, so the blackness was inky and unsettling.

"Right?" Sandy prodded from where she lounged on the pink bed.

"Wrong," Casey finally answered. "How could I leave when Eric's putting himself in danger?"

At that, Sandy sat bolt upright. "He's putting *you* in danger, you idiot. That guy didn't climb in here tonight to get decorating tips."

Casey waved her off, her own churning emotions distracting her. "I can't desert him."

"Casey," Sandy insisted, walking up to her. "We've gone way beyond blue eyes and great wardrobe here. You're starring in an Alfred Hitchcock movie, except that nobody's bothered to tell you how it's going to come out."

"As long as I get the handsome prince," Casey muttered half-heartedly.

"Casey..."

Casey turned on her friend, her patience disappearing. "Sandy, I already told you. I'm staying. I know it's a dumb thing to do, but I've done my share of dumb things before."

"Can't argue with you there."

"Then don't argue with me now. And don't run right over to my mother's when you get home and tell her what's going on. It's going to be hard enough to believe coming from me."

Sandy surrendered with a shrug. "You're the one paying for this shindig. I just wish I felt better about the whole thing."

Casey smiled as she got to her feet, weariness dragging at her. "I know. I'll try and be as logical as I can, Sandy. It's just that..."

"I know." Sandy smiled fatalistically. "I just wish I could stay and help."

"I'll be okay. I think I'd like to get some sleep now."

Sandy's silent reaction left Casey in no doubt as to her friend's opinion. But the goodbyes were given in hugs just the same. Then Casey was alone with memories of the kidnapping attempt and the unhappy realization that she'd caused Eric's injury.

After taking just enough time to soak out the first consequences of her struggle, Casey slipped out of the ruined garments and into one of Cassandra's less outrageous nightgowns. The sheets on the great mahogany bed were crisp and cool, and the eiderdown quilt as comforting as soft slippers on a cold night. Around her the palace sighed, its ancient walls whispering of the generations of emotion that had battered at it, the floors creaking beneath remembered weight. Casey lay in the luxurious bed and stared at another scrolled ceiling, unable for the first time in her life to get to sleep.

Soon the fear set in, the terror that hadn't had time to be fully realized while she'd battled her assailant and then struggled to maintain her composure before all those people. Her stomach churned and her chest grew hollow. Her hands began to shake until she clenched them in the soft quilt to keep them still. Her eyes stung with unshed tears.

Then the anger rose. Someone had actually tried to snatch her! Worse than that, he'd tried his best to make a soup bowl out of Eric's head. Lord, to remember her panic when she'd seen Eric go limp. When she'd called to him and he hadn't moved.

She'd really been afraid he was dead. The only reason she'd struggled so hard at first was to try to get to him. She hadn't really understood that the man was trying to take off with her. She just knew that Eric was hurt and some bozo in nylon and black leather was trying to keep her away from him.

And then they'd let him get away. Casey wanted to get her hands on that bastard. She wanted to pay him back for the blood she'd washed off her hands. And she wanted to pay the queen back because she'd let her relationship with her son wane to the point where she couldn't even hold him when he was hurt. She'd never even touched him.

Finally the frustration took over. Just what did she think she was doing here playing games with a country's future, doing Barbie Does Moritania while real hoodlums with real weapons were threatening its royalty? Was this the way it always was for Eric? Was he so calm because he was used to it? Maybe they got these kinds of threats all the time.

Well, she didn't. She was just a lousy secretary from Brooklyn with aspirations to someday graduate from law school and represent small claims if she was lucky. Nowhere in those dreams was there room for designer dresses and tiaras and customs about when you could be touched and talked to and people bowing and flinching at the sight of you for fear you'd do something to hurt them.

If she were going to be really honest about the whole thing, where did it say she had any right to somebody like Eric? She'd been telling herself that all along and hadn't believed it. She was born to marry a bus driver and have a few children to send off to school and ballet lessons. Her grandmother had been the last person she'd ever known who had even cared whether it was appropriate to wear white gloves or a hat to a function. Instead of attending high tea at the Savoy, Casey had grown up dining on hot dogs and soda at Shea Stadium.

But oh, Lord, how she wanted to have a chance. There had been such a life-giving incandescence in Eric's eyes tonight when he'd confessed that he wanted her. Such a heart-stopping hunger.

It didn't matter. She was going to be on that flight tomorrow with Sandy. She didn't belong here. Nobody really wanted her here. They hadn't even offered to clean up the mess once they'd escorted Eric off to be patched up. One little set-to and you really found out who mattered. She was going home where she meant something.

When Casey heard the door click open, she didn't move. She didn't have to. She knew just who it was, and her pragmatic resolutions flew right out the window. The hall light spilled over her, silhouetting her approaching guest. Then he closed the door, and the soft darkness enveloped them both once again.

When he reached the side of the bed, he stopped short. "I thought you'd be asleep."

Casey smiled ruefully. "I was just lying here thinking how I wasted a perfectly good vase earlier this evening. This is when I should be pitching things against the wall."

She sat up and scooted over, offering Eric a space to sit. He sat and leaned over to flip on the lone surviving table lamp. The pool of light surrounded them, glittering softly off the shards of glass clustered against the far wall as if they were paved gems.

Eric turned to take Casey's hands in his, his eyes tortured. "All you really all right?" he asked. "I wanted to be sure."

Casey sighed, furious that she couldn't better protect her determination from those sweet blue eyes. If only his forehead didn't crease just that way when he worried about her, or the crow's-feet appear when he smiled. If only he hadn't told her he was falling in love with her.

"It has been kind of an emotional day," she finally acknowledged, her gaze briefly straying to where her hands lay cradled within the warm strength of his.

"It has that." He nodded, and damned if those crow's-feet didn't show up. And that crease. Casey was losing ground fast.

"Maybe Sandy's right," Eric said quietly. "Maybe you should go home tomorrow with her."

Casey's eyes shot up. "How did you know about that?"

His smile widened. "There's not a whole lot that goes on around here that I don't know about."

Casey scowled. "Wonderful. I suppose you also know that she thinks I'm overdosing myself on make-believe."

"That's not why I think you should go. If anything happened to you, I don't know if I could survive it, Casey. I wanted to kill that man tonight."

"So did I," she admitted with a rueful grin. "Especially after he tried to dent your head." At the thought, she lifted tentative fingers to the area that had been hurt. His hair was freshly washed and combed, and there was no visible indication that the good doctor had been at him. "How is the royal concussion, by the way?"

He chuckled. Casey felt that sweet languor begin to steal through her limbs. "Probably just enough of a nuisance that I'll have to bring the royal aspirin to the functions tomorrow."

Casey's eyes sought his in outraged indignation. "Functions?" she demanded. "In my neighborhood, if you get a crack like that you spend the next day calling out for pizza and playing couch potato."

Eric's eyebrows lifted. "Possibly. But then, if Brooklyn had a finance minister he would not have the luxury to play any kind of potato. Especially if there were a big conference going on."

"Don't bet on it."

"I've put you through a lot," he admitted, his thumb drawing lazy patterns across her palm. "I just can't ask you to do any more."

Casey's eyes widened. Eric's were serious. He wanted her to go home. A great emptiness threatened to open within her. "You can't do that. Who's going to pretend they're Cassandra?"

He shook his head. "I'll worry about that."

"And if I say no?" She tried not to think about the fact that she had made the same decision no more than milliseconds before he'd walked into the room.

Still he wouldn't back down. "Then I'll deport you. You'll be on that flight tomorrow, Casey, so I know you're safe."

"And what about you?" she demanded, the tears threatening again. "How will I know *you're* safe?"

He kissed her hand with a gentle wistfulness that tore at her. "As soon as Cassandra is recovered, I'll be on a plane to Brooklyn to visit."

"And what about the meantime?" she asked. "Just how do you think you're going to manage without me?"

His smile was intimate. "I'll muddle through. It will give me something to occupy my time until I see you again."

Why was she so sure that if she left tomorrow she was never going to see him again? Was it just the fact that she could never envision Prince Eric Karl Phillip Marie von Lieberhaven walking into the drab little rooms on her street? Or was it the fact that when she left, all those ladies with their fine jewels and worldly demeanors would still be here to distract him?

Before she gave herself time to consider it, Casey turned her hand so that it could caress his face.

"How am I supposed to say goodbye to you tomorrow with all those people around?" she asked, her voice strained with the decision she'd just made.

Eric's expression softened, and he reached out to entwine her hair in his hand. "You could say goodbye tonight."

"Like we were going to do before?" she smiled. "Is your head up to it?"

His answering smile was so deliciously suggestive that it alone ignited the slow fire in Casey's belly. "My head doesn't have to be up to it," he assured her, his hand dipping around to trace the plunging neckline of Casey's ivory silk gown. "Especially if the rest of me is."

Casey rubbed her thumb over the rasp of his beard, thinking that this was the roughest she'd ever felt it. Thinking that she'd have to tell him that she liked it that way. And then praying she'd get another chance. If only the servants would understand and help her.

"In that case," she whispered, the beguiling smile on her lips drawing him closer, "let's part friends."

Nine

Oh, my God..."

Casey's fingers slowed at their task, the buttons of Eric's crisp linen shirt only half-undone. She had demanded the privilege, never having known the satisfaction of undressing a man. As Eric nibbled at the sweet flesh at her neck, she had managed to undo two or three of the tricky devils, made all the more difficult because the wildfire ignited by the touch of his lips set her hands to an unbearable trembling. His skin was so warm beneath his clothes, his muscles so tight and lean. And the golden hair that curled across his chest so delicious to the touch.

"What's the matter?" Eric mumbled against her neck, his words tickling.

Casey giggled, trying her best to draw in a stabilizing breath. He had pulled her down next to him on the bed, nestled atop those cloud-soft comforters, his hands at once taking command of her. She felt as if she was melting, her body reduced to a glowing, molten light stoked by the heat of his kiss and the hunger of his hands. She had never known her body could feel like that. Had never anticipated such agonizing delight at another's touch. Practical Casey Phillips was completely at Eric's mercy.

"You have a hairy chest," she managed with a smile, rubbing against him like a cat. Even through the silk of her gown, the feeling thrilled her breasts to a taut attention. She smiled and stretched again, surprised that she could elicit a moan from Eric by the action. "You never told me."

"You seem surprised," he murmured gruffly, his fingers twined in her hair, his lips teasing the base of her throat.

"I usually notice... that kind of thing sooner," she tried to explain. The buttons were all free, and she took to slipping his shirt off over his tight shoulders and hair-roughened arms. "But you never get casual enough that I can get a look at your chest."

Eric chuckled, deep in his throat where it vibrated against Casey. "Isn't this casual?"

She placed her hands flat against his belly, running up over the ridges of his ribs, the clean lines of his chest. He was so hard, so angular. The feel of him against her incited more fireworks—more of the molten fire that was turning her insides into water. "You have a beautiful chest," she murmured, dipping her mouth to it, tasting the throb of his heart. "You should show it off more."

Eric pulled her lips back to his, his eyes hot and possessive. "And you, my lovely Casey, have the most beautiful breasts—" he smiled, savoring the dark flavors of her as he discovered with his hand how her breasts anticipated him "—and the most lovely eyes, the most enticing mouth..." His fingers swept her nipples, dancing over the silk and lace and skin like the tongues of a spreading fire. His lips trailed after, along the edges of her gown, the moist tracks of his kisses sending her gasping.

Casey's head came back, her hands up to span the tight expanse of his back. Eric's head was just over her breast, the soft light glinting off his sleek brown hair, glowing off the tanned planes of his back. He bent to take a breast in his mouth, suckling against the slick silk. The hot possession of his mouth was agonizing. Sliding his other hand down along the contours of Casey's body, he explored her slightly concave belly, the ridge of her pelvis, the firm length of her thigh.

Casey was paralyzed. Nothing could have prepared her for the effects of his touch, nothing could have predicted this spiraling exhilaration. Eric brushed the filmy material away from her breast and just as easily slipped out of his remaining clothes. Casey watched with breathless wonder, intoxicated by the play of ivory light along his skin, desperate to know the hard, lean feel of him against her.

When he lay next to her, Casey felt him full and hard along her and her heart skidded. She held on to him, not even able to explore the delicious mysteries of his body as she wanted to. His mouth descended again and tore away her reason. All she could do was answer the urgent need Eric unleashed in her.

His hand moved up against her and her hips rose, pushing full against the flat of his hand. She ached for him, for the touch of him inside her to quell the fierce molten fire he had ignited. Her breathing was ragged against him, her heart racing. When Casey felt the gentle exploration of his fingers as they slipped beneath the tumbled skirt of her gown, she moaned, anticipating him, opening to him so that he could purge that agony.

"Oh, Casey," he gasped against her when his hand reached the dark recesses of her. "I've wanted you since the moment I saw you."

She could hardly draw breath to answer. His fingers plumbed her, dipping and stroking until she couldn't hold still against him. The agony was fierce, uncontrolled, a pain of yearning that only he could assuage. When he lifted his head to her, she managed a wild smile, her heart stolen by the tousled, unshaven face above her.

Casey didn't feel Eric ease up her gown. He bent to reclaim her mouth, and she became lost in the taste of him, the pressure of his hand against her leg. Wrapping her arms around him, she welcomed him to her.

The stab of pain didn't surprise her. It became lost within the explosion of sensation he ignited when he thrust into her. The firestorm broke over her, searing her, blinding her, bringing cries of release to her throat. Eric shielded them with his mouth, his own urgent groans mingling with hers. Casey felt her body begin to rock against him, arching against the fire that consumed it, molding with the overwhelming strength of Eric's. When he shuddered against her, his arms closing around her as if afraid to let her go, she held on to him. Felt him spill himself in her, knew the fulfillment of love.

Silence returned to the old room. Outside, the breeze rustled at the window and skittered through the trees. The floor of the room spoke again, and the walls answered. On the high mahogany bed, Casey and Eric lay intertwined, lost in the glow of contentment.

He lifted a hand to brush the hair away from her forehead. "You didn't tell me," he said with a little awe.

"What?" she asked with a smile. "That I was a virgin? Serves you right for not showing me your chest."

She surprised a smile from him. "Why?"

"Why didn't you show me your chest?" she countered, her own fingers splayed across his belly. "I don't know. Maybe you didn't trust me. Which was good judgment, actually. One look at it and I would have done this a lot sooner. Possibly right in the middle of that formal banquet the other night."

Eric scowled, running a finger down her nose. "You know what I mean."

Nestling a little closer, Casey sighed. "Did you ever hear about the little boy who didn't talk till he was three?"

"Pardon?"

"Not a peep, all that time. Then one day at breakfast he suddenly says, 'Mom, the toaster's on fire.' When she asked him later why he hadn't talked before then, he just shrugged and said, 'Because I didn't have anything worthwhile to say before now.'"

Eric chuckled, enfolding her in his arms. "You do have the most unique view of life, my lovely Casey."

"Just pragmatic." Casey smiled. She'd never really thought about her "state," as Sandy would have called it. It was just something that had never come up. She had always known in the back of her mind that there would be a time when this was right. Even two days ago she hadn't known that this would be it. Now, lying against the warm comfort of Eric's chest, she was glad she had waited.

"Pragmatic women don't push princes into lily ponds," he retorted. "Or let themselves be talked into parading themselves as a princess just to save the economy of a small country."

"They do if they were raised on the movies," she argued. "You've just been overdosed on duty all your life, my Prince. It tends to warp your sense of fun."

"Not totally," he said. "I know for a fact that what we just did was fun."

"A move in the right direction."

"It doesn't change what's going to happen tomorrow."

Casey nodded, hoping he didn't see the new light in her eyes. "I have no intentions of changing the plans."

Eric's hold tightened a little. "How would you feel about coming back when it's all over?"

"How would you explain me?" she asked, for she'd never had the nerve to ask before.

"As a long-lost cousin who just happened to show up."

"Right."

"I'm coming to get you, Casey," Eric warned, his hand absently stroking the satiny length of her hair where it tumbled over his chest. "I want you to know that."

Casey had to close her eyes against the hope that blossomed in her chest. The hope that he really would brave the streets of Brooklyn to find her. But in the last couple of hours she'd changed her mind about all that and decided not to give him the chance to back out, making the point moot anyway.

Eric didn't have a good morning. After slipping back into his own room just before dawn, he'd lain awake remembering the life-giving feeling of Casey in his arms, the worth of the gift she'd given him. Then he'd begun his day by issuing the orders that would send her away from him.

She didn't come down to breakfast. Eric sat alone at the great table, thinking how cold the room suddenly was, how bereft of the life her quick wit and irreverent manner brought. When Werner showed up for work, all Eric could think of was that Casey hadn't been able to believe he was guilty. She had given Eric the gift of seeing the people around him in a new light, and now he had to face them without it. The world he had inhabited because of station and duty suddenly seemed a less challenging one without Casey to share it.

"You've been seen in the pantry on more than one occasion," Eric said to Werner as the two of them sat in his study, the early-morning light honey-yellow on the warm wood. Eric kept waiting for Casey to walk into the room.

"Why, yes, Your Highness." Werner nodded, perplexed. "Is there some difficulty? I only thought that since the status of the palace is on alert, my services would be better utilized if I took less time for meals."

"Where were you last night, Werner?"

The older man frowned, leaning forward, his hands on his knees. "Have I done something to displease Your Highness?"

Eric eyed the pencil he was tapping against his desk. "We seem to be missing the stock of Beluga caviar that was kept for the princess. The local shop is also out. You have been seen at the pantry."

For a moment, Werner smiled. "Oh, sir, I can't tolerate the stuff. I've been eating the salmon, maybe some herring. Never the caviar."

"But the princess does eat the caviar, Werner. Caviar from that pantry."

The room fell silent. When Eric looked up, it was to see the hurt disbelief in his employee's eyes. Werner couldn't even seem to form the words to protest, so deep was the insult.

"I just had to ask, Werner," he said, feeling better. "Someone is getting that stuff to the princess, and right from under our noses."

Werner's astonishment could not have been manufactured. "A spy in the palace?"

"A kidnapper in the palace, I think. I'd like to quietly ask all the kitchen staff if they've seen anything unusual."

Now Werner could afford a weak smile. "Like my eating out of the pantry."

Eric allowed his own smile when he nodded. "If you would start now, I can help after the luncheon. I hate wasting time on that thing, but I'm afraid I have no choice. I have to make Cassandra's excuses."

Werner's eyebrows lifted again. "Miss Phillips won't be going with you?"

"She's not here, Werner. I sent her back home this morning."

"But she's down in the kitchens, Your Highness."

Eric's head came up, his eyes sharpening. "That's impossible. Her flight was scheduled to leave Zurich half an hour ago."

Werner shrugged. "I don't know, Your Highness. I just saw her on my way up here. She and Helga were concocting some kind of pastry."

Eric didn't say another word as he got to his feet and stalked out of the office.

It had been quite a while since he'd been down to the kitchens, since he'd snitched treats from the old cooks as a child. The room didn't seem quite so cavernous as it had when he'd been young. The walls still gleamed their immaculate white, and the flagstone floor shone spotlessly.

Activity in the great room stopped when Eric walked through the door. He didn't even see the ten or so people bow. Nor did he see the grins of anticipation on every one of their faces.

"Just what do you think you're doing?" he demanded, coming to an abrupt halt by a gleaming steel countertop.

Her nose smudged with flour, Casey looked up at him without noticeable discomfort. "Showing Helga how to make soda bread," she smiled, giving her dough another sound thump. Standing alongside, Helga didn't look quite so unconcerned. She dipped a quick curtsy, then kept her eyes firmly on Casey's work. "At least I think I am," Casey scolded. "I'm doing this all by memory."

"I told you to go home today," Eric persisted, his eyes as stormy as the North Sea.

Casey raised innocent eyes. "Now how can I do that?" she asked. "I have a luncheon to attend with the conference delegates and a cocktail reception this evening. And we still haven't found my caviar yet. Werner didn't take it, did he?"

Eric's breath escaped in a frustrated sigh. "Casey..."

Assuming an elaborate pose, arms akimbo, Casey mimicked his tone of voice. "Eric..."

"You can't stay. You could be in danger."

"You could be in danger, too," she countered. "I don't see you on the next flight from Zurich."

"You could lose your job."

She flashed a challenging grin. "You could lose your policies."

Eric turned on all the servants, his brows knit. "I suppose you all helped her."

Another round of bows and curtsies. "Yes, Your Highness."

"Fine," he snapped. "You can keep her in line. I give up."

"Excuse me, Your Highness," Maria spoke up from the door. "The seamstress is here for the fitting on your dress."

"And you," Eric said accusingly, whipping around. "I expected more sense from you, Maria."

"Yes, Your Highness."

"Don't go blaming Maria," Casey objected. "I strong-armed her."

Maria's placid expression belied the statement, but there was nothing to be done about it. Eric turned on Casey again.

"I could have you arrested, you know."

"Arrest your own niece?" she asked, eyes wide. "What for?"

"If you please, Your Highness," Maria said diffidently. "The fitting is important. We only have so much time."

"Casey," Eric tried one last time in a reasonable tone, "there really isn't any reason for you to stay."

"Yes, there is," she argued with an infuriating smile. "I decided that I can help you step off that throne a little more often. See how the real world lives. Who knows? Maybe it'll make you a better prince."

"I'm a finance minister," he shot back. "I know perfectly well how the real world lives. I control the economy of this country."

"Big deal," she retorted. "Have you ever tried to get a bus transfer in Manhattan? Find your luggage at LaGuardia? You have a hundred people to take care of you. You can't get a good taste of reality living like that. You can't even have any fun. It is my duty to change all that, Your Highness. I even found you a pair of jeans to wear." With a powdery hand, she pulled her long apron aside to exhibit a well-worn pair of denims and a cotton blouse from her wardrobe. "Just like mine."

"We'll talk about it later," Eric snapped, knowing perfectly well that he'd let her stay. "Now, go with Maria. You only have three days to get your dress fitted."

"Four," Casey automatically countered. "The coronation's Sunday."

He allowed a sly smile. "But the wedding is Saturday."

Casey's face fell. "What?"

"Your wedding to Rudolph. By law, you have to be married to rule. The wedding's Saturday and the coronation's Sunday."

She gaped. "You didn't tell me."

"Still want to stay?"

For a long moment Casey stared at him, then around at the staff, who had carefully gone back to their tasks. Finally she faced Eric again. "Do you promise you won't keep from rescuing Cassandra in time just to get even with me?"

It was rather disconcerting to see her sly smile mirrored on his face in answer.

The luncheon was held in the formal dining room, patrolled by Simmons and his cadre of servants and organized by Werner's accomplished hand. By the time Casey showed up to fulfill her duties, the guests were already seated and chattering among themselves. When she entered, they all stood and paid obeisance.

"Nice to see you all," she said, privately amused at the arched eyebrows. She'd refused Maria's help today, and satisfied herself with a simple French braid for her hair, and an unornamented Adolfo suit of raw emerald silk and matching pumps.

"A hat," Maria had very nearly wailed, the suggested implement in her fluttering hands. "The princess would never attend a luncheon without a hat and her gloves."

"Well, it's about time she did," Casey informed her, and headed for the door.

Eric appeared now to guide her in to eat, his own expression a study in bemused control

"Asserting your independence?" he asked under his breath.

"You're lucky I got the whole-wheat flour out of my hair," she smiled sweetly.

He got back at her by seating her directly across from the little woman from the other night. An ambassador's wife, it turned out, Countess Brader was not one to let a few days interrupt a train of thought. As Eric settled himself in next to Casey, the woman plopped down on her chair, returned to her half-finished roll and waved it in the general direction of Casey.

"Did you think about what I said the other evening, Your Highness?" she asked. "I was sure that once you did you would come to the only logical conclusion concerning the abysmal surrender to the crass Americans this country has arranged."

Bracing herself against a surge of irrational fury at this pompous, bigoted woman, Casey smiled with glacial control. Alongside her, Eric turned a warning eye on her.

"Indeed I have, Countess Brader," she announced, and quite a few heads turned. Most of the people here had been at the banquet. "I can well understand the pain you feel about having to converse in such a dismal language. Unfortunately it is the law, passed by my dear late father, so I am not at liberty to alter his intents. At least until I am on the throne. Therefore, since I do not wish to cause you any discomfort, nor do I wish to dishonor the memory of my father, I have come to a decision."

The woman's eyes brightened with cautious triumph. Casey smiled back.

"You do not have to speak in English. As a matter of fact, you do not have to speak at all."

The woman's face crumpled. "But, Your Highness—"

Casey raised a hand, seemingly oblivious to the delighted grins of the rest of her guests. "No, Countess Brader, it would not be fair to you. From this moment, I think it would be better if you never speak in my presence. That would suffice to satisfy both our problems, I think."

As Casey turned to begin her salad, she had to admit that she had gotten quite a kick out of the power she had just wielded. She'd never had the wherewithal to make a person she didn't like shut up, and to see that woman red-faced and silent was enough to make up for all the discomfort of charading as Cassandra these last few days.

She didn't think she'd done a bad job of carrying it off, either. Turning to take a sidelong glance at Eric, she found her hopes confirmed. His eyes were dutifully on his meal, but it was all he could do to keep a straight face. Others on down the table were having less luck. Casey could hear amazed chuckles ripple through the room, then the buzz of surprised conversation. Within moments the atmosphere of the room was just as it should have been for a state luncheon. At least the kind of state luncheon Casey would want to attend.

Eric spent at least the first fifteen minutes of his meal trying to maintain his composure. All he could think about was how glad he was that Casey had outwitted him and stayed off that flight. He wouldn't have wanted to miss this scene for all the world. Until now, no one in either Countess Brader's country or his, including her precise, pleasant little husband, had been able to put a curb on her sharp tongue. To see that woman reduced to frustrated silence was a satisfaction that he would enjoy for years to come.

And to think that the secretary from Brooklyn had been the one to finally discover the diplomatic words to shut her up. He couldn't believe it. The girl was brilliant. She was outrageous. And, he realized anew as he stole a look over at her in her sleekly simple attire, she was more beautiful than Cassandra could ever hope to be.

"Nobody looks you in the face," she complained later as they walked back down the long halls from the reception area.

Startled from his own reverie, Eric looked over at her. "What?"

"The diplomats," Casey elaborated with a frustrated little sigh. "They haven't once gotten their eyes higher than the level of my collarbone. Doesn't that drive you nuts?"

His hands in his pockets as he walked, Eric gave a little shrug. "I never really thought about it. It's the way they are."

"But if they won't look you in the eye, how do you know whether they're lying to you?"

He chuckled. "My dear Casey, in government you simply assume that *everyone* is lying to you and go from there."

Casey shot him an outraged look. "That's silly. You should make a law or something to change that."

"Don't forget," he advised, "you're dealing from centuries of tradition. At one time your head couldn't even be level with mine."

"Yeah, I know," she nodded offhandedly. "I saw *The King and I.*"

Eric smiled, hooking his arm around hers as they strolled the long corridors of the first floor. The hallway was wide, the floor a checkerboard tile. Alcoves were spaced along the walls with old Greek and Roman statuary, anonymous torsos that had long since lost limbs and faces to the ravages of time. It had been a place he'd enjoyed in his childhood, conjuring ghosts of dead centurions and popping out from shadows to scare the servants.

"Have you ever thought of getting used to the customs instead of just arguing about them?" he asked with a mischievous smile.

"Not when they don't make sense." Casey shook her head. "Can't touch a princess, for heaven's sake. That's one of the most archaic things I've ever heard of."

"Could you get used to them for me?"

That stopped her, the echo of her clicking footsteps dying along the corridor. "That's like my asking if you'd mind having the neighborhood over when you show up for dinner at my house. That's the custom there, you know. Especially if a native daughter makes it to twenty-five without prospect of marriage."

Eric laughed. "I'd be delighted to meet the neighborhood. What would I wear?"

Casey smiled back. "It's a dead cinch that you wouldn't get a block in black tie and tails."

"Then I'll wear some jeans," he said. "Just for you. Will you allow people to wait on you—just for me?"

"I am," she argued.

"Now—" he nodded "—because it fits your role. What about later when we're married and you have to keep house and grace those social functions?"

Casey had been all set to turn on down the hallway for the Rose Room, where the dowager queen awaited them. Eric's words first stopped her, then swung her on her heels.

"Did I ever tell you that this was my playground when I was a child?" he asked offhandedly, looking around with fond eyes. "I didn't have the luxury of a neighborhood park I could attend or a mother who had the time for me. So I played in among the statues. They became my friends." He paused a moment as the ghosts returned, both happy and sad. "I'm glad I won't have the pressure of ruling. My children will be able to lead a more normal life."

Casey finally found most of her voice. "I thought you weren't getting married."

"No." He shook his head. "I said that until now I hadn't had the time to get married. I guess what I should have said was that I hadn't found the woman I wanted to marry."

When he turned his gaze on her, Casey felt the impact of his decision. His eyes were bright, alive, almost merry. His whole being radiated anticipation. He really meant what he'd said.

Trying to remember how to breathe and stand up at the same time, Casey said the only thing that came to a mind unable to come to grips with his words. "Eric, I think your plane just overshot the runway."

Ten

Eric laughed, taking Casey into his arms. "It never fails to amaze me how you cut to the quick of an issue."

Casey was glad he was holding on to her. She had serious doubts about whether she could stand. His smile, even more than his surprise words, had robbed her of any strength. As for her brain, it had gone straight into meltdown. She couldn't pull a lucid thought from anywhere to dispute or agree with anything Eric said. Except one.

"You're nuts!"

"I believe we established that a long time ago." He smiled, his delight in her growing. "This time I think my insanity could save me."

"But Eric," she protested instinctively, "I have no business being married to a prince!"

"Why, just because you have more sense and style than half the people who were in that room today?"

"When somebody asked me how I thought Schmidt did in Germany, I told them I didn't know they played baseball in Germany!"

"A technicality."

"I told the Minister of the Exchequer how nice I thought it was that England provided clergy for old grocery clerks!"

"He thought you were cute."

"Oh. Is that what 'I beg your pardon' means?"

"Do you love me?"

That stopped her cold. Casey looked up into those azure eyes and knew she was lost. All she could think of was how Eric's arms felt more like home than anything in her life ever had. How he had supported and goaded and cherished her until she almost felt as if she belonged here.

Long ago, when she was a daydreaming teenager, she had anticipated what it would feel like to love a man. She hadn't had any idea what that really meant. A heady anguish was building in her chest, the pain of hope, of possibility. Eric had just threatened to make dreams come true she'd never even known she'd had.

"Do you love me?" he asked again, his voice just as gentle.

"Love?" She tried to bluff. "That's not love. I always blush and stammer like a high school sophomore when a handsome man with a continental accent touches me. Or it could be all the pink in that room. I wake up and think I'm in a Barbara Cartland novel. And the outfits—you can't count out the outfits. Dinner jackets were invented to drive women into frenzies. You can't count on anything I do when I'm in the same room as a dinner jacket—"

"Casey..."

"Yes." She finally wound down with a stunned little shake of her head. "I love you. I have from the first moment I laid eyes on you."

"Then what is the problem?"

"Eric," she objected, finally finding the hurdles, "if I weren't playing the role of your eminent niece, I couldn't even touch you. I couldn't talk to you without being asked. Doesn't that say something about how appropriate our marriage would be?"

Just saying that word ignited a new ache in Casey's chest. She pulled away, walking over to one of the statues. It was an armor-clad torso, its navel just level with her eyes, the long years having smoothed the marble into a mere suggestion of anatomy. Casey saw it and thought of the tight power of Eric's sleek muscles, the delicious taste of his skin. She flushed and turned away again.

"I don't mind," he said from behind her. "Why should you?"

"Marriage," she moaned, closing her eyes. "Boy, you do move at a brisk pace, don't you? Just the other day we were talking affairs. And if you'll remember correctly, I was having trouble with *that*."

"You weren't having any trouble last night." He smiled with just a touch of roguish charm. His troubles earned him a scowl. "I've been alone for thirty-five years, Casey. I realized it when I met you. I don't see any reason to wait anymore when I know I love you."

"But you're a prince!" she retorted, turning toward him. The fact that they'd known each other such a short time no longer seemed relevant.

"And if your ancestor had been handy when the crown prince disappeared back in 1870, you might have been in line for the throne instead of Cassandra. You have as much right to be here as I do. Probably more." He grinned rakishly. "You have at least one *legitimate* royal line in you."

Casey couldn't quite bring herself to look at him. "You really didn't have a playground to go to?"

Eric smiled, pulling her to him. "I really didn't. I had the stables, of course, and the nursery. But I never had a set of swings."

"My kids are going to have swings," she said. "Every kid deserves the chance to get stitches by the time he's four."

"I agree." Eric nodded, easing her closer to him. "And a pony."

"And a baseball team to belong to."

"We'll start a league."

"What about piano lessons?"

"We have several. Mozart played on one of them, come to think of it."

"I can't marry you."

"Why not? We agree on how to raise children."

"What about your mother?" she asked, closing her eyes against his chest. She felt so content in his arms. "What would she say?"

"She has no say in how we raise our children."

"Eric..."

"Besides, she loves the piano."

"But would she like Brooklyn accents in the ballroom and baseball on the TV?"

"Why don't we go find out?" Eric challenged, holding her back to get a good look at her. Casey's eyes were wide, glittering with the maelstrom of emotions he'd unleashed. He brushed a thumb across the soft edges of her lips, remembering their taste with new yearning. He wasn't about to give her the chance to back out.

"I know just what she'll say," Casey argued with a futile shake of her head. "She'll look way down at me and say, 'Indeed.' Just as if I'd told her there was a mouse in the throne room."

Eric found himself laughing. Casey had once again painted a scathingly accurate picture. It was just what his mother would do. But he wasn't in the least worried, he had the feeling that Casey was more than a match for his mother.

"Come on," he coaxed, slipping an arm through hers and guiding her down a side hall. "We'll go by way of the nursery."

"Your other favorite spot as a kid."

He grinned. "Kind of a foregone conclusion, wouldn't you say? I really wish our children could enjoy it like I did. Of course, we'll move elsewhere."

"Children." She sighed with another shake of the head. Repetition of pertinent words sometimes helped clear an overloaded brain. It wasn't doing much for her this time.

The hallway they took ended in a short flight of stairs and then another hallway. Just as airy, this one was decorated with paintings. Portraits, the subjects decked out in a progressive series of costumes from the time when men had first charted the oceans. Casey scanned the paintings in passing, wondering if these were family or friends or maybe enemies hung in a back hall to remind the ruling government what they were on alert against. Maybe some of them had been related somehow. Noting the patch of powdered wig on one rather dandified gentleman, Casey almost hoped not. He would be kind of hard to explain back on the block.

Suddenly she stopped. "What is this, the Corridor of the Butlers? What's his picture doing up there?"

Eric came to a halt beside her, his eyes following hers. "Whose picture?"

"My great-great-grandfather."

Eric's eyes were still on the stiff features of the young man, the large dark eyes and the bristling blond mustache, the formal morning suit and the pearl stickpin in the cravat. Eric's eyes slowly swept around to her.

"Who's your great-great-grandfather?"

Casey pointed toward the eyes that watched timelessly over her head. "Him. I have an old picture of him from New York. That's him, even down to that funny scar on his face."

"The Heidelberg scar."

She turned then, to see Eric stunned for a second time. His eyes were also on the portrait, but they weren't examining. They were introspective, calculating.

"What's the Heidelberg scar?" she asked.

"From dueling," he allowed, still not facing her. "It was quite popular. Are you sure this is your great-great-grandfather?" he demanded. "What was his name?"

"Mmm, let's see," she mused, counting back generations on her fingers. "He would have been . . ."

"Berthold," Eric said for her.

Casey turned, surprised. "Yeah. How did you know?"

"Berthold Phillips," he said, his eyes widening as much in humor as surprise. Casey saw a true delight take hold in him.

Casey scowled at him. "How did you know? You sure as heck couldn't pull that one out of the air."

"I didn't have to." He grinned excitedly. He'd just dropped a kiss on her forehead when he suddenly backed away, his hands up in the air, his lips curling with wry delight. "Oh, excuse me, Your Highness. I exceeded my privilege in touching you without your permission."

"Eric, knock it off." Casey scowled. "What are you talking about? How did you know his name?"

"Casey," he said, grinning broadly, "the gentleman in this picture was the Crown Prince Berthold *Phillip* Karl Eric von Lieberhaven, the rightful heir to the Moritanian throne. He disappeared in the year 1870, and my ancestor took over."

Full realization took her a moment. "You mean *I'm*—?"

"The legitimate heir to the throne. You are a crown princess, my lovely secretary."

"In-deed," the queen said when they told her sometime later. Neither Casey nor Eric could face each other for fear they'd laugh.

"And what was your great-great-grandmother's name?" the old woman asked, her eyebrows still raised in stiff disbelief.

"Oh, gosh." Casey sighed, thinking back. Names weren't a long suit in the Phillips family. "Kurtz? Is that the one? I remember hearing that her first name was Genevieve."

Mother and son exchanged enlightened looks.

"So that's where he went." Eric grinned. "After all these years, we finally know." Turning back to Casey, he continued. "Berthold disappeared during a border dispute between Moritania and Austria. There was a faction within the aristocracy that sided with Austria. The Kurtzes were such a family."

"So old Berthold ran off with one of the bad guys?"

Eric shrugged. "It would seem so. The marriage was probably forbidden by his family and hers, and they ran off rather than give in."

Casey couldn't manage much more than a raised eyebrow. "Indeed." She turned to Eric as if the queen weren't seated just across from her. "Does this mean we really don't have to ask your mother..."

Eric's laughter echoed around the small room. "It means we probably have to get permission from *your* mother in order to get married."

To her credit, the queen picked up on that right away. "Eric," she snapped, her eyes swiveling frostily to Casey. "Explain yourself."

"Quite simple, Mother." He grinned, enjoying himself much more than Casey was. "I plan to set all your long-standing fears about my bachelorhood to rest. Casey and I are going to be married."

Casey and the queen objected in unison, Casey because Eric was making rash assumptions and the queen because he was making those assumptions about Casey. The queen won out.

"But she's—"

"The rightful heir to our throne, dear." He smiled. "If she pressed it, she might be able to dump the whole lot of us right out in the snow."

"Be serious," Casey objected. "That couldn't happen. Could it?"

Eric shook his head. "Not really. But I can't wait to threaten Cassandra with it. She'll go mad. Speaking of which, I have to make a few calls on that very sore subject. Would you ladies excuse me?"

Dropping a kiss on Casey's forehead, he strolled on out of the room, oblivious to her rather desperate eyes. The door closed, and the room fell into silence. Gathering her courage, Casey turned to the queen. The diamond-hard gaze that met her was enough to make her flinch.

"You may pour tea," the old woman announced, her posture, if possible, even more regal. She wasn't going to let a little change of plans throw her off. After all, in her mind it wasn't *her* family that was illegitimate. "We shall discuss this rather startling news."

"Startling's a good word," Casey nodded halfheartedly as she got to her feet. She missed the glint of calculating worry in the queen's eyes.

Almost two hours later, Casey found Eric back in his study.

"You left me alone in the lion's den," she accused, plopping down into one of the leather armchairs and kicking her shoes off.

"And I wager you did beautifully," he said, smiling.

"Well, she didn't bite me. Then again, she didn't offer to come to Brooklyn to meet my mother, either." Rubbing at a set of sore feet, Casey tilted her head to the side. "Actually, it isn't that important. Seems to me we're getting way ahead of ourselves here."

Eric's head was still bent over some paperwork he was doing. "Ahead of ourselves?"

"Yes. As in 'the bride-to-be hasn't said yes yet.'"

He looked up then to see the sly mischief in her eyes. "She will," he assured her with a maddeningly complacent smile, and returned to his work.

She matched his complacency. "What's it worth to you?"

"Me?" he countered easily. "Nothing. You? Now that's a different story."

"Why?"

Eric didn't say anything. He just held up a suspiciously familiar-looking passport.

"That's kidnapping!"

He snatched the little book away just in time. "That's such an ugly word. We in government prefer . . . protective custody."

Casey's eyes narrowed. "And what are you protecting me from?"

"Your own misconceptions. I was wrong to want to send you away. You belong here with me, and I'm afraid I'll just have to keep a watchful eye on you until you realize that."

Casey was going to protest, possibly even go after the passport again, when his next words brought her up short.

"Well, actually Werner will for the next day or two."

Casey straightened. "Werner? Why?"

Eric smiled, and Casey found herself caught in the throes of an overriding desire to throw him on the carpet and reexplore that hair on his chest.

"After the reception tonight, I'm going to be...out of touch for the next day or so."

Something clicked when he said that. Something Casey didn't like. Eric was looking suspiciously pleased with himself, and the last thing he'd said he was going to do was check up on Cassandra.

"Explain 'out of touch,'" she suggested carefully.

"I'm taking your suggestion to get to know how people live a little better," he announced. "I'm going out into the real world."

That was when Casey realized something else. Eric was dressed all wrong. He didn't have his suit on, nor his tie. He didn't even have on one of those hand-tailored linen shirts she'd grown so fond of. He was clad in a dark gray Aran-knit sweater. Casey's eyes narrowed even more. Her heart rate also took a quantum leap. How could anyone possibly look so good?

"See?" he said, pushing his chair out. "I even found those jeans you got for me."

Find them he did indeed. At any other time or place Casey would have been mortified to find herself staring in such a southerly direction at a man as he got to his feet. It wasn't, after all, very polite. But she truly couldn't help herself. Eric, who had virtually redefined elegance for her, should not have looked quite so nice in casual clothes. After all, he had been born and bred to fine tailoring and expensive materials.

Not true. The jeans hugged his lean frame as if they had been painted on, outlining any number of powerful muscle groups with breathtaking effect. Combined with the sweater, the outfit made him look twice as handsome, twice as sexy. Casey found herself shaking her head, her palms already slick.

"What's wrong?" he asked. "Don't I look right?"

She couldn't help a rueful laugh. "It's not fair."

"What isn't?"

Her grin broadened. "Give me an hour or so and I'll show you."

Eric's answering smile was broad. "So you think I'll blend right in."

"Nope."

"But you said . . ."

"I said you looked great. And I meant every word. The problem is you still don't look like anything but a prince."

Moving around to her, he slid his arms around her waist. "And you, of course, have a suggestion."

Casey did her best to ignore the rising temperature in the room. Eric's denim-clad thighs were insinuating themselves against her silk-clad ones, and it was the most interesting sensation. Tantalizing . . .

"Where are you going?" she asked abruptly, trying to ignore the tongues of flame snaking their way up her thighs.

Eric's smile was enigmatic and enticing. "Out."

She would have no part of it. "Out where?"

"I'm not about to tell you. You'll just try and tag along."

She tried to make her shrug nonchalant. "Walk out like that and you'll be spotted in a flash."

Eric was doing his best to keep his mind on the subject. He'd made a mistake when he'd taken hold of her. His body couldn't care less for Cassandra's problems and the duties of the country when it got this close to Casey. It simply wanted to satisfy that age-old need that kept men and women having the next generation of men and women.

The whisper of Casey's silk-clad legs against his was setting off warning bells, the soft fragrance of her hair filling his nostrils and driving all logical thought before it. He wanted to bury his face in its honey-hued depths, exploring the dark treasures of her delectable body with his hands. The fierce ache for her flared hard in him, almost taking his breath. For the first time in his life he very nearly shut the door on his obligations and spent his day exploring the delights of afternoon lovemaking on an Oriental carpet.

"Eric?"

"What?"

Casey smiled, sure of her power over him, an instinct that needed no practice to surface. It didn't hurt that the evidence of his arousal was so obvious, either.

She rubbed against him just a little. "You were going to tell me where you were going."

Just in time, Eric reeled his senses back into the safety zone. "No, I wasn't," he disagreed with a grin, dropping a kiss on her very pliable lips. "Witch."

Casey's voice remained soft. "Does this have anything to do with Cassandra?"

"It has to do with us."

Her eyebrow lifted. "I think I'm going to enjoy this."

The corners of his lips curled. "The sooner Cassandra's back on the throne, the sooner we can uncover your existence and arrange a proper wedding."

"I still haven't said yes."

His next kiss was not as fleeting. "You will."

"I'll say yes faster if you tell me what's going on."

"You don't give up easily, do you?" Eric had to smile at the determined look on her face. It would probably be easier in the long run to let her know now. "Simple. I got in touch with the shop owner, who said that the same man comes in for the caviar each day. He gets there right about five. I'm just going to see where he goes."

"Why can't somebody else do it?"

At that, Eric's face shadowed over a little. "Let's just say I have some questions that I need answered for myself. Don't worry. When I find out what I need to know, I'll call in for help."

A strange chill chased down Casey's spine. "How could General Mueller agree to such a thing?"

Eric's smile didn't quite touch his eyes. "Princes outrank generals."

She didn't feel any better. There was a whole lot of something Eric wasn't telling her, and she had the feeling that it would put him in danger.

"How about if I come along?"

"No. I'll be back in time for dinner."

She scowled. "That doesn't mean anything. They hold dinner for you. We could still be sitting there at four tomorrow...."

"Casey. I'll be fine. Let me have my moment of excitement."

She deliberately eased back into his embrace. "I thought I was your moment of excitement."

Eric would have none of it. "Go on and get dressed for the reception. I'll escort you before I go."

She made a face. "'And the condemned man ate a hearty meal.'"

For the first time since she'd been playing this little game of Cinderella goes to Moritania, Casey snapped at Maria. Then she snapped at Werner and Simmons. It had all begun with her decision to stay. Somehow, just that action had changed her participation in the game from a passive to an active role. If they wanted her around, they were at least going to have to let her have her two cents' worth.

She turned a bit surly when Eric insisted on playing detective without her right after asking her to marry him. Casey still hadn't figured out just how she was going to break the news of the wedding to her mother, and now he was putting the whole thing in jeopardy.

The worst part was the effect his proposal had had on her emotional stability. From the moment she had realized he was serious, an explosion had ripped through her. A tremor that could surely have been felt on the Richter scale. Within the period of—what, days?—she had progressed from lusting from afar to yearning from close up to the frustration of futile hope to the shock of certainty. She had, quite literally, fallen in love at first sight, and amazingly, unbelievably, so had he.

It wasn't supposed to happen this way. That only happened in fairy tales and movies. Her mother had known her father for five years before she'd "known," as she put it. How could Casey know in a week? How could Eric? But, inexplicably, she did.

And how had she managed to outsmart reality by meeting and falling in love with Eric in the first place? It couldn't be real. It just couldn't. And yet every time she looked at him, she fell even harder. Every time he reached out to touch her as if to make sure she really existed, she felt his power over her grow. She melted before the intensity of his eyes and ached for the touch of his skin. No matter if he'd been a cabdriver who'd picked her up on the way to the airport, she would have loved this handsome, vital man.

But, and this was the final twist that fueled even more emotional quakes, he was a prince. The kind who lived in a palace and played polo just for fun. The unreality of it only fueled even more Casey's unconscious decision to make her own place in the palace while she had the chance.

So when Maria had come to inform her that it was unseemly for her to sit sipping coffee with the cooks while dressed for a formal occasion, Casey had informed her that since she was willing to show up on time for the functions they needed her to attend, the least they could do was to let her pass her time her way in the meantime. Especially since it wasn't bothering anybody to begin with.

Then Werner and Simmons approached to apologize for a few glitches in the proceedings, and she had told them both to chill out a little.

"What are they going to do if the flowers don't get here for their reception, overthrow the throne?" she demanded. Swinging on her heel, Casey shook her head in exasperation. "Everybody takes things to damn seriously around here."

"Certainly not you," Eric said, smiling tolerantly as he approached.

Casey turned to see him in yet another three-piece suit, this one gray with a scarlet silk tie. All of her irritations fled as if just the sight of him were soothing water where one bathed one's fevered brow. Eric did have the knack for settling her feet a little more surely back on earth and putting her priorities back in order. After all, what could be a problem if she could be with him?

"How long are you going to stay?" she asked, her voice unaccountably husky. Casey was thinking suggestive thoughts again, which inevitably led to the devious ones. He did look so delectable in gray.

"Just an hour or so. That's all that's expected of us."

She nodded and took his arm, and he turned with her into the main ballroom.

The doors slid open to the glittering assembly of the rich and famous, all suspended in the mirrors along the walls. The chandeliers sparkled and the late sunlight slanted in, gilding the room. The chatter echoed down the marbled floors and back again from the great portrait that hung at the far end of the hall. When the doors opened, everyone stopped.

Casey ran a nervous hand down the side of her mauve sheath dress, thinking how if Eric had his way she was going to have to get used to this. Then she decided that Eric couldn't possibly be serious after all. He couldn't really mean that she could fit in here.

They were announced, and Eric let go of her arm. The crowd turned to her and bowed, only the sporadic tinkling of ice against glass betraying the fact that they'd already started the party.

Casey scowled. "Eric, this is ridiculous," she said under her breath.

He turned without speaking.

"I'm getting real tired of this bowing garbage," she elaborated. "I've seen more bald spots than a toupee salesman!"

His abrupt chuckle brought some heads up. Casey's next announcement brought up the rest, most with startled expressions on their faces.

"Oh, for heaven's sakes, let's dispense with this," she announced, trying to catch the attention of even one pair of eyes. "I'm not going to banish anybody just because they didn't bow. It's a waste of time."

"But Your Highness . . ." one voice said automatically.

"Look me in the eye when you speak to me," she snapped. "Nobody looks me in the eye. How can I possibly know what you're thinking?"

Their first reaction was to bow acceptance. Half the room hesitated halfway down and straightened with some embarrassment.

"Thank you." Casey nodded briskly. "This is the way I'll conduct business from now on. It'll keep me from getting a swollen head."

Before she moved into the room, Casey turned on a very amused Eric. "Let Cassandra straighten out *that* when she gets home," she said, grinning wickedly.

Eric was still chuckling over Casey's actions two hours later as he finished dressing for his little journey. Lord, wasn't she just what this place needed? She was right. Cassandra would have a seizure when she got back and no one thought to bow when she stalked past. He couldn't wait to see it.

First, though, he had to get her back. He knew Casey was right. He shouldn't be playing amateur spy, but until some things were settled he saw no other way. Once he discovered where they were keeping Cassandra, he could gracefully back away and let someone else handle it, just as he'd planned to do all along. Then he'd come back and thoroughly ravish the young lady he'd just asked to marry him.

He was just buckling his belt when he heard the knock on his door. His attention still on the task, he walked over and opened the door. Casey never gave him the chance to protest.

"This is just what I expected from your room." She smiled brightly as she kissed him with determination on her way past. "All dark wood and teal blues. Very masculine. Very sexy."

"You're supposed to be at the reception," he accused, one look at her denim-clad figure enough to stir objection. "And just where do you think you're going?"

"With you," she replied, stuffing the cap she'd borrowed from Simmons, and was saving for the end of negotiations, into her back pocket. "You need an operative familiar in street work."

"I need to put a guard on you," he retorted. "You can't come."

"You can't go like that," Casey assured him with a practiced eye. Walking up to him, she unbuttoned the two top buttons of the cotton shirt he'd opted for, arranging the edges just so that the hair that curled at the base of his neck was visible. "*Very* sexy," she said. Then she mussed the shirt a little to negate the meticulous care the servants took of his clothes.

Eric couldn't help reaching out to gather her into his arms. "You think that will make the difference?" he asked skeptically, his mind more on the deliciously soft feel of her against him.

"No. But this will." And then reaching up with her hand, Casey proceeded to completely rumple his hair. It looked so good that she found herself wrapping her arms around his neck.

Eric's eyes immediately yielded, a languid heat rising from their depths. He pulled her closer and dipped down to claim her lips, thinking how honey-sweet they were. How eagerly she responded to him, opening her lips to him and curling her fingers in the hair at the base of his neck.

Eric groaned, the need flaring sharp and insistent. Casey's breasts pressed full and were against his chest, the nipples taut. He could feel the sudden staccato of her heart against him, counterpoint to his own. His hand strayed to it, his fingers cupping the swell of her breast and searching upward to claim the button-hard pleasure of her nipple. Stretching, she eased herself more fully into his grasp. The passion he had controlled for so long in deference to his position threatened to overwhelm him with just the satiny feel of Casey's hair against his fingers, the soft mewling sounds he tore from her throat, the bold evidence of her arousal in his grasp.

Just as he was about to lose all control and lift her onto the heavy canopied bed, Eric pulled away, his breathing still ragged.

"No." He shook his head at the desire in her eyes. "I have to go."

Casey's expression crumbled, her eyes still filled with the fierce desire Eric had unleashed in her. He held his hand against her breast as if unable to pull completely away from her. She felt the tingling contact of him spread throughout her and knew she didn't want him to leave.

"I've never said this before," she managed, her voice husky, "but if you go now, just know that I fully intend to encourage you to finish this later. I . . . think I'm addicted to you."

Eric's smile was intimate and soft, his eyes intense. "I'll hold you to that, my lovely Casey. And then I'll have the time to make love to you thoroughly and tenderly, just as you deserve. We'll make it a joint addiction." His smile grew slightly rakish. "Now what is that in your pocket?"

Chuckling at Eric's deliberate choice of words, Casey reached for the cap and set it square on his head. It brought the picture to an attractive completion. With the cap on, he looked more like a tourist than a prince of anything.

Stepping back, she considered her handiwork. "Sunglasses and a camera would help. Do you have cash?"

Eric pulled out his money clip with a grin.

"Where's your wallet?"

He shook his head. "I usually don't carry one."

"Are you kidding? Where do you carry your credit . . . ?" Reason kicked in. "Never mind. I don't suppose you need identification, either, do you?"

His smile said it all.

"Maybe I wouldn't mind living with you so much after all. When do we leave?"

"I leave now. Alone. I'm not a total idiot, Casey. Believe it or not, when I fulfilled military training, I took a bit of espionage."

"You still haven't ever grocery-shopped for yourself. Besides, if you leave me here, I'll just continue to embroil myself in one scandal after another until you return." Casey's eyes grew lazy. "You might not even have a throne to come back to after I get finished with it."

Eric stared at her, thinking how beguiling she looked with her beribboned, full-flowing hair and how infuriating her determination was. "You would, wouldn't you?"

It was Casey's turn to smile.

"Maybe I *am* crazy." He sighed in resignation, taking her by the hand and pulling her to him. "Because I think I am going to do it."

Eleven

I didn't know you wore glasses."

"Only when it suits me." Casey pushed the offending lenses up on her nose and took another look up and down the street. She and Eric were seated at a sidewalk café just next door to the gourmet shop that sold Cassandra's caviar. After convincing the shop owner to point out the caviar buyer for them, they had taken seats beneath the colorful umbrellas to observe. Their conventional tourist attire and Casey's exaggerated Brooklyn accent made them all but invisible to the average Moritanian eye.

"I still can't believe no one recognizes us," Eric offered as he took a drink of his beer.

"People see what they expect," Casey told him. "We're the last thing they'd look for in a sovereign. Take pictures everywhere we go, and remember to let me do the talking. Another preconceived notion about tourists."

Eric grinned and raised the camera to snap a shot of her biting into a pastry. "Only if you'll promise to stay out of the way when we finally get where we're going. That's my area of expertise."

Casey nodded, pushing the wide-brimmed straw hat back a bit on her forehead. With her hair knotted up under the hat, it was virtually impossible to see the telltale locks, and her face looked noticeably different with the owlish glasses she wore for distances.

"So," she said after letting the delectable chocolate-and-sugar confection dissolve to her satisfaction. "What do you think of your country from the other side?"

Eric flashed a smug smile. "Pretty well-run place, if you ask me."

Casey giggled. "The romantic out-of-the-way spot for the tourist who wants something different from his vacation."

"Or the investor who wants something different for his money."

Eric's eye strayed to a long-legged Slavic beauty who strolled by with a matching set of Afghans on leash. The street was lively with foot traffic, and the specialty shops were decorated in traditional Bavarian motifs, painted gingerbread and leaded windows. A white-gloved officer stood on a box at the intersection directing traffic—and watching the blonde with the dogs—and a flower vendor paced the corner behind his bright wagon. Overhead, great puffy clouds skirted the mountaintops and chased lengthening shadows along the narrow streets. If they hadn't been here to follow a possible kidnapper, it might have been an idyllic afternoon for two lovers to spend in the small Alpine community. Soon the cowbells would begin to clatter as the herds moved to their food, and the citizens emptied the streets for their homes.

"He's here."

Casey's head snapped around. "I thought you were watching the blonde over there."

A fleeting grin touched Eric's lips, his eyes resolutely on the wide window of the gourmet shop. "A good sovereign is an observant one. Let's go."

Casey's eyes followed around to get a quick impression of a slightly scruffy young man in fatigue jacket and jeans. Nothing, really, to set him apart from any of the other wandering youth in Europe.

"Eric, wait," she warned as he got to his feet, intent on the young man who was just nodding thanks over his package.

Eric turned to her. "C'mon, Casey. We don't want to lose him."

"We also don't want to draw attention to ourselves," she retorted quietly. "Which we will do if we don't pay."

Eric had the grace to offer a rueful smile. But when he pulled a ten-pound note out to drop on the table, Casey shook her head.

"This country should be bankrupt," she groused, exchanging the ten for a one and standing up after him.

That was when she bowed to Eric's area of expertise. She was going to walk right after the young man. Eric held her back until their prey had rounded the corner.

"Give him a little room to move," he suggested. "He won't be so suspicious."

"Hey, yeah." She nodded enthusiastically. "That's the way they always do it on TV."

Taking her by the arm, Eric turned down Wilhelminstrasse and around to the little side street, Kirkenstrasse, where the cathedral sat. The crowds thinned out a little bit here, since there weren't as many shops or businesses and no services were scheduled. It was more of a residential street, with old gabled homes sharing space with more modern apartment buildings. At the center of the block, St. Cyril's jutted in soaring gray stone. Just like anywhere else in the ancient cities of Europe, the modern auto accommodated itself to streets laid for horses by parking halfway up on the sidewalks. A walk along the street was a bit claustrophobic.

Casey immediately spotted the young man half a block up as he walked resolutely along past the old Gothic church. He held the bag to him as if protecting treasure, his attention alternately on his way and the street around him. He was obviously anticipating unwanted company along his trek.

"I wonder where he's going," Casey mused.

"Nothing down this way but..." Eric's voice trailed off a moment, his own eyes scanning briefly around as if to reacquaint himself with his capital. "Of course."

When he wasn't forthcoming with an explanation, Casey nudged him. "Of course what?"

"The train station. It's another block down."

Casey nodded, a strange exhilaration blooming in her chest. The anticipation of the hunt, the thrill of adventure. For a midlevel secretary from New York, she had had more than her share of adventure for a lifetime, yet here she was on another escapade that made her feel like a movie heroine. First she wondered just when she was going to wake up. Then she had what she considered to be the good grace to wonder whether having a good time at Cassandra's expense was quite proper.

"Casey."

Casey turned to see that Eric's attention was still resolutely on their target. "Yes?"

His eyes never shifted. "I'm having a hell of a good time."

"Chasing a kidnapper?"

"We're going to have to do this again sometime."

She couldn't help but giggle. "I'm not sure Cassandra will be so anxious to cooperate just so we can play cops and robbers."

"Not just that," Eric retorted with a quick shake of his head. "This is probably the first time I've been out without the entourage. Even in school I had servants and attendants and spies to let my family know whether I was behaving myself. This is . . . well, liberating."

Casey grinned as his eyes strayed briefly to her. "It is, isn't it? If we could only throw in a passionate interlude on a white rug in front of a fireplace where Rolph can't find us, it would be damn near perfect."

"Don't even suggest it," he begged, his eyes alight. "I might be sorely tempted to let this guy go."

The train station had been built with the kind of ostentation that made one think of Roman temples. This was a temple to transportation, with crowds gathering at regular intervals to worship progress, and trains clattering and wheezing like great behemoths captured to entertain the populace.

Casey and Eric followed their young gentleman straight through the great vaulted lobby and out the back door to the platform. The young man was heading for the waiting train.

"He bought his ticket ahead of time," Casey marveled. "Good planning."

Letting a respectable number of people come between them, Eric and Casey followed the young man onto the train just as the conductor pulled in the steps. The cars were about half-full with tourists and commuters. The young man took his seat at the very back of the car so that he could keep an eye on everyone else. Taking hold of Casey's hand, Eric walked blithely past and sat in a seat farther up.

Settling into a window seat, Casey turned to him. "So how do we keep an eye on him?"

"He can't go far," Eric retorted easily. "At least until the train stops." The station was already sliding slowly past the window as they picked up speed. "Do you have a compact?"

"A what?"

He motioned with his fingers. "Powder. Makeup."

Casey scowled. "I'm not Doris Day, Eric. The first time I wore powder in ten years was when Maria made me. Why?"

He scowled right back. "The mirror."

Reaching into her purse, she couldn't help a wicked grin. "And if I hadn't come along, how were you going to keep an eye on him? Or do *you* have a compact?"

Eric didn't dignify that with an answer. His eyebrows did raise a bit when Casey handed him a small mirror in a plastic case.

"I do brush my hair on occasion," she retorted before he could get a word out.

"Then do it when we pull into the next town."

"*Guten Tag*, your tickets please."

Both Eric and Casey turned to the congenial voice at their elbows.

"Tickets," Casey breathed in surprise.

Eric turned to her, then back to the conductor. "What?"

"We forgot."

"You don't have a ticket?" the gentleman asked. Gray-haired and short, like the classic image of a brewmaster with a ruddy nose and sparkling little eyes, the man didn't seem terribly upset.

Eric leaned close to Casey. "What do we do now?" he asked quietly, his gaze slipping out the window to where the narrow valley was speeding past in a pleasant blur.

Casey motioned to the old man. "Buy them."

That seemed interesting news to Eric. "We can do that?"

Casey's eyes rolled. "Oh, for heaven's sake. Excuse him," she said to the conductor. "He's been in the monastery a little too long."

"For what stop?" the little man asked, bringing out his ticket book.

"For what stop?" Eric echoed.

Casey couldn't come up with any ideas. "It's *your* country."

"Not anymore." Eric smiled at her. "We've just crossed into Switzerland. Moritania has a special provision that allows free travel between the two countries."

"What stop, *Bitte*?" the conductor prodded patiently.

"Lucerne," Eric replied. "I've always wanted to see it."

"Lucerne," the little man repeated, nodding.

"I don't want to go there." Casey whined in her best Brooklynese. "We've been going to all the cities you want to go to,

Howard. I want to go someplace different. Conductor, is there anyplace that's on the way that's not so big?''

''Oh, *ja*. There is a festival in Holman this week, and quite a few lovely *hofbrauhausen* in Thusis or Haustock. Almost any town along the way is lovely.''

Casey made the pretense of thinking. ''We-e-e-ll. Maybe we can go to those on our way back to Italy. What I'd really like to find is a plastic cuckoo clock with a silhouette of Elvis on it. Don't they make clocks somewhere in Switzerland?''

The poor little man didn't know quite what to think. Eric didn't give him the chance. ''Lucerne will be fine, thank you. How much?''

The little man returned hesitantly to his book. ''For the two of you, eighty-four francs.''

Eric looked up from his money. ''That much?'' he retorted sincerely. ''Why, that's outrageous.''

Casey just rolled her eyes and kept silent.

A moment later, Eric cast a jaundiced eye in her direction. ''Howard?''

She graced him with her best hundred-watt smile. ''Do you like it?''

He smiled right back. ''I love it. Mildred.''

The scenery they passed was, as promised, lovely. Breathtaking. The tracks followed a river through the valley, the water glinting sharp cobalt and magenta with the setting sun. The mountains thrust up beyond, sudden and majestic, their crowns still mantled in the pale blue of late snow. The farms they passed were neat and tidy, the fields carefully tended and the animals robust. A perfect pastoral scene. Casey found it difficult to believe that such prosperous, ongoing rural life could exist in such peaceful fashion in the same small country with great cities like Zurich and Geneva.

Alongside her, Eric's attention was alternately on the man who sat six rows behind them and Casey's profile as she looked out the window. The longer he knew her, the more Eric wondered how he could have so completely mistaken her for Cassandra that first afternoon. She was as different from Cassandra as a brightly feathered bird from a cat. Casey was all light and laughter and common sense, scattering her offhand compassion before her like a rainbow from a prism. The sun had been caught in her, and it shimmered from the depths of those soft hazel eyes. And standing within their gaze he suddenly felt like a man freed after years in his own prison.

For the first time he knew that his secrets would be safe with someone. That his insecurities would be attended and his accomplishments celebrated in such a way that their intangible worth would be greater than any riches he had ever known. True, he still had to convince her to say yes, but as he sat alongside her, away from the fishbowl of the palace, he couldn't believe that she would ever say no. He loved her far too much to consider a life without her.

When Eric took hold of her hand, Casey turned bright eyes on him. He knew she was enjoying herself as much as he. Now all he had to do was convince her that she could enjoy herself as much as his princess.

The train passed through three towns before their quarry made his move to get off. Eric spotted it as they were pulling into Holman, the little village all decked out for its summer wine festival.

"This is the spot," he muttered, his eye on the scrap of glass in Casey's hand.

She turned surprised eyes on him. "How do you know? We haven't stopped."

"He's getting nervous. Picking the bag up and putting it down. He hasn't done that before. And this is the first time he's been interested in what's outside."

"What do we do?" Casey asked, trying to decipher the same signals Eric seemed to see.

"We get off first. Doesn't that look like an interesting little town?"

"Oh, Howard," she immediately whined, picking up the cue. "Look at all the people. I don't want to go all the way to Lucerne tonight. I'll bet we could stay here. Let's go to their fair. Maybe they have the clocks here."

"Mildred . . ."

"Well, I'm getting off. If you don't want to, fine."

Pulling her purse over her shoulder, Casey stood just as the train came to a shuddering stop. Grumbling about women and whims and trying to find available rooms on the spur of the moment, Eric clambered to his feet and followed her down the aisle. Sure enough, their friend followed right behind.

Tucked alongside a narrow lake in the high Alps, Holman was alive with celebration. Even as the sun set and the sky lost its crisp edge, crowds of people wandered streets lit up by

Japanese lanterns and decorated with fresh flowers and bunt-ing. The buildings were all immaculately whitewashed, every window boasting a flower box overflowing with geraniums. The untidy swell of voices spilled from open beer halls, where the revelers were already sampling local fare and music. Stepping onto the platform, Eric and Casey were greeted by a young woman in Tyrolean attire who handed out flowers and smiles. The picture was enchanting.

Casey wished she could stay here and show Eric what life was like in the real world. But, as they stood basking in the young woman's smile, their quarry was heading down the main street. They had no choice but to follow. Eric took hold of Casey's hand and began to weave his way through the crowd.

They would have been successful if it hadn't been for the ebullient partyer who wanted to share his bonhomie. Just as the suspect was turning down one of the streets halfway up a winding hill, a man stepped from one of the open doors that spilled music and took Eric by the hand, then by the shoulder. Casey couldn't understand his German, but she did under-stand the universal body language. Here was a man who felt happy with the world and wanted to know that everybody else was. He offered some of his beer, then some companionship inside the noble establishment and then, when Eric struggled to get away, a rebuke for wasting such a wonderful festival.

By the time they broke free, their prey was gone. Hurrying up to the cross street, they turned, only to find an even denser crowd. Eric strained to see something familiar. He dragged Casey on through the crowd, then up and around several side streets. He even asked some of the partyers if they'd seen the young man. They struck out at every turn.

"What do we do now?" Casey asked, their failure gnawing at her. They'd been so close.

Eric took one more look around to see that nothing had changed. His shoulders slumped and he shrugged. "Try again tomorrow, I guess. He has to go back."

"Maybe we can get a microtransmitter or something," Casey offered.

Eric grimaced. "That only happens in movies, Casey. We have to rely on footwork."

"But what do we do tonight?" she asked.

"Get back on that train."

She shook her head. "Not tonight, we don't. There isn't another train going our way until morning. I heard the conductor tell one of the passengers."

Eric made another sweep. "Then I guess we stay here."

It turned out that their friend the happy partyer was the one who guided them to lodgings for the night. After exhausting all his luck at finding a place to stay on his own, Eric had opted to rest at a little *hofbrauhaus*. Their friend had chosen the same one to move on to.

Apologizing for their earlier rudeness, Eric and Casey found themselves sitting with him and sharing a drink. And that was when he gave them the good news. It just so happened that his cousin Gerta had lost a customer that very evening in the finest of the rooms she kept over the restaurant. If they'd like, he'd introduce them as his very dear friends—after they'd all had a drink together, that is.

Four drinks later, Eric and Casey finally climbed the steps to a cottage on the slope above a little restaurant. Of typical chalet construction, the cottage had a balcony that overlooked the celebration and the lake below, and two complete little apartments for guests. Frau Voelker showed them into the one with the fireplace.

Casey stepped over the threshold and came to an abrupt halt. "Oh, my."

Eric stopped next to her. "A rug."

"A *white* rug." She nodded with the beginnings of a smile. "Right in front of the fireplace."

"I suppose we'll just have to settle for this place."

She nodded again, chills of anticipation already racing through her. "I suppose."

After Eric paid Frau Voelker in cash, the little woman didn't mind in the least bringing the magnum of champagne he requested up from the restaurant. She didn't even mind adding a few hors d'oeuvres. The festival was a good time to sample the local food, she reminded the couple gently. Eric assured her that they would. Later. She smiled and backed out the door.

The apartment consisted of one small sitting area and a bedroom, both filled with heavy old furniture. The walls were whitewashed and the fireplace was stone. Casey immediately fell in love with it.

"Well," she mused, looking around, "it's not the palace...."

Eric slipped his arms around her waist and pulled her against him. "We also don't have to worry about Werner interrupting us, or Rolph, or another intruder...."

"Enough said," she murmured, rubbing her cheek against the crisp cotton of his shirt. "Just what did you have in mind for that champagne?"

Eric flipped her hat off and sailed it across to a chair. "It's to be sacrificed," he said wickedly.

Casey looked up at him, her heart already beginning its erratic acceleration. "Sacrificed."

He nodded very slowly, his hot blue eyes boring into her with relentless intensity. "I plan to offer it up in the hopes that I can talk you into marrying me."

"Planning on getting me drunk?"

His attitude was all innocence. "Never. It is merely a—"

"Bribe."

"Refreshment. Our negotiations could, well, become...heated."

As Eric spoke, he reached up to unpin her hair, pulling it down to cascade over his hands. He ran his fingers through its satiny lengths, igniting fresh shivers along Casey's spine. She couldn't seem to breathe correctly, and her heart was pounding.

"And what about poor Cassandra while we're...arguing?" she asked, her eyes ensnared within the sorcery of his.

Eric smiled, and the message of his smile shot through her like hot, living fire. "She has caviar. We have more important things to discuss."

His hands had strayed from her hair, making slow sweeps along the curve of her spine and the gentle swell of her hips. Where his hands traveled, her skin sang, the music seeping into her very core until she felt her entire body thrumming with the special song of his touch.

It was as if her body was a stranger to her, it responded with such frightening intensity to Eric. Casey had never felt that white-hot explosion from just the dance of fingertips against her throat, never known the sudden keen lightning in her belly that flickered throughout her limbs with only his glance. When Eric bent to take her lips, she went liquid and rigid at once, burning to hurry his touch, terrified of the pleasures he was unleashing. She had always been terrified of what she couldn't control, and there was no controlling the firestorm this man was unleashing in her.

"How 'bout that champagne?" she stammered, straightening abruptly.

Eric let his hands rest at the small of her back where the skin was so soft and intimate beneath the material of her blouse, where nerve endings sent rippling messages down Casey's legs. She tried to pull from his grasp and couldn't. Her legs had lost the will to leave.

Eric's smile contained his full power. "I thought I'd like to see you in the firelight first."

Casey started. His words had sent the lightning through her again.

"Casey." His voice was soft. "Look at me."

She had no choice.

"What are you afraid of?"

Trembling before the onslaught to her senses, she was afraid she was going to cry. "I . . . I don't know. It's just so much. . . . It scares me to feel this good."

His smile turned to a low chuckle, brimming with comprehension. Casey could feel his need for her, the steely strength of him alongside her. But his hands were patient, his temper gentle.

Instead of answering right away, Eric gathered her to him once more and recaptured her mouth. His lips were so sweet, like the water from a spring. His beard chafed her cheek with delicious effect. Casey could taste the smoky flavor of alcohol and smell the tang of his after-shave. He eased her lips open to fully explore the dark pleasures of her mouth, and she sank into his embrace.

Just the communion of his mouth, the hungry plundering of his tongue, sapped Casey's resistance. Her blood rang in her ears and her knees trembled with the effort to stay upright. The winds took the fire in her and spread it.

"I need you, Casey," he whispered into her ear, his tongue flickering against the soft shell and igniting shudders of pleasure. "I've never needed anyone like this before. Tell me you're not afraid of me."

Casey's hands clutched at the steely contours of his back. Her chest heaved with the exertion of control, the panic that couldn't be told quite so easily from exhilaration anymore. She squeezed her eyes shut against the spell of his, but she could feel that piercing blue right through to her core.

"No, Eric," she managed, her face against his chest where she could feel his heart and the strength of him around her.

"I'm afraid of me. I've never let myself go like this before... before you, anyway."

"Doesn't that tell you something?"

"Yeah. It tells me that you cast spells. I'm not normal around you."

Gently Eric lifted her face to him, and she saw the full scope of her power over him. "Maybe you're just beginning to realize what normal is. I love you. Tell me you love me."

Casey couldn't manage it. His words compelled tears, tears that lodged in her throat and stung her eyes. She clung even tighter to him.

Eric wouldn't be dissuaded. He returned to claim her mouth, exploring it with a thoroughness that left Casey moaning against him. Then he let his lips trail to her throat, his touch unleashing showers of sparks that settled in her breasts and brought her nipples to attention.

"Tell me you love me," he repeated.

"I love you...." She couldn't think past the heat of his touch, the intimate play of his hand along her back. Then his lips discovered the soft hollow of her throat and his hand roved upward toward her breasts.

"Tell me you'll marry me."

"Eric..."

His fingers rasped against her blouse, teasing her breasts with fleeting contact. His fingers circled her nipple and then swept outward again. Again she moaned. Eric's tongue was drawing designs of fire at the base of her throat, and Casey's head was thrown back to better receive it.

"You'll marry me."

"All right! All right, I'll marry you.... Oh, that feels so wonderful."

"You won't be afraid?"

She brought her own hand around to seek out the hair that curled at the base of his throat. When she found it, she let her fingers luxuriate in it, thinking that she had never known how delicious the texture could feel. How enticing. Casey wanted to stretch against it like a cat.

"Terrified," she finally admitted with a hesitant little smile. "But I don't think I care. I want you, too."

Taking her face in his hands, Eric brought her hesitations to an end. "Well, my beautiful Casey," he murmured, "you have me."

Easing Casey back onto the soft white rug, Eric settled himself over her. The wait was difficult for him, but he knew that this time was for Casey. This time he wanted her to understand what he wanted to be able to give her, what lovemaking would be between them. When he undressed her, he did it slowly, his eyes devouring the soft, sleek lines of her body as he uncovered it layer by layer, as his fingers sought to come closer to the core that fueled the hot light in her half-open eyes.

She was softened with her arousal, her lips puffy with his attentions, her breasts straining against the lacy bra that contained them.

Eric ran his hand up the firm lines of her calves, her thighs, only her panties keeping him from that mysterious silken flower that beckoned. He swept trembling fingers along her hips, her belly, the line of her ribs, aching to taste the muskiness of her as he excited her. She reached up to unbutton his shirt, but he restrained her. That would come later. Later when he'd thoroughly maddened her and he saw that entreaty for release in her eyes.

Casey writhed before his touch. Eric pinned her beneath his weight, his mouth commanding hers, his tongue tasting her lips, her throat, sketching shivers along her shoulders and down her collarbone. His hands finally savoring her breasts, he rubbed the tender nipples with thumb and forefinger until lightning leaped to her toes.

The fire spread; the tremors began to build. Casey arched against Eric's touch, only to find that his mouth had replaced his hand, his tongue and teeth drawing out new moans as they teased and tasted and tempted her breast through the filmy material. She ached to feel him bare against her, to feel his passion-heated skin alongside her, to touch him. To open to him and ride the crest together with him. The fire crackled in the fireplace and seared her with his touch.

When Eric slid his hand in past the material at her hips, Casey writhed against him, desperate for his fingers against that sweet, hot ache he'd ignited. So warm against her, they dipped into her, fled, then dipped in again. She was whimpering now, desperate, her hands clutching at him. She swept his hips, his legs, the straining power of him where it met her thigh. Her eyes open and barely seeing, she rushed to free him of his clothes.

His hands never seemed to leave her, but suddenly he rested above her, naked, his lean body golden in the firelight. Casey let her hands discover the hard muscles, the whorls of golden hair on his chest that tapered toward his flat belly. She devoured his body with her hands, much as he had hers with his eyes, taking it to her as if she might never have the chance to have it again. The sight of his arousal awed her. The smile in his eyes captured her.

Casey felt his hand on her thigh, an invitation and a command, and she opened to him, letting him ease the panties free and away. Then the bra, so that her breasts were free for him. He tasted her skin, then, the soft mound of her belly as it curved toward her navel. He reclaimed her breasts with his tongue and let his fingers dance against the satin petals he sought to enter. Casey eased tentative fingers to bring him to her and he groaned, a sound that maddened her even more.

She couldn't bear the agony any longer. Her body was now screaming for release. She had to have him in her, feel him drive into her and fill her with himself.

"Eric, please..." She strained against him, rocking against the exquisite pain of his touch. "Take me. Please take me."

And then his hand was gone, his mouth, which had so sweetly tormented her. She looked up and found that he would return to her, easing over her, his eyes trapping her with their incandescence. She opened her lips and her thighs to welcome him, and he entered her.

This time there was no pain. But the hot fullness of him in her sent her into shudders. A rhythm took over she didn't understand. She rocked against him, her breasts crushed against his chest, her mouth ravaged by his, her entire body quaking with the climax that swept nearer.

Eric sheltered Casey's cries and offered her his harsh groans, his hands tight against her buttocks, driving her closer against him, driving him deeper inside her. Casey's head went back; her fingers dug into Eric's back. Convulsions of fire racked her body, torrents of shattered light and heat, as the world whirled away into a liquid center where she and Eric embraced. Then he shuddered against her and called her name, and she collapsed within his hold, where a floating euphoria filled her like late-afternoon light in summer.

Twelve

———

And to think," Eric mused, running a finger along the edge of Casey's breast, "I didn't even have to resort to the champagne."

"Don't make rash assumptions," she warned from where her head rested in the hollow of his shoulder. The fire still crackled, and the white rug cushioned them with its thick, delicious warmth. Outside their window the moon was just topping the mountains across the lake, the sky that sheltered it a deep indigo. Casey couldn't remember ever having been so content.

"Resort to champagne for what?" she asked a moment later, lifting her head. A shower of honey-colored hair cascaded over Eric's chest.

"For getting an answer to my proposal," he said with smug satisfaction, his finger straying to outline Casey's softly pouting lower lip.

She frowned a moment, trying to remember what she'd said in the previous few minutes. She hadn't exactly had all her senses in working order. Most had been on Receive instead of Send.

But send she had. It came back to her in a rush. Not only her promise, but his method of extraction.

"Coercion," she protested with laughing eyes. "No judge in the world would honor a promise made under duress."

"Duress?" His eyebrows lifted. "Are you telling me you were tortured?"

"Tormented is a closer word. I never stood a chance, Your Honor. The plaintiff used underhanded and foolproof methods of extracting the promise."

"And just what were those?" he goaded with a smug grin.

Casey looked up as if in thought. "Well . . . severe and prolonged kissing . . . expertly applied embraces . . ."

"Are you telling me you won't marry me?"

"Are you telling me I don't get any champagne?"

"You can have some if you'll marry me."

"Then it *is* a bribe!"

"A reward," Eric retorted.

Casey grimaced. "All right."

He grimaced right back. "All right what?"

"All right, I accept your lame argument *and* your proposal."

Eric laughed, pulling her tightly against him in a hug that was almost fierce. "That has to be the most unique acceptance I've ever had."

Casey looked up slyly. "You've had others?"

He deposited a kiss on her upturned nose. "None I've enjoyed half so much. Now after we decide when we'll have the wedding, I say we should go down and get something to eat."

"Champagne first," she retorted.

Eric scowled at her. "You'd almost think you liked the stuff."

"I never had the chance to find out until a couple days ago. No wonder jockeys drink it for breakfast."

His eyebrows rose again. "How do you know that?"

"Books," she said. "The one really democratic place in New York is the library. Anybody with a library card can get in and get all the knowledge they want."

"And you wasted yours on jockeys."

They were both grinning, enjoying their moment of freedom. It seemed the first time their conversation wasn't governed by what Cassandra did or where she was.

"And Irish and Russian history. Want to know about what Cromwell did to Ireland?"

"I know, thank you. Interesting combination of interests."

Casey shrugged, her breasts brushing against his chest. "I'm weak on geography—which you know—and social graces. And I wouldn't know a Picasso from a pizza. But I can quote the opening line from just about everything Dickens and Breslin have ever written." She considered him with calculating eyes. "You know, you really don't know that much about me."

He brought his hand up to stroke the soft skin of her cheek. "I know that you speak your mind, that you aren't afraid of anything and that I love you."

"But for all you know I could paint myself blue and worship trees. All I've done since I've been here is play Cassandra."

Cupping her chin with a gentle squeeze, Eric eased both of them to a sitting position. "In that case, I can't think of a better way to use up champagne."

And they did just that. Drinking the first half over questions of Casey's life story and preferences in pastimes—baseball and swimming coming quickly to mind, and horseback riding still a strong dream—they sat side by side on the rug, voices and companionship quiet and completely comfortable. The second half was saved until after dinner was obtained down the slope in town.

It was there that Eric really opened up. It might have been the champagne, or the fact that he was just another anonymous reveler in the happy crowd, but by the time the two of them climbed back up to their chalet he'd made seven or eight friends, joined in any number of community sing-alongs and come away with someone's Tyrolean hat. When Casey saw the sparkling life in his eyes, she knew he had never been so totally free.

As she'd watched him lose an arm-wrestling contest with a farmer, she'd promised herself that if she really married him, she'd see he got out for these little weekends regularly.

"But my home is in Brooklyn," she said quietly some time later. They sat on an old cushioned couch on the balcony, the champagne propped in a bucket at their feet. Eric still wore the hat, now at a rather acute angle so that the little feather at its crown was close to his ear.

Steeped in the champagne, the beer from the festival and the gemütlichkeit of the day, he looked drowsily over at her. "Would it be so bad to live in Moritania?" he asked.

Casey shook her head, her eyes suspiciously misty. "I don't know," she admitted. "I haven't had the chance to miss the old block yet—my friends, my family."

"You have a lot of cousins?"

She nodded. "Oh, yeah. Tons. And they all come over for Christmas and St. Patrick's Day. We all grew up within a few blocks of each other."

"Then we'll invite them to the wedding."

She turned to him. "Eric . . ."

He made his decision with a definite shake of his head. "If they are important to you, they will come. Your cousins, your friends, Sandy, your mother . . ." He nestled closer to her, slipping an arm around her shoulders and resting his head against hers. "I want our wedding to be the happiest day of your life."

Casey didn't even notice the tears that started to trickle. "I don't know, Eric. I just don't know."

He faced her, his eyes far more sober than they should have been. "Do you love me?" he asked very quietly, his own avowal there in the depths of his eyes, lighter than a morning sky.

Casey didn't flinch. The soft mountain breeze tickled her hair and carried the sound of distant music and the cowbells that were so much a part of the mountains. She'd come to love those sounds, so tranquil and pristine, so much a part of Eric. Somewhere in town a church clock chimed eleven, its notes rolling gently out over the water. It surprised her to realize that she didn't even miss the cacophony of traffic anymore. She wondered whether walking through downtown Manhattan would ever be the same.

"Yes," she whispered. "I love you. I love you enough to give up Brooklyn without a second thought. But my mother's there, too, Eric. And she's alone."

"Then she'll come stay with us."

"You don't know if you'd like her."

Eric's eyebrows went up. "The woman who thinks hugs should be world currency? How could I not like her? Casey, there is nothing I wouldn't do for you."

Her voice grew very small. "You really mean that?"

When Eric smiled, the entire worth of what Casey had given him reflected in his eyes, she knew his answer without words. "I can't wait to meet your cousins," he said simply. "Or your mother."

She felt the tears then, hot and sweet as they coursed down her cheeks. She felt Eric's arm tighten around her. Their lips met. Soft, probing, intense. He eased her mouth open and plundered the honeyed depths with his tongue. Casey never felt her empty champagne glass slide from lifeless fingers, but did recognize the sharp shaft of light that ignited in her belly as Eric's other hand reached for it.

She braced herself against him, her hands flat against his chest where she could feel the suggestion of curling hair beneath his shirt. Her fingers immediately went to work on the buttons, and this time he let her. Casey ached for him, for the remembered lightning of his touch, the soft seduction of her name on his lips. She wanted desperately to feel that cherished union with him, to hear his hoarse cry and feel him shudder against her as he gave himself completely to her in a way no other man had. And then she wanted to fall asleep within his embrace and watch him wake next to her in the morning. You don't miss what you've never had, they said. Suddenly she missed it fiercely and knew that Eric was the only man who could provide it.

When Eric lifted Casey from the couch, he carried her in to the antique bed to lay her amid the soft embrace of goose down. And then he returned to claim her.

It amazed Casey that Eric could be again so different in his lovemaking. Tonight there was a kind of desperation to his touch, an urgency to his kisses, as if he had to make up for lost time or protect them from an uncertain future. He slipped her clothes off quickly and let his follow close behind. When he had her beneath him, he let his hands and mouth prowl over her as if to memorize every hollow and curve. His hands cherished her, stirring her skin to a fresh molten glow and feeding the fierce ache in her belly. He bent to taste her breasts, one after the other, nipping at the tender skin, suckling and caressing until the nipples rose taut for him. He let his hand foray down past the downy triangle at her thighs to once again inflame her to begging.

Casey's body thrilled with the mounting shudders, the breathless, bright incandescence Eric's hands provoked. Her own hands roamed as hungrily, tracing muscle and sinew as a sculptor would his own perfect creation, her fingers curling in the hair on his chest and sweeping across his flat, hard belly. She tested the turgid length of him, his brutal groans at her touch making her bolder. She teased and tormented him much as he did her, learning just what would drive him mad and what would bring him to her. Finally Eric shifted on top of her, and

Casey looked up to see the blue of his eyes. She took the privilege of guiding him home.

His mouth claimed hers. He wrapped her within steely arms, entered her with the pent-up longing of a man who had waited his whole life for the one woman he would claim as his own. Casey gasped at the intensity of his entry, at the fierce, primal rhythm he set, crushing her to him and capturing her moans with his fevered mouth. She wrapped around him, his fever infecting her, his drive compelling her until she rocked with him, faster, faster, her fingers clutching helplessly until the nails left scratches, until her moans became gasps and her gasps cries, her eyes open to Eric's and her body brilliant with his fire.

Slowly the night returned, and Casey could hear the cowbells on the wind and a few boats out on the lake. The world outside was peaceful, sheltered in starlight and bathed by the moon. And inside, cradled within the comfort of Eric's love, Casey slowly fell asleep.

She woke the next morning before the sun. Curled in the protection of Eric's embrace, she watched the day slowly take hold and thought how very much she had grown to love the mountains. They began the day in shadow, indigo like the distant night and stark against the brightening sky. But as the sun rose behind them, their shape and hue began to change. The snow was eared soft, muted robin's egg that edged the peaks in severe slashes. Then the mountains themselves, blue, then gray, then green, the high crags a nutmeg brown. The lake mirrored the sky, wisps of coral skimming the azure surface, soft morning mist rolling off it and obscuring the edges.

The town woke slowly, first the roosters, then the cows, strolling out from their barns to the tune of their bells, and then the people. Casey thought that she had never been so content to hear so little. Not one plane, not one ambulance keening off to disaster. Not a single screaming neighbor or blaring television. Of all the things she would miss, she realized those wouldn't be on the list.

She didn't realize Eric was awake until he reached up to stroke a hand through the tumbled mass of her hair.

"Quite a nice day outside," she ventured softly.

"Then it will be the day we call your mother and invite her to the wedding," he decided.

The hesitation returned with his words. The feeling that no matter what she wanted there was no way this all could come true. "What if she won't come to live with us?" she asked, her hands up to the solidity of his arms as if steeping herself in his strength. "She hasn't even left Brooklyn her whole life. Her family's there."

"She will," he assured her with a kiss to the top of her head. "We'll convince her. Right after we figure out what to do with Cassandra."

"Oh." Casey grinned mischievously. "Her."

"I imagine Sandy's told her by now."

"Cassandra?"

"Your mother."

"Then we should get our buns in gear and get her back."

"Your mother?"

Casey giggled. "Cassandra. Don't you have cousins?"

Eric didn't seem to have any trouble following her train of thought as his fingers roamed along Casey's bare arm. "Distant ones," he admitted. "The von Lieberhavens weren't great propagators."

"Should have had a little Hapsburg blood in you. They propagated half of Europe."

"We do."

"Oh. What about your sister? The one who played the harp?"

"Anna Marie," he said, his voice suddenly wistful. "She was like a second mother to me. Never married. She died when I was ten—a plane crash. It nearly did me in." His words were a lot more matter-of-fact than his voice. The woman who had inspired such regret in the dowager queen's eyes must have been a special person. Eric still missed her.

"You're an only child?" he asked.

"I didn't say that." Casey's voice suddenly sounded defensive.

Eric's hand stopped moving. "You're not?"

Casey kept her eyes on the mountains. Solid, unchanging, dependable, unlike some people.

"I have an older brother. Paul."

"You sound angry."

She sighed, snuggling more deeply into Eric's arms. "Confused, I guess. Hurt. He, uh, left home quite a few years ago, and we haven't heard much from him since."

"He ever say why?"

"Why he left, or why he hasn't bothered to find out his father died?" Casey pursed her lips for a moment, angry that she'd let her voice rise. "He never said," she admitted. "When he left he just told me he had to do it and that I'd be all right."

"I'm sorry, Casey."

Lifting her face to his, she smiled. "Well, at least if I live in Moritania I won't have to worry about his dropping in unexpectedly. He always thought the country was a joke, too."

Eric rewarded her with his first kiss of the day.

The first train to Moritania was at eight-thirty. After making certain they purchased their tickets, Eric and Casey wandered off. Hand in hand, they strolled the winding little streets, sometimes stopping at shop windows, or pausing to greet someone they'd met the night before. Casey couldn't remember how, but quite a few people had found out that she and Eric were engaged and had ended up being invited to the wedding. She couldn't wait until they got their invitations.

Frau Voelker insisted on serving them breakfast since it came with the price of the room, so they dined on hard rolls and cold cuts, the Germanic version of the continental breakfast. To be perfectly truthful, Casey had gotten to the point where she looked forward to the fare each morning. It went well with the strong coffee and tea that were so popular in Europe. After serving them in the timbered-and-plastered room that Casey was sure dated back to the Hundred Years' War, Frau Voelker extracted her own invitation to the wedding.

"This is going to be one of the most novel royal weddings of the decade," Casey confided to Eric with a grin as they finally left, fortified with the Frau's blessings and hearty handshakes.

"It's *our* wedding," Eric returned with a mischievous grin. "Why shouldn't we be allowed to invite whomever we wish?"

"What's your mother going to say?"

He rolled his eyes. "Don't worry. Since you don't speak German, you'll never know. It's the only language she uses to curse."

The day was another sparkler, the sun climbing fast over the mountain peaks to burn off the mist and a fresh breeze swirling along the brightly decorated streets. A few shop owners were already out sweeping their stoops, waving a greeting as prospective customers passed. Tourists strolled along aimlessly, and out on the lake a flock of birds lifted into the sun.

Eric took Casey's hand as they walked toward the train station, each of them eking out their last moments alone. It seemed as if the world was conspiring to make these last peaceful moments bittersweet in their beauty. In this tiny Alpine town, for at least these few hours, they were no more than a young couple in love. They had no tradition to uphold, no honor to consider, no title to think of. It made Casey just a little more frightened of what Eric was asking her accept for him.

"The post office," he said suddenly. "I have to call the palace and let them know our schedule."

"Don't let them suggest sending a car," she advised.

"Don't worry." He gave her a quick kiss. "I won't. I'm not telling them where I am, just that I'm on my way back."

Casey elected to stay outside, preferring the view there to the precise paneled cubicles inside. Leaning back against the whitewashed wall, she let her gaze wander aimlessly. She saw the meat shop where the butcher spread wood shavings on the floor, the flower shop with its riot of color and scent, the town square with its expertly manicured garden. All around her she heard German and English, Italian and French, Japanese, Arabic, Swedish. It was a delicious symphony of sound, a delicious bouquet of aromas on the mountain breezes.

Suddenly she froze. Jeans and a fatigue jacket. No, it couldn't be. He was walking right toward her, right into the post office where Eric was making his call to the palace. Casey's heart started thumping and her hands dampened. It was definitely the man they'd tailed the night before. And here he was walking right at them.

Looking around wildly, Casey tried desperately to think of something brilliant. Should she hide? Should she brave it out and stand her ground, pretending she'd never seen him before? She took a quick look into the dim interior of the post office to see Eric at one of the phones, his back to her. At least he was keeping his voice down. If their friend wandered too close, he wouldn't find out too much.

When she turned back to the street, he was almost on top of her. Keep calm, Casey, she told herself. Take slow breaths and look right through him like you don't know him.

He was walking right into the post office!

Summoning all her courage, she took a slow breath and nodded an impersonal greeting as he passed. He nodded back, his features pleasant and noncommittal. Then he walked in the door. It was all Casey could do to keep from following him. She wanted to throw something at Eric to get his attention, but his back remained resolutely to her.

The young man walked up to the window and greeted the teller like a friend. The teller smiled and handed over a batch of envelopes. Replies from other kidnapping attempts, Casey thought blackly. How could he seem like such a nice guy? He had a crown princess stashed someplace. Throwing a familiar wave and farewell over his shoulder, he headed out of the building.

Casey barely let him get by before she whipped into the office.

"That young man," she said to the official, "I think I know him. Does he live around here?"

The man shrugged easily. "For the summer, you know. I think he's been up in the old Gasthaus Reifsteck on the Lake Road."

She nodded. "Has he?" Then she turned to watch his progress through the window. "I could swear I know him. Do you know his name?"

"Of course. Hans Gerdman. I believe he's Dutch."

"Thank you." Casey smiled brightly at the tall, very bureaucratic-looking man with uniform buttons that had been polished to a blinding gleam. "I'll have to look him up while he's here. I think we went to school together."

The man smiled a vague response and returned to his work. Casey turned to Eric. "Get off the phone," she muttered, an eye to the official.

Eric looked at her, still speaking to someone on the other end about quotas and deadlines.

"He was just here," she insisted, making motions toward the desk and then out the window. "The—" her voice lowered dramatically "—kidnapper."

Eric's eyes widened. The young Herr Gerdman could be seen chatting with the florist across the street. Without so much as an "Excuse me," Eric hung up the phone and followed Casey toward the door.

"He's living up at the old Gasthaus Reifsteck on the Lake Road," she said quietly. "Now all we have to find out is where that is."

Eric turned amazed eyes on her. "How did you find that out?" he asked.

Casey couldn't help but grin. "Another lesson from TV."

The young Herr Gerdman didn't seem to be in any kind of hurry. Picking up a handful of flowers, he wandered a few stores down and haggled with the baker over some fresh-baked pastries.

"Stoking up for his next encounter with Cassandra, no doubt," Eric said dryly. "Well, let's go out ourselves and do some quiet questioning. We might just make it back to the Gasthaus before our friend there."

The Gasthaus, they discovered, was in the process of renovation. A group of very nice men had spent the summer working on it, supervised by a quite proper gentleman who spoke very practically about his investment and his relationships with the town nearby. Set on a bluff above the lake, it was an old lodge built in the 1400s and since then in service as any number of restaurants and hostels. The town was glad to see an energetic group of people working on it. The quickest way to get to it was via the footpath at the edge of town. The scenic route, of course, was along the lake.

Eric and Casey chose the lake. It was a cinch Herr Gerdman didn't consider scenery a high priority, so there would be less of a chance of them meeting unexpectedly. Setting off at a brisk pace, they walked along hand in hand. No one paid the slightest bit of attention.

"All I want to do is assure myself that Cassandra is indeed in the Gasthaus," Eric said as they topped the first rise, where the lake spread out in a long finger beyond them, the sun glistening off its waters.

"And if she is?"

"We come back and call for help."

Casey nodded, as satisfied as she could be.

"You will not get involved," he warned. "I plan to set you in a safe place while I search the area. Is that understood?"

She turned anxious eyes on him. "But I can help...."

"No." He came to an abrupt halt, pulling her to a stop alongside him. "I let you come along this far because you insisted that you could help with the everyday world."

"I have, haven't I?"

"Yes. You have. But I will not expose you to any more danger than I can. I would have left you back in town if I'd thought you wouldn't hotfoot it right down that footpath to meet me.'

Casey had to allow a sheepish grin. "You *do* know me pretty well, don't you?"

With a flash of affectionate frustration in his eyes, Eric delivered a quick kiss. "Yes," he said. "I do. So I want you to promise me that you'll stay where I put you until I come back to get you. No matter what."

"What if—?"

"Promise!"

Casey pouted, a real four-star lip-curler with an added bonus of downcast eyes. "All right. I promise. But don't fool around and take too long. I have a much-too-vivid imagination."

"I won't." Eric knew he was taking a chance by trusting her, but he couldn't think of another way to appease her and still keep her from getting too involved.

Fifteen minutes later, they turned to see the Gasthaus Reifsteck tucked back in the trees to their right. An uninspiring structure, it was a basic block with open timbers and plaster, the windows now boarded up. Behind the main building, just as at Frau Voelker's, a few lesser buildings spread out up the hill to accommodate guests. There were stacks of lumber and equipment scattered over the area, making it look as if it would be a beehive of activity on a working day. This didn't seem to be one of them.

"There are people living in the guest houses," Eric said quietly, pointing out open windows and intact power lines. "I wonder if anybody's in the restaurant proper."

"Only one way to find out."

Eric took Casey by the hand and led her across to the front door of the main building. They had just reached it then they heard someone approaching. Eric yanked on the door. It came open easily and the two of them slipped inside.

The restaurant was empty, old and half-renovated. Tarps lay everywhere, and plaster dust coated every exposed inch. Most of the walls and parts of the floor were finished. The two fireplaces appeared to be in the process of a major cleaning. Casey could imagine the enormity of the job. You could pack a lot of soot up those babies in five hundred years.

Their footsteps echoed hollowly across the floor. No one appeared to challenge them. Casey felt some of the tension ease out of her chest. She started breathing again.

"Well, looks like nobody's home," she whispered. "Can we go now?"

She'd no more than said it then they heard a grating sound along the outside front wall. Eric wasted no time. Pulling Casey into the kitchen, he found a pantry and threw open the door.

Somebody was using it as a cleaning closet, hiding brooms and mops and cleaners. Eric shoved Casey right in.

"Stay here," he ordered. "If anyone comes along, make a noise like a broom."

She didn't even get a chance to throw him a scowl before he closed the door. All right, she thought disparagingly. Here I am in a broom closet. What do I do now? Casey felt absurdly like a clandestine lover trying to hide from the wife. She prayed she wouldn't be found. Not so much because of the danger—she refused to consider that—but because of the embarrassment. How do you explain standing all alone in the broom closet in a closed restaurant?

Casey had only been in there a few seconds when she first smelled it. Pine. Somebody had left a big bottle of pine cleaner in there. She stood very still, her hands stuffed in her jean pockets, and wondered how long it was going to be before her body ran amok.

The restaurant's front door opened. Casey froze, the pine already tickling at her nose. She wrinkled it up in defense, but that didn't help. Somebody was coming, and she was in desperate danger of sneezing.

She heard approaching footsteps, heavy, precise, measured. No panic, so they hadn't found Eric yet. She wondered where he was. She wondered why she'd insisted on coming along. Then the floor creaked out in the kitchen and she lost interest in everything but holding her breath.

That pine cleaner. She had to do something, push it out of the way, bury it under something, dilute it in water. If she didn't she'd give herself away.

The footsteps grew nearer. The burning grew along her nasal passages. Casey's entire face wrinkled involuntarily. She opened her mouth to cushion the blow.

And then, just as her visitor drew abreast of her very door, her body betrayed her. Casey let out the sneeze of the century.

Immediately the door flew open. Light flooded in, silhouetting a tall, ramrod-straight figure. Delicately rubbing at her still-burning nose, Casey managed a sheepish smile.

"You know, you Swiss really know how to organize a broom closet," she bluffed heartily, stepping right out and trying to get past her visitor.

"But I'm not Swiss," the man said, and Casey turned toward him, recognizing his voice, sparking unhappy recognition.

There before her, one hand on the open door, his other on her arm, stood General Mueller. He had a smile on his face that told Casey he had visions of dollar signs dancing in his head.

"Uh-oh," she moaned, "is Eric going to be mad at me now."

Thirteen

—

Eric had never meant to get this involved, but it had been so easy. Coming out of the restaurant, he'd spotted a thin, blond young man heading toward the nearest building, possibly a sentry inspecting the grounds. Eric followed discreetly until the young man entered the building to join another person for what looked like an ongoing card game. They never noticed as Eric skirted around to complete his reconnaissance.

The other chalet was in use but presently empty, the phone working. After calling the palace for a little backup, Eric returned and took care of the two guards, a simple matter of making a little noise and greeting the responding man with a gun to the back. He'd carried the small automatic without Casey's knowledge and without intending to use it, but it turned out to come in handy in a situation like this.

It also fortunately turned out that these particular band members weren't the stuff of action-adventure films. When the one saw his partner with his hands up, his hands did a matching salute, his playing cards fluttering forgotten to the floor. There hadn't even been any guns in the room.

From that point it had been quite easy to find out that Cassandra was closeted in a third-floor bedroom in the restaurant proper, guarded by a third man. Hans, it seemed, hadn't made it back yet.

After getting the rest of his answers, Eric tied the guards securely, stuffed them in the cellar and prepared to return to the restaurant. He'd send Casey to meet the guard team when it reached town and guide them back. Then he'd position himself to make sure nobody entered or left the restaurant that held Cassandra until help arrived to free her. After that, he'd deal with General Mueller.

Just as Eric had come to suspect, the general was behind the whole plot. The general had contacted the MSM with the idea for the kidnapping and had helped them set it in motion, claiming to adhere to their principles. Eric had an idea that it had a lot more to do with the million-franc ransom. The general might be wily and crooked, but there was one thing Eric would swear to in court. Politically, the general placed himself just a bit to the right of Genghis Khan, and that end of the spectrum had little room for socialists.

While keeping an eye on the upstairs window, Eric crept across the yard and up the back steps to the kitchen. He couldn't wait to get his hands on Mueller. And not so much for endangering Cassandra. Knowing her, he felt sorrier for the cardplayers, who had undoubtedly had to put up with her tantrums. He was furious because he had trusted the general only to be made a fool of. If he hadn't had that itch to call the gourmet shop and double-check on the caviar, he never would have discovered that the general hadn't questioned the shop owner at all, much less followed up on the tip any other way. Eric might have trusted the general enough to have paid out the million in ransom.

Eric cracked the back door and peered through. No one was inside. No sounds, no movement. There were plenty of footprints on that dusty floor, but nobody to immediately claim them. He slipped inside and headed carefully over to the broom closet.

"Casey..."

No answer. Eric opened the door, expecting to have to fight off a barrage of her questions. The mop was crammed to the side of the closet, and the pail was upended. But Casey was gone.

He'd told her to stay where she was. What the hell had she disappeared for? She'd better not have tried to follow him. There was still Hans and that third man to account for.

Preparing to slip the gun back beneath his sweater, Eric suddenly stopped. His head turned as a frisson of fear slithered down his neck. What if she hadn't disappeared on her own? What if that third man had somehow found her? What Eric had seen so far didn't exactly add up to a top-notch terrorist operation, but all the same she could be in danger. He let the door swing silently shut behind him.

Looking quickly around, Eric tried to decide what to do, his heart suddenly in his throat. He couldn't wait for the team to get there from the palace. It could be an hour or more. He had to find Casey, and find her now.

Eric crept through the room, looking for a possible hint as to where Casey was and whether she'd gone voluntarily. The footprints were no help. There were too many of them, accumulated over too long a period of time, to follow one set. He decided to check the two sets of stairs that led up from either end of the front room.

The sound of footsteps brought him to a halt. Crouching low along the wall, he raised the gun. There was somebody coming downstairs. Eric prepared to greet him.

Then he saw who it was.

The general came into view, slowly taking each step as if trying very hard to maintain a difficult balance. Eric immediately saw why. He had Casey.

Mueller carried her in his arms, a gun in one hand pointed so that it could kill her. Casey's hair swung limply alongside him as he negotiated the steps, her neck arched over his arm, her face pasty-white and slack. She was unconscious. Eric came to a shuddering halt, his heart dying in him.

"What have you done!"

"Ah." The general smiled in genuine delight. "You're here. I wondered."

Only that gun, pointed right at Casey's face, kept Eric from going for Mueller's throat. If the General had done anything to hurt her, Eric would kill him.

"Don't be a fool, General." His eyes struggled to stay away from the pale face in the man's arms. "The team is on its way. You can't have the ransom. You know that now."

"I know no such thing," he said agreeably, coming to a stop at the last step.

"If you hurt her..."

"Prince Eric," the general said indignantly, "I am an officer and a gentleman. I do not *injure* innocent ladies. I do pacify them, however. It makes then so much more agreeable, don't you know."

"Bring them both down now, and it will go easier on you."

He shook his head. "I don't think so. But I will make a deal with you. I will give you one and keep the other."

"But there's no way out." His expression carefully nonchalant, Eric was feverishly trying to think of some way to neutralize that gun. After that, he could maybe get past the general to get both Casey and Cassandra. An impossible task, with Casey unconscious and Cassandra in who knew what condition? But he had to do something.

"If you would be so kind as to drop the gun, I won't be forced to do something...disagreeable," the general threatened in an absurdly congenial voice. "After all, I'm in a most unpleasant position. It makes me seriously consider acts I would otherwise have no part in."

It was the cold amusement in Mueller's eyes more than the words he used to threaten Eric that convinced him to drop the gun. The general had no qualms about doing what he had to to save himself.

"Now you may let me by," he continued with a grateful smile, "so I can conclude the hasty negotiations you and the young lady have precipitated."

"Know this," Eric snarled. "If you harm her, I'll come for you."

"The queen mother was right, then. You are quite besotted with the girl."

"You heard me."

There was a scuffing sound out back, and the general's eyes momentarily strayed to it. It seemed to be a signal, for at the sound of it a great smile of triumph bloomed on the general's features.

"In that case," he said happily, "here. I give you a gift."

Before Eric could move, the general pushed Casey directly at him. Eric leaped forward to try to catch her. The general had outsmarted him, though. Eric was able to get his arms under Casey, but the momentum was too great, and they ended up sprawled on the floor. With a great laugh, the general scooped up Eric's gun and scooted right past.

"The other one is now worth two million. And I know you'll pay it."

Eric pulled the limp body into his arms, desperate to find a pulse. His fingers went to Casey's throat, when his eyes wid-

ened. Suddenly he was unceremoniously dumping the still form
on the floor.

"Mueller!" he howled, coming to his feet. "I'll get you!"

One hole. There had been one hole in the earlobe. The
general had kept Eric's attention with Cassandra while his co-
hort had somehow gotten Casey out of the house. Suddenly she
was the hostage, and Eric was truly frightened. Frightened and
enraged.

The general might correctly assume that Eric wouldn't think
twice about paying an exorbitant amount to ensure Casey's
safety, but he didn't realize that Eric's feelings for her transcended state and family honor and responsibilities. Eric would
gladly kill Mueller with his bare hands.

His only thoughts now on rescuing Casey, Eric turned to
search out some kind of weapon, leaving Cassandra in an ungainly heap on the dusty floor. Absurdly enough, the only thing
he discovered was a set of fencing foils over one of the fireplaces. Marvelous. The best he could hope for was for the
general to run quickly out of bullets and for none of them to
end up anywhere in him. Eric pulled one foil down and headed
for the door. It was better than nothing.

The general hadn't taken the time to free his two men from
the chalet. He and one other man were hustling Casey back
down toward the Lake Road, possibly to where they had a car
waiting. She was gagged and her hands were tied behind her,
the partially buttoned raincoat Mueller had supplied flapping
around her like a sail in an uncertain wind. Without a thought
for his own safety, Eric ran after them.

"I'll shoot!" the general shouted.

"Go right ahead!" Eric shouted back, gaining ground.

Her eyes like saucers at Eric's wild taunt, Casey managed an
outraged shriek behind her gag. Her arms were pretty well tied
up, but she did land a couple of good barefoot kicks at her
captor's knees.

The man who pushed her was none other than the mouth-
breather she'd gotten so acquainted with at the palace a few
nights before. Even without the stocking mask, she'd recognized him right away.

"Well, hi there," she'd said brightly when the general had
pushed her into the room. "Nice to see you again."

He'd liked her witty repartee so much he'd stuffed a gag in
her mouth. Then the general had told her to take her clothes
off. It hadn't, in truth, been the high point of her day. Casey

had seen Cassandra asleep in the bed across the room and had wondered if that was how dying people felt, looking on at themselves as they drifted away. She'd even pulled the gag out and objected, but Bubba—she'd decided to dub him—had taken care of that with dispatch.

"Either you take your clothes off," the general had said without much agitation, "or he will."

Casey had gone right for her buttons.

So here she was stumbling along in her bra and panties and somebody's raincoat, wondering whether it would be worth it to sell the story for a miniseries and then realizing that she'd been right the first time. Not even Hollywood would buy this one.

Another shot echoed behind her, and she whipped around, throwing Bubba off balance. Eric bobbed and weaved, the sun glinting off the long sword he carried.

Casey's heart sank lower. Swords were impressive. She'd seen Douglas Fairbanks trim all of a castle's candles without putting out a single flame. But in any book in the world, a gun still beat a sword. She was terrified that she was going to see Eric stumble to his knees, a crimson blossom appearing on his shirtfront. Bubba grabbed her by the arm and she landed another kick.

The general hadn't picked Bubba for his patience. Letting out what Casey was sure was a curse, he flipped her over his back and headed off again. She took up kicking at his chest, her hands helpless behind her. The general got off another shot over his shoulder before following. Ducking behind a tree, Eric could be seen edging closer.

Eric gained ground as the one man labored to stay up under Casey's struggling weight. The general fired two more shots just as they turned onto a path a few hundred feet shy of the road and headed away from town. Eric ducked successfully both times, weaving in and out of trees to keep the general's target at a minimum.

He wasn't quite sure what he was going to do if he got close enough. The general seemed to have an unlimited supply of bullets. But Eric had the overwhelming feeling that if he didn't free Casey right now, he wouldn't be able to again. It was a lot more difficult to work up the courage to kill a crown princess than it was a secretary.

Eric saw the car as he rounded a corner, parked a ways up the path and facing the road. Mueller would have reached it by now if Casey hadn't managed to plant both knees in her captor's solar plexus and get him to drop her.

Casey was fighting tooth and nail now, knowing somehow that once she got to that car it would be all over. Eric still stalked them. She could see him through the trees, approaching relentlessly even as the general continued to fire shots. Would Mueller really try to kill him, she wondered, or just injure him to make a point? Somehow the latter thought didn't make her feel any better. An injured Eric, here away from the town, could die before help got to him. And she'd be the cause of it. The fire that lit in her chest propelled her limbs faster against the implacable Bubba.

The general had had just about enough of it. Turning briefly to her, he threatened, "Either stop or I'll hurt you, young lady. I have plenty of ammunition for the both of you."

Only the gag prevented Casey from telling him just what she thought. She even tried to land a kick in his direction, but Bubba wrapped a steely arm around her struggling frame and dragged her toward the car.

Turning back to Eric, Mueller fired off another shot. Eric dived for cover, not even feeling the sudden sting on his shoulder for the pounding his body took trying to go to ground. Why didn't somebody hear the shots and call the authorities? Scooting across from tree to tree, he advanced as the general struggled with his companion to get Casey into the car.

A vehicle rumbled along the road below them, and Eric heard her get the breath to let out a muffled scream. The general hit her for it. That was all Eric needed. Discovering a log just in front of him, he opted for it over the sword. Hefting it before him, he made the final run for that car.

The general turned and aimed. Eric heard the report and felt a thud in the wood he held. He ran faster. The general fired. Nothing happened. It was like an old movie. The general looked at the gun as if it had betrayed him and considered throwing it at Eric. The other man was still struggling with Casey's flailing arms and legs in the back of the car.

Smiling, Eric stopped. The wood was heavy in his hand, a satisfying feeling of justice. The general stared at him and then the gun as if in a daze.

"Why don't we be civilized about this?" Eric offered one last time before the impulse to crush the general's head overtook him.

Mueller suddenly smiled back. "Absolutely not."

He raised the gun again. Eric shrugged, and began to swing with the wood. The general pulled the trigger. The log connected with the gun just as it went off.

Bubba stopped just long enough to see which man yelled behind him and why. Casey needed just that long to kick him hard where it counted. Screaming in agony, he hit the ground and stayed there. He deserved every groan. But the silence beyond that car terrified her, and she had to discover its outcome.

Her heart thundering in her ears and her breath coming in ragged gasps, Casey made herself peek out over the window. Then she screamed.

She did have the courtesy to step over the writhing man before she launched herself into Eric's arms. The general lay dazed at his feet. He'd landed there after he'd made the enraged rush at Eric's throat, only to be met with a well-swung log to the side of the head. Eric opened his arms to Casey, gathering her trembling body to him as if afraid that she weren't really there.

"Are you all right?" he asked, his voice rough-edged and hesitant. He should never have let her talk him into taking her along. He'd almost lost her. "Did he hurt you?"

It wasn't until he held her back to see the disdainful look in her eyes that he remembered that she was gagged. He immediately beamed.

"You know, it does occur to me that I might prefer you this way. At least I won't get any back talk from you."

The threat in Casey's eyes grew dramatically direr the longer Eric chuckled at her. He paused only long enough to pick up the guns so that he didn't have to worry about trouble from that quarter, before reaching around to pull down the gag and remove the wad of cloth from her mouth.

Casey immediately took to spitting. "I think they used Bubba's old socks. Blah!"

"Bubba?"

She grinned up at him. "Our late-night visitor over there. Since he didn't have the manners to introduce himself, I made up a name for him. Untie me, Eric. You're bleeding."

Eric looked down in surprise to see that she was right. There was a ragged hole in his sleeve just below his shoulder, and a lengthening scarlet stain on his shirt. He supposed he was going to feel it soon. He didn't now. All he felt now was relief.

"I'll make a deal with you," he said easily. Both of them ignored Mueller's groan. Eric pointed the gun in the appropriate direction, his eyes still on Casey. "I'll only untie you if you promise, once and for all, to marry me."

"You're doing it again!" she protested.

Dropping a kiss on her very tight lips, he smiled agreeably. "I know. It seems the only time I can get you to make sense is when I have the . . . advantage."

Casey struggled to keep that scowl on her face. Eric deserved a resounding no for his smug attitude. But she couldn't refuse him. Relief and giddy joy bubbled through her like that champagne she'd gotten to like. She hadn't made any sense around him so far. Why should she change now?

"Oh, all right," she snapped, turning to let him at her hands. "I'll marry you." Bending down, she nudged the still-dizzy general at her feet. "Did you hear that, General? He's going to want a witness."

The general groaned.

"He heard it," she said over her shoulder. "Now let me loose."

"Just a minute," Eric said, his hand to her neck. "I'd better check."

Casey shot him a look that somehow bordered on the lethal and the delirious all at once. "Check what?"

Eric fingered the soft little lobe of her ear. "He fooled me once already, and I certainly wouldn't want to let Cassandra out of such a manageable condition. I wouldn't want to marry her, either."

"Neither would I."

He bent for a closer examination that somehow entailed the flicking of his tongue against her skin. Casey almost ended up on the ground next to the general. "Hmmm," he murmured. "Three holes. Who won the 1986 World Series?"

She allowed a certain amount of exasperation. "The Mets. If you don't let me loose right now, I'm going to make sure you bleed to death."

Eric not only let her loose, he whirled her around for a resounding I'm-glad-you're-safe kiss that left her dazed.

"Yes." Eric nodded, his eyes happy and bright. "You're all right. You scared me for a while there. I was afraid he wasn't going to be as nice to you as he was to Cassandra."

"He made me take my clothes off!" Casey retorted indignantly, a self-righteous eye on the general's still form on the ground.

"To give him time to get you away. He dressed Cassandra up in them."

"What a ridiculous idea." Then a grin teased the corner of her mouth. "Speaking of which, what happened to the sword? I thought this was going to be a real swashbuckler."

Eric nodded sagely. "A good prince is also a flexible prince. Besides," he added, easing her more tightly into his grasp, "I couldn't see myself eulogized as the prince who lost a duel between a foil and a .38."

"The last of the great romantics."

The sunlight sent feathered shafts through the trees, gilding Casey's hair and warming Eric's face. The day was really going to be a beautiful one, full and sweet, just like the life that now stretched ahead of them.

Eric stood with Casey in his arms, wondering how he was going to keep the general and his crew peaceable until the team arrived, when he heard the crashing through the trees. Letting go of Casey, he turned to see Hans come to a sudden stop, the deer in sight of the hunter. Without more than a second's hesitation, the young man whirled around and was gone. Casey moved in his direction.

"Forget it," Eric suggested. "Let's just get home."

"What if he goes back for Cassandra?"

"Then he's either a lot dumber or braver than I think."

"Speaking of which," she said, "where is Cassandra?"

"You certainly took your sweet time looking for me!" Seated regally in the back seat of the limo as it sped across the countryside, Cassandra once again checked her appearance in Casey's hand mirror. "And then to leave me just lying there in all that . . . dust while you went gallivanting off after . . . her!" The sidelong glance she shot at Casey said it all.

Casey looked over at the woman opposite her and then at Eric. "Yeah, Eric. We're going to get along just great."

Cassandra didn't deign to notice the comment.

"Be careful, Cassandra dear," Eric said, "or we'll give you right back."

"Don't be absurd, Eric. I am the crown princess."

"And Casey's been impersonating you for a week without anyone being the wiser."

This time she did cast an eye on Casey, albeit a jaundiced one. Lifting the royal chin with icy disdain, Cassandra returned to the mirror. "Hard to believe."

"I agree," Casey said evenly. "I'm much thinner."

They pulled through the sleepy streets of Braz to scattered waves and smiles, and proceeded to the palace. Casey looked forward to seeing the lovely old forest again, and the gardens and, surprisingly enough, the queen. Today, she knew, she would finally break the news to her own mother. The sun was settling onto the tops of the western Alps, shedding a liquid golden light over the valley and gilding the palace windows. Eric had his arm around her, and they were coming home.

Eric spoke up as they came to a stop at the front door. "Cassandra, I think you'll find that there have been some changes since you've left."

"Changes?" she challenged. "Dear Eric, what could change here? An invasion by Austria, a foreclosure of the banks? Nuclear confrontation?"

Cassandra waited until the chauffeur opened the door before stepping out. Behind her, not only Eric and Casey but the chauffeur smiled.

"Worse," Eric assured her. But his niece didn't hear.

A moment later, the assembled staff greeted their crown princess without so much as a nod of the head, and she began to shriek.

"I hope the staff doesn't mind the fireworks," Casey apologized with a barely suppressed smile as she and Eric stepped into the foyer.

"Certainly not, Prin—Fraülein Phillips," Rolph said from behind her. "It does the young princess good to be unsettled once in a while. Welcome back, Your Highness."

"Rolph," Eric said with a smile, "I assume everything has been going well since we've been gone."

"Yes, Your Highness. Her Majesty the queen would like to see you—and Fraülein Phillips—in the Rose Room. And then the kitchen staff is expecting Fraülein Phillips in the kitchen to taste-test their attempts at making soda bread."

Casey reached a hand out to the very proper little man's arm. "Thank you, Rolph. I'll be there."

Eric took her hand and led her into the Rose Room, where the queen sat alone by the fireplace. The old woman didn't acknowledge their presence until they were seated a moment.

"Cassandra is safe?" she asked without preamble.

"You mean you didn't hear her?" Eric asked incredulously.

"It was a foolish risk you took, Eric," she snapped. For a second her eyes strayed to the patched arm he held gingerly by his side. Then she returned her attention to the fireplace. "General Mueller has been dealt with, I assume?"

"He has. And now, if you don't mind, Mother, I think I'd like to shower and change. There is still a government to run."

Her hand came up even as he moved to get to his feet. Eric eased himself down again. "Another matter. We must talk, I think, about the marriage."

"What marriage, Mother?" Eric asked. "Cassandra's? Mine?"

"Do you really think the country would be served by your flaunting a twin to the queen so soon after this incident? Do you think Cassandra would tolerate it? Surely it would be better if no one knew Miss Phillips existed."

Casey, for one, couldn't think of anything intelligent to say. Eric maintained his princely control.

"What are you driving at, Mother?"

She turned to him, her eyes the eyes of a queen who must make a difficult decision. "We do not have the luxury of some countries to have comic-strip princesses and tabloid royalty. Our country depends on the stability envisioned in our government by very conservative business leaders. If they thought we were susceptible to blackmail, we would lose their trust and their business. If the people of this country thought we would deceive them we, the royal house, would lose their good will. And we would have at best a puppet royalty."

"I assume there's a good reason for bringing this up now," he said with tight control.

"To be frank," the queen admitted, "I am . . . fond of Fräulein Phillips. I did not wish to cause her pain. But I hoped that the two of you were merely caught in an emotional thrall of the moment, and that once Cassandra was back you would realize how impossible it is for you to continue your relationship. I have gone to the lengths of consulting Frau Phillips concerning my decision, and she agrees with me. Neither of us advise this marriage."

It was Casey who stood first. "You talked to my mother?"

"It was only in your interests, child. I have a car and a plane standing by to take you safely home as soon as you are packed."

Casey turned to Eric, her eyes filled with pain where they had been so bright only moments before. "But we haven't even told her."

"I want you to consider this, Eric," the queen said. "You have more than yourself to think about. You have a country."

Standing to face his mother, Eric smiled icily. "I *have* been thinking of my country, Mother, my entire life. It's about time I think of myself for once."

"But as queen, Cassandra surely won't allow it. Think of the damage to her."

He shook his head. "I don't really care. If Cassandra thinks she can run this country without me as her finance minister, that's fine. I'm going to marry Casey, and that's final. I don't care if it means I have to renounce my title and move to Brooklyn with her." His voice softening, he turned to smile encouragement into Casey's stricken eyes. "Maybe I could learn to play Space Invaders."

"Oh, Eric . . ." Casey protested.

He silenced her by taking her hand.

"Surely you can't dismiss the situation so blithely," his mother objected, her own eyes now uncertain. "Why would you even consider making such a rash sacrifice?"

When he smiled then, it was at Casey. "Just because I want to." Eric turned to level an uncompromising gaze on his mother and all she represented. "It's your decision. I'll stay long enough for Cassandra to be installed, but if my wife isn't welcome in my family, then neither am I."

Fourteen

Eric had been right when he'd said that Moritania was rife with good taste. Cassandra's wedding was the proof. Filling the cathedral with bright and beautiful guests, the event galvanized the little country into a day of widespread celebration. Garlands of fresh flowers decorated the buildings, and the citizens dressed in the bright hand-sewn finery of traditional costumes. Flags and bunting flew, banners hung from the gray stone of the cathedral walls, and every policeman and guard member had been shined and pressed to a razor-sharp finish.

Braz was alive with color and music and life. Even though Cassandra was not a favorite in the royal family, even though no one really anticipated her becoming the queen, it was still a chance to reaffirm the ancient traditions that helped bind the small country together. The royal family belonged to each and every citizen of Moritania, and they were pleased to show them off. Even the camera crews from the cable company had been situated so that they didn't mar the scene.

At precisely noon, the procession started out from the palace. The Moritanian Guards led on horseback, then the palace guards on foot and the intricately designed carriages that carried the royal family.

Eric sat alongside his mother, resplendent in the full uniform of the guard. As the prince, he was the traditional head of the unit and entitled to its benefits. He sat regally straight in the pristine white uniform with its polished brass buttons and high-crowned cap. A saber lay at his side, and his feet were shod in glossy black boots. More than one female citizen could be seen blowing kisses at the handsome prince. His mother, alongside, was attired in traditional queen's garb—a matronly blue dress and an awful-looking feathery hat. Casey figured it must be some kind of tradition of its own.

After the last of the procession wound its way into town, the chauffeur helped Casey and James McCormac into the back of the limo. Eric had asked James to escort a now-silent Casey so that she could at least enjoy the festivities before she left. From the expression beneath her wide-brimmed hat, Casey wasn't at all looking forward to it. Even the addition of James, now even more attentive than when he'd thought she was Cassandra, couldn't lift her spirits. Casey had the depressing feeling that once Cassandra was queen, she had every intention of dropping the last sandbags into Casey's hot-air balloon.

There was a crowd all along the route, and by the time they reached the narrow Kirkenstrasse there was no way to get through. The people packed the available space along the street and down the two blocks to the station in the hope of hearing the ceremony through the loudspeakers outside the church.

Quite a few tourists swelled the crowd, good for the economy of the little country. Casey only knew that the cheering rose precipitously when Eric stepped from his carriage, flowers arcing through the air toward him from his adoring subjects and tourists alike. After that, Cassandra's reception was something of an anticlimax.

Cassandra noticed it, too. Stepping from her carriage with the help of her uncle, The princess stopped to bathe in her people's adoration, only to realize that it wasn't quite as forthcoming as it had been a moment earlier. Breathtakingly beautiful in a satin-and-beadwork gown and a tulle veil, she seemed distracted and nervous, something Casey had noticed the last few days. The staff had noticed it, too, speculating on its causes over the coffee they shared with Casey. Even James had commented on it, noting that Cassandra's usually perfect porcelain complexion seemed a bit wan, her bare shoulders sagging above the expanse of the exquisitely designed gown.

"Maybe she finally realized just what she's in for," James said, smiling wryly as he guided Casey along to a side door in an attempt to miss the cameras.

"Being queen?" Casey asked, her hand held firmly in the crook of James's arm. She should have been swooning by now. He was in a morning suit and top hat, his famed brown eyes sparkling and seductive. And his attention was all on her. Why couldn't he have managed to do all this before Eric dropped into her life?

With a flash of white teeth, James motioned to the front of the church, where Rudolph, Baron of Austerlitz, waited. "Being married."

He almost succeeded in getting Casey to giggle as the two slipped into a side pew about halfway back. Casey could see heads of state from where she sat, royalty, jet-set luminaries and what she assumed were the wealthy and notable of European society. Her marriage to Eric would have been different, she thought with a rueful little smile beneath her concealing veil. They were going to invite whomever they wanted.

High above them, the organ swelled to a thunderous crescendo that echoed through the soaring church, and heads turned to see Cassandra standing at the back. Candlelight flickered, rich ornaments glittered in the yellow light streaming in from the huge rose window behind the altar. The scene was magical. Casey should have been properly awed, as she'd been the first time she'd attended one of these functions. Instead, she watched Eric walk sedately up the aisle alongside his niece and thought that her heart would break at the sight of him.

Casey turned away, her eyes on the ice-blue kid gloves in her lap, which matched her tailored dress, a soft geometric print in blues and greens and ivories that fell from padded shoulders and skimmed her figure with delicate attention. The sleeves were long and fitted, the matching hat a delicious shade of blue-green that matched the ocean on a sunny day.

Casey would never have the chance to wear something this fine again. She would never be invited to functions like this or be treated with quite the same deference by the people who ran the world. But she didn't care. The Russians and the Irish were right. It all ended. Even while you were enjoying it, savoring it, it was coming to a close.

"What the—"

Casey's head came up at James's bitten words. He pointed over toward the center aisle. Confused, she followed to find that everyone's attention was ahead of her. A hush had fallen on the crowd.

Just shy of the steps to the altar, Eric stood with his head bent toward Cassandra's. She was at a dead stop, her head shaking, making some kind of point. From the angle of her face, Casey could see that she was watching the less-than-impressive Rudolph.

The organist faltered, then picked up the melody again with a bit less enthusiasm. The bishops and priests who crowded the altar waited with frowns on their studious faces. The audience began to shift in their seats. Rudolph waited at rigid attention.

Suddenly Cassandra pulled herself free of Eric's hold. "No!" she shrieked, loud enough for the cable viewers to hear. "I won't do it! He's a worm!"

Casey's eyes rolled. Beside her, James did his best to maintain his composure. Up on the center aisle, Eric was doing his best to talk some sense into his niece.

"That girl does know how to throw a tantrum," Casey admitted under her breath.

James heard and chuckled. Outside, the crowd had grown very quiet. Casey looked up to the balcony to which the commentator had been relegated. He was hot at his microphone, his avid commentary probably more appropriate for a title bout than a wedding. Maybe if Casey waved now, her mother would see her.

"Oh, the hell with the crown!"

Casey's head came back up with a snap. You could have heard a pin drop as Cassandra's peevish words echoed throughout the cathedral. One of the priests had taken to mopping his brow.

Without warning, Cassandra turned on the audience and flipped her veil back. To everyone's surprise, the famously composed face was tear-stained.

"The crown isn't worth it!" she shouted to everyone. "Free yourselves of it! I am! I'm renouncing this sham of a marriage and that anachronistic title of queen to become Mrs. Hans Gerdman! People of Moritania, unite behind me!"

Before Eric could catch her, she fled down the aisle. Actually, Casey wasn't sure Eric wanted to try. The look on his face left her in no doubt as to his opinion of Cassandra's latest little act.

"Hans?" she squeaked in delighted surprise, a hand to her mouth.

"Who's that?" James demanded in her ear.

"One of the dissidents who kidnapped her," she giggled, thinking of the thin, earnest young man who had spent so much time at the florist's. She hoped Cassandra could find him again. The way he'd been running when he'd gotten away made Casey suspect that he wasn't about to stop until he reached the Mediterranean.

"Well, leave it to Cassandra to throw out the baby with the bathwater." James grinned, easing back in his pew to enjoy the proceedings.

Up at the side of the altar, Rudolph had gone white. He was looking around as if planning the least public means of escape. The archbishop looked as if he was going to faint. The commentator up in the shadows almost fell off the balcony in his excitement as his cameraman swiveled frantically in Cassandra's wake. As usual, it was left to Eric to rescue the situation.

Without noticeable agitation, he stepped up to the altar and turned to face the audience. "Excuse me," he said. "It seems we have an abdication on our hands."

Casey saw the sharp expression on his mother's face and knew that she was outraged. Roll with it, honey, Casey thought with a grim smile. He's probably the only person who can save your royal position right now.

"I do apologize for Cassandra's timing," Eric went on with a smile to the audience, carefully checking out the church. "She's had a rough week of it, though. I asked her to consider putting her decision off, but she refused—in her inimitable style."

A rumble of laughter could be heard from outdoors.

"So," he continued, looking for a moment at the plumed hat he held in his hands. "We seem to have a country without a monarch. I'm afraid that just leaves me."

When Eric looked up, Casey felt James move beside her. She turned a bit to see his hand lift just enough for Eric to see. Her heart leaped. What were those two up to?

"Stop that," she hissed, batting at his arm.

James smiled. His task had been accomplished. A great grin broke out over Eric's face as he stepped down off the altar and approached. Casey's eyes went very wide. So did the queen's. The commentator was speechless.

"I hope you as our guests at this most auspicious occasion won't mind," Eric was saying as he walked, "but I have to consult with my subjects on a matter of some import. I'll be right back."

He walked right up to the end of Casey's pew and held out his hand. A thousand pairs of eyes turned to her. She blushed scarlet beneath the veil, frozen to the spot.

"Casey?" he asked, smiling with those beguiling eyes.

"Go on." James nudged from behind her.

Before she knew it, she was on her feet walking toward Eric, and a fresh buzz of excitement broke over the audience. She had no idea where Rudolph had gone, but the bishops were toughing the whole thing out.

The crowd that met them was jubilant. They knew better than anyone what Cassandra's abdication would mean. The minute the door opened, pandemonium reigned. Flowers filled the air and adults held their children up to see. Some were clapping, stamping their approval. Some were singing and crying. Eric silenced them all with a raised hand.

"As I'm sure you've all figured by now," he began, "if Cassandra refuses to rule, it's up to me. I have always been willing to serve my country any way I can."

A fresh wave of cheering attested to that.

"But now," he continued, "I must ask for something in return. I must ask for your understanding in a matter that has been transpiring for the last week." With one last, lingering look at Casey, he turned back to them and went on. "You see, I'm afraid that the reports of Cassandra's kidnapping were absolutely true. She had been held all week, only having been freed yesterday. As you may also know, she has been seen repeatedly at functions in Moritania. I'm afraid that we, your government, sought desperate means to preserve the stability of the country, and had to do it behind your backs. I ask your forgiveness. I would also like to introduce you to the young woman here, a distant relative of the family, who flew in to help us in our hours of need."

He never gave Casey the chance to object before whipping off her hat. Beneath, her hair was swept up and she had pearls at her ears. The crowd gasped at the resemblance. Casey stood rigidly still beside Eric, torn between the desire to run and the desire to collapse into a little pile right there on the stone steps.

"Now, certain advisers claim that revealing Fraülein Phillips's identity would be deleterious to the benefit of the country. Under normal circumstances, I would agree. But you see, I have decided that unless she can be my queen I cannot rule. I ask your permission.''

The man was pure magic. He barely got the words out before the crowd went wild again, now showering Casey with the flowers and the well-wishing. There was very little question about their feelings concerning her, especially since she'd come in contact with quite a few of them the week before.

''Now just a minute,'' Casey objected to Eric.

''You promised,'' he said, eyebrow raised.

''I didn't know you were going to be a king.''

He shrugged. ''The vagaries of power. Take it or leave it.''

''What about the wedding we'd planned? My mother and Sandy?''

Eric held up his hand again and received the crowd's attention. ''One thing. My lovely fiancée wants to wait for our wedding so that her family and friends may attend. Can we put this marriage off a bit?''

They cheered.

''What about my career?'' she asked then.

His hand went up.

''College,'' he said. ''She demands that she be allowed to finish college and practice law.''

''Before the wedding?'' somebody asked.

He turned to her with inquiring eyes.

''No.'' She smiled sheepishly, then turned to the crowd and repeated herself. ''No. After.''

That was fine with them.

Eric laughed. ''Fine, then, if it's all right with you, how about a coronation instead today?''

''Coronation?'' Casey demanded. ''How can you be crowned without being married? I thought it was the law.''

It was his turn for a sheepish grin. ''Only for women,'' he admitted.

Casey bestowed her best scowl on him. ''Now I *know* I'm going to finish college. You guys have quite a few laws around here that could use a little updating.''

Her audience approved. Eric approved even more heartily. Turning her into his arms, he bestowed the first official, public royal kiss, which had not only Casey but every other woman in sight weak-kneed.

The crowd went wild.

* * *

Early the next morning, before anyone else was up, Eric and Casey went out riding. He presented her with a roan mare with a very solid disposition to carry her, and Casey fell in love a second time. The two of them cantered over the grounds back to the manicured lawns beyond the gardens. As the sun appeared to first burn off the dew, they settled on a blanket under a vast oak tree and considered their future.

"Your mother wasn't far from a stroke yesterday," Casey grinned from where she lay nestled in Eric's arms watching the brightening sky.

"She'll grumble about it for at least a week," he said, his hand already fingering her hair. "Then she'll go along, just as always. Especially when she realizes that the country will survive."

"There's no chance Cassandra will change her mind and dethrone you?"

"Why?" He grinned. "Looking forward to wearing that crown at all those state functions?"

Casey grinned back a bit dryly. "I'm already measuring her old room for a couple of Space Invaders machines. Beats all those pink ruffles."

"Cassandra is long gone," Eric assured her. "And quite impotent to change things once the entire staff lined up to witness her statement of abdication. Werner admits to having signed twice."

Casey chuckled. The picture was an amusing one.

"She's gone. Off to live on love," he assured her. "And the fifty thousand pounds she took from the office safe."

"Love comes expensive these days," Casey admitted. "Good thing I have simple tastes."

"Hot dogs instead of caviar."

"Beer instead of cognac."

"I can't wait for our first barbecue."

She giggled, her fingers seeking out the delicious expanse of hair that curled through his open shirt. "I can't wait for the wedding."

"When does your mother get here?"

"Friday. She refuses to make any decisions about moving. Says maybe *I'm* going to be a queen, but that doesn't mean *she* wants to live like one."

"All in good time," Eric murmured soothingly, feathering kisses across her cheek. "All in good time. After all, look how far we've come in a few days."

"Yes." Casey sighed, Eric's touch suddenly stirring the embers that glowed in her belly. "Just last week I was a frog." Her legs were shot with sudden fire, her arms reaching for him. "Now I'm going to marry one."

Eric chuckled. His finger trailed along her throat to the open neck of her blouse. "I'm the king now, remember. I can have you beheaded."

Casey stretched against the sweet lightning of his touch. "I thought you were going to ply me with wine and take me on the royal yacht."

Eric's mouth followed the trail, eliciting surprised little gasps. "That's only for mistresses," he said, his tongue descending the valley between her breasts as he mastered her buttons.

With a wicked grin, Casey twisted her fingers in his hair and gave a yank. "What about queens?" she asked with deliberate sweetness when he yelped.

"They get this."

His mouth descended to her breast, hot against the cotton and succulent against her flesh. Casey gasped, arching, the fire crowning without warning, liquefying her with impatient desire. She scrabbled at his back with her hands, dipping to slip them in beneath his shirt, pulling at it to free his chest to her. He leaned against her, his own impatient fire burning the length of her thigh.

Eric dipped a hand to her jeans, sneaking in flat against her belly and tempting the curve of her thigh. Casey moaned, the sun bright in her eyes, Eric's body hot against her hands.

"Eric . . . won't somebody . . . find us . . ."

He lifted his head long enough to answer. "Just poachers. Everybody else knows exactly where we are and why."

"Wonderful . . ."

It was, though. She didn't care who knew. Her body had already sought its new rhythm, arching against the torment of Eric's touch, seeking the feel of him with hungry hands. Casey ran hands along his thighs, the tight square of his buttocks, so firm and tempting, then up the sleek expanse of his back. She buried her mouth into the delicious texture of his chest and let the rasp of it against her tongue and lips inflame her even more.

She felt his hands at her hips, sliding her jeans down. His fingers galvanized her. She lifted to him, aching to feel his hard, strong hands against the soft, sensitive skin there. Impatient to lie naked and vulnerable before his sight.

It was the light of his eyes that praised her the most, their smoky arousal prowling her skin like the touch of a hot wind.

Every time he aroused her, Casey wondered how such a flame could be quenched. And yet it was, again and again, and she found herself aching just to awaken the fire again, each time better, each time special for the loving passion in Eric's eyes; in the steely length of him within her.

Her skin was moist with his kisses, her legs trembling for the control, for the fever that raged in her. He bent to take her mouth, mingling sighs and savoring taste and texture. His body was hard against hers, his hair-roughened chest agonizing the tender nipples that strained against him, his thigh chafing hers. His fingers danced in a maddened flight against the hot, slick center of her until she cried out in agony. Casey's body quivered with the impending cataclysm. Her eyes opened to Eric and the sun. Her heart, long lost to him, swelled to bursting for happiness.

"Ah, my fair king," she gasped with a smile, her hands tangled in his soft golden-brown hair, "I am yours. I only ask the chance to try and provide a worthy heir."

For just a moment, Eric's eyes went wide. "You're . . ."

"I said try. Again and again . . . and again . . ."

Her hand blindly seeking, Casey found Eric rigid and waiting, and taunted him even more. He gasped at her bold touch and returned the favor. Easing his hand down her thigh, he invited her submission. But again it was Casey who took the initiative. Rolling a surprised Eric on his back, she eased herself on top of him. Then, her eyes wide and tempting, she began to rock. Eric groaned. He brought his own hands up, to her breasts, to the hair that shimmered in the sunlight like rare gold, to the soft, milky skin of her shoulders.

"Witch," he groaned again, the light of laughter in his eyes. "You're a witch. You've cast a spell on me."

"Damn right," she moaned, the hard power of him inside her filling her with light, with unspeakable agony and joy. "And I'm not going to let you go again, either."

They reached the peak together, their names intermingled on the soft summer wind, their arms tight around each other as the light broke over them in shimmering waves like the summer sun.

At the edge of the clearing, a doe appeared and stopped. Paused in that breathless moment before flight, she considered the intertwined couple across the lawn with wide, curious eyes. And then she bounded away, startled by the renewed whispering.

"So I guess I'll have to be queen," Casey said softly, her hand once again stroking Eric's silky hair.

"Do you mind so much?" he asked.

Casey was surprised to see that he was serious. She kissed him, once again nestled within his embrace, the sun warming her skin and the breeze cooling her heated body. Beyond them, the Alps rose in majestic silence and the sky arced into infinity. The calm in the air was palpable.

"No," she said, smiling. "In fact, I'd almost venture to say..."

"Say what?"

"Oh, you know, that we'll..."

His brows knit. "We'll what?"

"C'mon," Casey scoffed with a mischievous smile. "Don't you read fairy tales? What's the last line of everything from Cinderella to Snow White?"

Eric's eyes sparkled with mischief. "The end?"

She scowled. "And then Casey Phillips married her Prince Charming—"

"*King* Charming, if you don't mind."

"...and they lived..."

"In Moritania and Palm Springs."

"Eric!"

He mimicked her pose. "Casey!"

"You're not very romantic."

"I'm lying naked in an open field with you in the middle of the day when I'm supposed to be at the bank," he objected. "What would you call that?"

"Wanton."

Reaching over, he drew a lazy finger along her breast, raising a new crop of goose bumps. "I've always been a man of action," he explained, dipping to taste her swollen lips. "Not words."

She giggled, bringing her hand up to his cheek. "Can you interpret it for me then?"

An hour later, as Casey once again lay nestled in Eric's arms, she decided that she liked the way Eric ended a fairy tale a lot more than the way the Brothers Grimm did. After all, this Prince Charming did a lot more than dance. Now, if she could only teach him about baseball...

* * * * *

COMING NEXT MONTH

Silhouette Classics

The best books from the past by your favorite authors.

The first two stories of a delightful collection...

#1 DREAMS OF EVENING by Kristin James

As a teenager, Erica had given Tonio Cruz all her love, body and soul, but he betrayed and left her anyway. Ten years later, he was back in her life, and she quickly discovered that she still wanted him. But the situation had changed—now she had a son. A son who was very much like his father, Tonio, the man she didn't know whether to hate—or love.

#2 INTIMATE STRANGERS by Brooke Hastings

Rachel Grant had worked hard to put the past behind her, but Jason Wilder's novel about her shattered her veneer of confidence. When they met, he turned her life upside down again. Rachel was shocked to discover that Jason wasn't the unfeeling man she had imagined. Haunted by the past, she was afraid to trust him, but he was determined to write a new story about her—one that had to do with passion and tenderness and love.